NIGHTSONG

NIGHTSONG

AN HISTORICAL NOVEL: THE NIGHTSONG SAGA, BOOK ONE

V. J. BANIS

THE BORGO PRESS

MMXII

NIGHTSONG

FIRST BORGO PRESS EDITION

Published by Wildside Press LLC

www.wildsidebooks.com

DEDICATION

I am deeply indebted to my friend, Heather, for all the help she has given me in getting these early works of mine reissued.

And I am grateful as well to Rob Reginald, for all his assistance and support.

CONTENTS

PART ONE

CHAPTER ONE

"I'm telling you, you'll be murdered in your beds," Mrs. Blaise said, thumping her purple parasol on the hard-packed dirt of the floor for emphasis. "If you've got any sense, you'll come along with us right now, and not risk another night in this godforsaken place."

"If God had really forsaken this place, Cynthia," Sarah Holt replied, managing a sweet smile despite the tautness of her own nerves, "I doubt he'd have sent us here to preach to the natives."

"Well, he's managing to drive us right back out of here, isn't he? At least, *we're* going, as soon as Mr. Blaise finds a cart for our things, and you're blamed fools if you don't do the same."

"Lydia, dear," Sarah turned to her daughter, who was following the conversation with scarcely concealed interest. "Your father should be coming soon. Why don't you and Reginald walk out to meet him? He just might have something for you."

"Yes, Mama," Lydia said obediently, though she would far rather have stayed where she was. Mrs. Blaise's son, Reginald, was thin and pimply, and had a way of looking at her that she found disconcerting, though she could not say just why; anyway, Mrs. Blaise's conversation was far more fascinating, if frightening. The native Chinese were rioting against what they called "foreign devils," mostly missionaries like her parents and the Blaises, who were scattered throughout the country. The rumors had begun a fortnight ago.

"Scapegoats," her father, the Reverend Joshua Holt, had said. "The cholera's gotten bad. You'll see, as soon as that dies down, so will this other."

But the cholera—and the rumors—had worsened. A trader had been shot in Shanghai; the culprit had been arrested, but mobs of Chinese had demanded, and obtained, his release. Then a missionary and his wife had been killed at Hangchow.

Outside, "...don't want the girl frightened," she heard her mother saying through the window's shutters.

"...not safe anymore....," was all she caught of Mrs. Blaise's reply.

She turned toward the center of town, and the market, which was where her father had gone earlier.

"This way," Reginald said, turning in the opposite direction.

"Mama said...."

"I saw your father on our way over here," Reginald interrupted her. "And he won't be back for ages. Come on."

Somewhat reluctantly she went with him. The street was crowded and, remembering Mrs. Blaise's dire warnings, she fancied that the Chinese were looking sideways at them as they went along, though her common sense told her there was nothing singular in that. White people, after all, were still rare this far inland, even if it was 1870. Except for themselves and the Blaises, and a Scotch-American trader living a few streets away, the only other whites for a hundred miles were a couple in Mei Fu, the next town.

"You ought to come with us, you know," Reginald said, taking her arm to steer her around a pile of offal on the rough pavement. "We could have some fun in the back of the cart, couldn't we?"

"I don't know what you mean," she said, freeing her arm. "Anyway, Papa says God's love brought us here, and God's love will protect us."

"My pa says, the Lord helps them that helps themselves."

"Not very noble sentiments for a missionary."

"These people don't want missionaries, they want a good army to get them in shape," Reginald said. "And someone to clean things up. I'll be glad to get out of this stench, won't you?"

Lydia did not answer. It was true that the China she had seen while traveling with her parents was not very clean, though she supposed they were seeing only the poorer sections. And the food being prepared and eaten in the open stalls looked unspeakably horrible; she could not bear to think of what went into it.

Still, there was something—she hadn't quite find the words to define it, though "romance" sprang to mind when she tried.

Above the streets, mats were stretched between the eaves of the buildings, so that the light was dim. The streets were thronged with noisy, jostling crowds. She had an idea that they must have looked like this for centuries, as if she were seeing right into some ancient fairy tale. Over there was a turbaned man with a one-eyed ass. Surely she had read of just such a sight. At any moment the crowd might part to make way for a sedan chair borne by jogging coolies, and in it might be—a prince? A singsong girl whose beauty was hidden from all but the honored and the wealthy?

A green and yellow parrot flew up from a window. The breeze set wind chimes tinkling, and loosened a shower of white blossoms from above, like perfumed snow falling upon their shoulders.

"Wait, listen." Lydia stopped short, cocking her head. Above the noise of the crowd she heard a baby crying, but this was not the sound of a hungry child, or one impatient for a nap; rather, this was a sound of ageless terror.

"Come on, we don't want to get into any trouble," Reginald said.

"This way," Lydia said, ignoring him. She turned down one of the narrow, twisting streets. They had gone no more than a few feet when they rounded a corner and saw before them a small child, sitting naked in the street, screaming.

The reason for the infant's terror was evident, for it was surrounded by a pack of wild-looking dogs. From the marks on the child's arms and legs, the animals had already bitten her once or twice, and they were now circling the child as if making ready to rush upon her.

"Stop that," Lydia cried. She picked up a stone and threw it, catching the biggest dog on the rump and making him yelp.

She threw another stone and ran forward. The dogs backed away, but only a short distance, yapping and snarling as she snatched the baby up in her arms.

"There, there," Lydia said, cradling the infant. "It's all right, you're safe now. Where do you suppose the parents are, anyway? This child might have been killed."

"I think that was the idea," Reginald said.

Lydia's mouth fell open. "But—surely, you don't mean...."

"It's a girl," Reginald said, pointing.

Lydia glanced down, blushing to have such an anatomical detail pointed out to her by a boy. In the next instant she was filled with horror, as the full import of Reginald's remark became clear to her.

Before she could speak, however, a group of Chinese burst from the house before which they were standing. The woman in the lead snatched the infant from Lydia's arms. She was speaking too fast for Lydia, with her scant grasp of the language, to understand much, but there was no question that she was angry with the foreign devils for "interfering where they had no business."

"Come on, we'd better go," Reginald said, taking her arm again and urging her back the way they had come.

Lydia went with him, though she kept looking back in dismay at the group, now grown to nearly a dozen. The Chinese were still scolding them angrily, the baby still crying, though less shrilly than before.

"It's horrible," she said, when they had gone round the corner and were out of sight.

"They're heathens," Reginald said matter-of-factly. "If a baby turns out to be a girl, they just put it out in the street for the dogs or the pigs to eat. I'm surprised they don't cook it themselves—"

"Stop it," she said sharply. "Papa says it's because they're poor. They can't afford to invest all the expense of raising a daughter, knowing that when she's grown she'll marry and go to work for someone else."

Despite her defense of the Chinese, however, the incident had left her badly shaken. It was one thing to be told that girl children were sometimes left to die by their destitute parents; it was quite another to see it being done, and to be able to do nothing to prevent it.

All of a sudden, China had lost a great deal of its romance for her.

* * * * * * *

Like all but the meanest of Chinese towns, this one was surrounded by a crenellated wall, and they had come to the gate.

"Let's go outside," Reginald said, taking her arm again.

"Do you think we ought to?" she asked. "Aren't you afraid of the Chinese?"

"There's lots fewer of them out here." When she still held back, he added in a pleading tone, "Come on, this may be the last I'll see you in a long time, maybe forever."

She shuddered, his words seeming to her a grim prophecy, but she relented. From outside, they could look down upon the rice paddies, crescent-shaped patches descending one below the other, so that they could be easily flooded, with firs and bamboos growing in the hollows.

Reginald led them to one of the little groves of bamboo, and when they had passed into its green shade they seemed quite removed from all the bustle and commotion of the city. This she had not resisted at all, for she found the bamboo groves enchanted places in which she could forget the horror that still lingered in her mind. Here she could imagine herself a princess, in the midst of fantastic adventures.

Reginald cleared his throat nervously, reminding her of his presence. If only, she thought, he were more of a prince.

"So today's your birthday, is it?" he asked.

His voice was higher pitched than usual, and she gave him a puzzled glance, wondering what on earth was making him so nervous all of a sudden. Maybe he was more frightened of the Chinese than he'd let on.

"Yes," she said. "Mama's making me a cake and Papa went to the market to get me a present, though of course he didn't say so."

"Sweet sixteen, and never been kissed," Reginald said, attempting a laugh that came out a gurgle.

"I don't think that's any concern of yours," she replied archly, her face coloring.

"Well, come on then, give us a kiss," he said, seizing her all of a sudden in a clumsy embrace.

"I won't," she cried, struggling to free herself. "Let go of me, how dare you, you silly boy!"

"I'm not a boy anymore, Pa said I could carry a gun on the trip back to Shanghai—and I'll show you, too, if you'll just hold still a minute."

She flung her head to and fro, avoiding his attempts to plant his mouth on hers. She had almost broken free of his arms when her foot slipped and, to her dismay, she fell to the ground. In an instant he was upon her, his weight threatening to crush her. It was harder in this position to elude him, and she felt his mouth at her throat, moving down toward her little breasts as he tore at the bodice of her dress with his hand.

"Let me go," she cried, almost in tears; how dare this pockmarked lout manhandle her like this! Papa would have him horsewhipped.

"Not till I've got what I want to remember you by," he said, his breath hoarse and rasping in her ear.

His knees were between hers and he forced them apart, rubbing his body roughly against hers. It was frightening and crude and at the same time she felt a mysterious tingling in her loins that she had never felt before, that both puzzled her and added to her fear.

"Stop it, I say!" she cried, pounding his shoulders. "I'll tell your pa."

"We'll be gone from here by nightfall," he said, laughing

again as one hand found the tender flesh beneath her skirt, "so there'll be no one to tell."

"Reginald, you wouldn't...." Even had she known the correct words, she could not have brought herself to use them, but there was little doubt by now in either of their minds just what he intended.

"What do you think?" he said, mocking her; his fingernails raked one silken thigh.

"I think," a masculine voice said from above them, "that you'd better do as the young lady says, and let her go."

Reginald shot to his feet, his already pale face going whiter. Over his shoulder, Lydia saw the face of Peter MacNair, the Scotch-American trader who had arrived in the city a few days ago.

"Wh-wh-wh—" Reginald stammered helplessly, unable to form a complete word.

"This isn't a very safe place for you youngsters to be just now," MacNair said. "Hasn't anyone told you there's been some trouble with the Chinese?"

"Yes, sir." Reginald's Adam's apple bobbed furiously.

"Well, then, you'd better scoot on home, your parents must be worried about you."

"Yes, sir," Reginald said again, gesturing to Lydia, who was still lying on the ground.

"I'll escort the young lady home," Peter MacNair said in a voice that brooked no argument.

"Yes, sir." Reginald was gone in a flash. Lydia had a glimpse of him racing pell-mell for the gate, without so much as a backward glance.

"Here." Peter MacNair gave her his hand and helped her to her feet. The bodice of her dress was torn, and she was grateful that he looked away while she adjusted it as best she could. It gave her, too, a chance to glance at him undetected.

How handsome he was, with his sandy brown hair that spilled carelessly over his forehead, and eyes so dark a brown that they looked black when he was scowling, as he was now. But why was he angry? Did he think she had encouraged Reginald?

"I thank you for coming to my assistance," she said aloud, hoping to put his mind at ease on that account.

"It was nothing," he said curtly. "Shall we go now?"

Intimidated by his cool manner, Lydia went wordlessly with him, out of the grove, and back to the city's gate, wondering as she did so what she had done to offend him.

In fact, Peter MacNair was annoyed not with her, but with himself for having intervened in something that was none of his business. The two had looked little more than children on a lark when he had seen them disappear into that bamboo grove. He had gone there only intending to warn them of the danger abroad, and when he'd seen what was afoot, he had very nearly turned around and gone on his way; what did it matter to him if the daughter of a pompous missionary entertained some lout among the bamboo?

But then the girl had started protesting, and she had looked so damnably young. He had spoken on an impulse, and having once taken such a stand, he could hardly have backed down from it without looking like an ass.

So now here he was, escorting the silly child home, and no doubt the righteous Reverend Holt would think he was the one who'd torn her dress in an attempt to have his way with her.

The idea having entered his mind, however fleetingly, he instinctively gave the girl an appraising glance, and as quickly chided himself for being foolish. She was every bit as young as he had thought at first sight, and on top of it, not even his type. That red-gold hair of hers, falling in a luxuriant cascade about her face and shoulders, was smashing, particularly with her green eyes, but he favored dark-haired women, and in due time those wide-set eyes would lose that look of enraptured innocence that made them so appealing just now. As for the rest, well, she had hardly any breasts, and she tended toward plumpness, though that might have been some lingering baby fat.

All and all, he'd much rather have one of the Chinese singsong girls, though truth to tell he had been hankering for a white woman lately. He had been in China nearly a year, and he was not a man noted for continence.

They had entered the city by now, but its teeming streets had lost their charm for Lydia. She walked at the trader's side with her eyes dejectedly downward. It was apparent that she had somehow offended her rescuer, though she couldn't for the life of her imagine how. She stole a quick glance up at his profile—he was taller even than Papa—but at the sight of his stern visage, she glanced away again at once.

She had been traveling with her parents since she was a mere baby, in one remote corner of the world after another. Cut off as she was from the usual social mingling, she had experienced none of the innocent flirtation, the tentative exploration of romance that was usual for girls of her age. Reginald was the only boy she knew near her own age, and she knew him only slightly. Her parents had even sheltered her from the romantic novels that might at least have given her some clue to why her pulse quickened whenever she glanced at the handsome man beside her.

All that she did know was that to be near him like this gave her pleasure, but one so intense that it was akin to pain. He moved with a certain cocksure manner that reminded her of a prize-winning stallion her father had once taken her to see. It gave her a peculiar thrill of excitement to see how he towered over the Chinese about them. If only he would take her hand again, as he had when he had helped her up from the ground; her palm still tingled from the memory of his touch.

"Oh, there's Papa," she cried suddenly, spying her father in the street ahead of them.

Reverend Holt had already seen them, and was waiting for them to come up, scowling at them. MacNair saw the father's eyes go to his daughter's torn bodice and return to him, glinting angrily.

"Reverend." MacNair lifted his topee, the pith helmet that whites wore for protection from the burning sun, in greeting; Reverend Holt made no gesture in reply. "I found your daughter outside the gates, and thought it best if I escorted her home."

Holt's eyes went again to Lydia's torn dress. "I tore my dress on some bamboo," she said hastily, her face reddening. Now that she was no longer in any danger from Reginald, she saw no point in causing trouble, though she hoped Peter MacNair would not refute her explanation and make her out a liar.

He did not, nor did her father question her explanation. "We thank you for your trouble, Mr. MacNair," he said stiffly. "It was foolish of my daughter to go wandering off alone. There are many unscrupulous persons who might be tempted to take advantage of her youth and innocence."

"Lucky she met me instead," MacNair said. "Good day to you, sir. Miss Holt." He tipped his hat to both of them again and, turning on his heel, strode off. The throngs of Chinese seemed to part before him as if before the prow of a ship.

"You are not to speak to Mr. MacNair in the future," the reverend said.

"But Papa, he was so kind to me," Lydia said. "You can't mean it."

Her father's jaw tightened; it was the first time his daughter had ever challenged one of his commands. "I mean it most assuredly," he said, his voice icy. "And we will not discuss it further. Mind what I say."

Despite his admonition, she was about to protest further, but she was suddenly aware of something unusual that was occurring. At first she could not grasp what it was, then suddenly it came to her that an abrupt silence, more striking in a Chinese street than it would have been elsewhere, had fallen. Her father, whose great height made it possible for him to see further, suddenly took her arm and drew her into the slight shelter of a doorway.

In a moment she understood. Four peasants passed through the street, moving quickly and silently, and they bore a new coffin between them.

Another victim of the cholera. The silence lingered briefly after the coffin had passed. Then, from somewhere behind, came a sudden din, the beating of gongs and the snapping of firecrackers, the Chinese way of frightening off the evil spirits that had brought the cholera.

It was odd but that unexpected silence, and the passing of the coffin, followed by that uproar, frightened Lydia more than all the talk of illness or murder had before, and when her father, still holding tightly to her arm, drew her from the doorway and began to hurry her toward their house, she went with him meekly, glad once more to be in the shadow of his domination.

CHAPTER TWO

Lydia was surprised when her father handed her a brown wrapped package somewhat later; with everything else that had occurred, she had forgotten that it was her birthday.

"Oh, Papa, it's beautiful," she cried, unwrapping the package to reveal a golden locket. Inside was a likeness of her father, taken only a few years before, and so lifelike, with his stern expression and his eyes seeming to see right into her heart. Peter MacNair had looked at her like that in the bamboo grove.

Her heart sank as she remembered her father's admonition not to speak to the trader in the future. It was unfair. Of course, she had known that the two weren't on very good terms. Her parents had gone to see MacNair soon after he had arrived.

The meeting had not gone well; they had returned out of sorts, and her father had pronounced the Scotch-American "not a Godfearing sort." And though she could not know all the circumstances, Lydia had an idea that this had something to do with the singsong girls she had observed going in and out of the trader's house with awesome regularity.

A sudden forceful knocking at the door interrupted Lydia's reverie.

"It's that mandarin," Sarah said, glancing from one of the windows.

"Lydia, go to your room," Reverend Holt ordered.

Lydia hastened to obey, though once in her room she glued her eye to the crack of the door to watch the proceedings. She saw her mother usher Ke Loo, the mandarin prince, into the front room, where her father waited.

It was rare for missionaries to meet the mandarins, though they could occasionally be seen traveling through the cities in sedan chairs borne by servants, with attendants marching before them striking gongs to warn the people that a great man approached, and others bearing boards upon which the prince's titles were inscribed.

The first time Ke Loo had appeared, unannounced, at their door, Lydia had been appropriately awed and dazzled by the elegance of his silk robe, elaborately embroidered with dragons front and back.

"Your daughter is old," Ke Loo had informed Reverend Holt, though at that time she had been only fifteen. "She should marry. I have need of a wife. I will marry her."

To Lydia, eavesdropping that time as well, it had been thrilling and certainly flattering, but she had been relieved when her father had haughtily rejected the proposal. For all of his obvious wealth and importance, Ke Loo had a cruel face, with hooded, leering eyes and a thin, austere mouth.

He had left in a pompous flurry, but Lydia had been right in thinking that the mandarin was not accustomed to having his demands refused, for he had come now to make them again.

"Daughter should be married," Ke Loo was saying in the next room. "I will marry her."

"My daughter will marry when and where we choose," her father said, his tone angry, for he was no more accustomed than Ke Loo to having his opinions challenged.

The mandarin gave him a smile that had nothing of pleasure or friendship in it. "Is not a good time for foreign devils in China," he said.

"Are you threatening me?" Papa said, jumping from his chair. "I'll talk to Colonel Wu—"

"Colonel Wu most busy now," Ke Loo said, unmoved by the show of anger. "The cholera, it strikes everywhere, soldiers must help bury the dead."

"This is outrageous! I won't be...." He stopped; to Lydia's

horror she saw her father suddenly sway to and fro. He steadied himself with a hand on the back of a chair. In an instant, Sarah was at his side.

"Papa," Lydia cried, forgetting propriety and dashing from her hiding place. Ke Loo's eyes widened in shock at the breach of etiquette; a maiden ought to remain chastely hidden from the eyes of her suitor. That did not prevent him, however, from greedily feasting his eyes on her, particularly upon the red gold of her hair, so unlike the hair of a Chinese maiden, and the pale smoothness of her skin, like the petal of a lotus flower.

It had been the merest chance that had brought her to his attention. He had been stopping only briefly in this city, on his way from Peking to his native city of Kalgan, in the shadow of the Great Wall, and he had happened to glance from the curtains of his sedan chair, to see what at first he had thought a mere vision.

He had made up his mind at once that he must have her, this strange pale girl whose hair burned like the first hot flames of a new-laid fire. And have her he would. He was unused to being refused what he wanted, and he could not understand these foreign parents, with a daughter already past the marriage age and unclaimed, who would not reach agreement with him. He was determined.

"I'm all right," the reverend was assuring his wife and daughter, but Lydia had discovered that his skin was hot to the touch. "I'm afraid I must ask you to leave us now," he said, addressing the Chinese prince.

"I will come another time," Ke Loo said, bowing from the waist.

"You'll only be wasting your time."

Ke Loo made no reply, but smiled his mysterious smile, and with a final nod turned and went out. In a moment they heard him shouting to his bearers as they started off along the twisting street.

"Joshua, you should rest," Sarah said.

"I'm fine, I say," the reverend insisted, glowering at the door through which the mandarin had disappeared. After a moment he gave a sigh, and turned his attention to the two women.

"I suppose this is as good a time as any to tell you," he said. "I've decided it's time we traveled down to the coast, to Shanghai. We'll get our things ready tonight, and start out in the morning."

"The natives," Sarah started to say.

"It's got nothing to do with that nonsense," he said, a trifle too emphatically. "There are things I need, some books I ordered, for one. And I rather thought you'd both welcome a change of scene. Of course, if you'd rather stay here...."

"No," Sarah said quickly. "No, we'll be ready in the morning."

"We'll leave at dawn, then," he said. "Might as well get an early start." He went out of the room. It seemed to Lydia that his gait was a trifle unsteady.

* * * * * * *

They did not leave at dawn, however. Hours before that, Lydia was awakened by her mother.

"Your father's been taken ill," she said, shaking Lydia from her sleep.

"Is it—is it the cholera?"

"I'm afraid so."

What followed was like a nightmare that seemed to go on and on without end. For three days Reverend Holt's condition worsened, while his wife and daughter ministered to him as best they could, and listened in dread to every sound from without. They could not know what turn outside events had taken.

Sarah dismissed the servants, fearful that one of them might let it be known that the master was dying, so the two women were left unprotected. Women did not count for much in China, and it was not unlikely that someone might try to take advantage, particularly in view of the anti-white uproar sweeping the country.

To add to their fears, Ke Loo returned once more to press

his suit.

"My husband is away at the moment," Sarah said. The reverend had the misfortune to utter a low moan just then. Ke Loo's eyes slid in the direction of the bedroom.

"One of the servants," Sarah said, alarmed.

Ke Loo left, but Sarah was certain he would return. It was horrible; she hadn't an ounce of courage of her own. She had always journeyed without question or hesitation anywhere her husband had chosen to go, but in doing so she had only relied upon her utter confidence in him and upon his own lack of fear. To travel with him into the interior of China had seemed no more alarming than any of a dozen other trips they had taken, without any harm befalling them.

To be left in China on her own was terrifying beyond belief. If only they were in Shanghai, or Hong Kong, somewhere where there were other Americans or English; but she had no idea even how to arrange their transport to one of those places. Her husband had never allowed her to trouble herself with such matters. She spoke not a word of Chinese, though Lydia had learned a smattering of the language. At any rate, it was unthinkable that two women could travel across the Chinese mainland without a man's escort. Yet they surely could not stay here, either.

Joshua Holt died on the third day of his illness. Lydia came into the room to find her mother weeping softly. Her father's eyes, looking ghastly in his pale, sunken face, stared unseeingly upward. Though it filled her with horror, Lydia forced herself to close his eyes.

"What shall we do?" she asked her mother. Sarah shook her head helplessly.

I shall have to be strong, Lydia thought suddenly, *for both of us.*

It was a new idea to her, and in a way more frightening than all the rest that had happened, or was still threatening to happen. Never before in her life had she really needed to be strong, for there had always been her beloved father to rely upon. Now, though, every instinct told her that it was on her shoulders, and not her mother's trembling ones, that her father's mantle of responsibility must fall.

"We shall go to the Cabots," she said aloud; the Cabots were the missionary couple who lived in Mei Fu, thirty miles away. "We'll wait until night, and travel by darkness."

Her mother meekly accepted her authority, and at Lydia's direction began to pack their bags. It did not apparently occur to her to ponder the one question that most worried her daughter: what if the Cabots had already left that city?

They were packed and ready to go by the time darkness fell, but Sarah would not leave without burying her husband.

"We can't just leave him here like that," she insisted. "Suppose they came in a mob, there's no telling what they might do to him."

"Yes, of course, you're right," Lydia said, though her common sense urged her to flee without any delay. "It will have to be in the garden, then. We'd better find something for digging."

The moon had not yet risen and the air was hot and heavy with dampness, threatening a storm. They found a pair of hoes, but no shovel.

"Under the plum tree, I think," Lydia said, indicating the straggly tree at the far corner of the enclosure. "It stays damp there. The ground will be softer."

The ground was indeed soft under the tree. Even so, it was hard work. Within minutes Lydia's clothes were clinging wetly to her. She had vowed that she would not think of the purpose of their labors, but it was impossible to judge the size of the pit they were scratching from the earth without considering what was to go into it.

The stillness of the night was broken by a distant sound of shouting. The two women stopped their work, cocking their heads, as a single cry of terror, like the soprano in a mass, soared high and clear above the others, ending abruptly.

"Bandits," Lydia said, straining at the silence that had rushed back over them; or was that a footstep beyond the garden wall?

Had someone whispered, or was it only the restless birds in the branches above them?

"Someone being slaughtered," Sarah said.

Lydia shuddered, trying to think of something to say, as her father would have done, to break the tension, and all too aware of her own inadequacy.

Sarah's hoe slipped from her fingers and dropped with a soft thunk to the ground. "I can't do any more," she gasped, swaying slightly.

Lydia steadied her with an arm about her shoulders. "It will do," she said.

It would have to do, or they would be too exhausted to travel, and go they must, for she was convinced that the longer they stayed here, the greater their danger, two women, alone and unprotected, in an alien and increasingly unfriendly land.

First, however, they must finish the grim task at hand. They went into the house. Almost at once, Sarah sank weakly onto one of the hard wooden chairs.

"I can't get my breath," she said.

Lydia came to her and wiped her brow; her mother's face was burning to the touch. The cholera? But if her mother died.... Lydia felt a fresh spasm of fear.

"You rest here," she said.

She went into the bedroom alone. The shutters were open and she closed them before lighting the oil lamp. In its flickering light her father's lifeless face had a waxen, unearthly look. Lydia knelt by the bed, meaning to pray, but her heart was gripped with fear and the words would not come. Finally, despairing, she got up again.

She put her hands under his arms, averting her face, and tugged at him. Though he had been lean, he had stood more than six feet tall, and now he would not budge.

"I'll help," Sarah said unexpectedly, coming into the room.

"You should be resting."

"You'll never move him alone," Sarah said matter-of-factly. She took hold of her dead husband's feet and motioned for Lydia to lift his shoulders at the same time.

It was done at last, the earth scraped back into place, the restless birds clucking a benediction. The moon had risen, then vanished behind a bank of clouds, and thunder rumbled in the distance as they started back to the house, breathless from their exertions. They had just reached the door when Sarah again swayed dizzily. This time she would have fallen had Lydia not moved quickly to her side.

"I'll be all right," Sarah insisted, though her limbs would not support her.

"Here," Lydia said, leading her to the cot in the other bedroom.

"We must go," Sarah protested feebly, too weak to resist being put on the bed.

"In a few minutes," Lydia said. "You rest while I get everything ready."

Almost at once Sarah's eyes fluttered closed. Lydia stared anxiously down at her. Surely her fever was worse, and she was so weak already, how would she ever manage to travel thirty miles over the hills and rice fields?

Their bags were sitting on the hard-packed dirt floor in her parents' bedroom. They were too much, Lydia decided. She would pack just the essentials into one small valise that she could carry herself. Later, if the uproar should die down—and that was possible; her father had told her that there had been outbreaks of anti-white sentiment before, but they had lasted only briefly—then they could come back for their other belongings.

Beyond that, her plans were necessarily vague. Her mother had a brother, Richard Whitley, in San Francisco. Once they traveled safely to Shanghai, surely they could book passage on a ship there. Brother and sister were not close, but he could hardly refuse to help them, could he?

She began emptying the freshly packed bags onto the floor, tossing things hither and thither. Her nerves were stretched taut and she gave a start at a sound from outside; this time she was certain she heard footsteps in the street. She held her breath, listening. The smoke from the lamp had begun to sting her eyes so that she saw through a veil of tears. She was holding the locket Papa had given her, and it slipped from her trembling fingers, falling open. Her father's likeness gazed up at her, his eyes seeming to reproach her.

A sob caught in Lydia's throat and she buried her face in her hands. It was hopeless. What could she do, a mere girl?

Another sound from outside brought her sharply back to reality. Yes, there was someone there. She jumped up and ran into the front room of the house, staring wide-eyed at the door. She heard voices and more footsteps, then suddenly an imperious rapping.

She held her breath. Who could it be? The Chinese hordes, come to kill them? Or someone to rescue them perhaps, the Cabots, or even the authorities?

The rapping came again, louder, more insistent than before. Lydia could neither speak nor move. Her heart pounding, she watched the door being tested gingerly at first, then shoved abruptly inward. Ke Loo came into the room, stopping when he saw her.

Lydia stared as if mesmerized. Ke Loo's glance went around the room, and came back to her.

"I wish to speak to the father," he informed her arrogantly. His expression as he regarded her was a contradiction. It was plain that he disapproved of being met by a mere female, for in a proper Chinese home they would remain out of sight when a visitor was present. At the same time, there was an unmistakable glint of pleasure in his eyes as he scrutinized her more boldly than politely.

"He—he's busy," she replied. "He's writing a sermon."

Ke Loo's eyes flicked from one end of the room to the other. There was not a sound in the house.

"The mother, then," he said, taking a step further into the room. "I will speak to her."

"She's busy also." Lydia's heart was pounding and she could barely trust her voice to speak.

Ke Loo came still closer. His lips contorted into a mockery of a smile. "You are alone?" he asked.

"No," she said, a note of hysteria giving the lie to her denial. His grin widened.

"The father, he is ill?"

"No, he's busy, I tell you."

"In China," he said, his voice as sleek and sinuous as the snake who lived in the little garden, "we honor the widow. I have much wealth. I am cousin to Dragon Empress. You and honored mother could live as queens."

He spoke as if he knew Papa was dead. His eyes held hers for a moment. They went to her hair, and she realized for the first time that he had probably never seen hair that color before. It seemed to fascinate him. She had let it hang loose, and now he put out one hand, taking the long curls in his fingers, fondling their silky luxuriance.

"No," she cried suddenly, jerking her hair from his hand. "I won't marry you, I won't."

His nostrils flared angrily, and again his eyes darted about the room. "Where are the parents?" he demanded.

"They're both indisposed," she said, fighting a wave of hysteria. "You must go, please."

She gestured toward the door. For a moment he hesitated, studying her as if reading the meaning of her actions. Then, without a further word, he whirled about and, silk robe rustling, went out the door. She ran to it, watching as he entered his sedan chair, the curtains falling to conceal him from view. His bearers, so thin and frail looking that she wondered how they could manage the weight, hoisted the poles onto their callused shoulders and set off at once with the peculiar jogging motion they used.

She slammed the door shut and ran into the room where her mother was sleeping. "Oh, Mama, Mama, wake up," she cried, shaking her mother's shoulders. "We've got to leave right away."

Though Sarah opened her eyes, she seemed to focus them with difficulty, and her skin was burning to the touch.

"Lydia? What...?"

"It's Ke Loo, Mama, he's been here, and he'll come back, I know he will. He knows about Papa, I don't know how, but he does, he knows we're alone. Oh, Mama, we've got to leave right away."

"Ke Loo, the mandarin?" Sarah's fever-wracked brain wrestled with this information. After a moment she struggled to sit up. "Yes, yes, you're right, we must go. He won't rest until he's carried you off. Help me."

With Lydia's help she managed to get to her feet, though she swayed unsteadily. Lydia left her a moment and ran to get dark cloaks for both of them.

"The bags," Sarah said, seeing them on the floor, their contents scattered about the room.

"There isn't time, we'll send for them later," Lydia said. "Hurry."

She paused just long enough to extinguish the oil lamps, plunging the house into darkness. Outside the moon had vanished again behind the clouds and the rain that had been threatening had begun to fall. Staying to the shadows, the two women stole from the house.

"Not this way," Sarah said, hesitating. "The gate's over here."

"We won't be able to go there," Lydia said. "You're not well enough to travel so far. We'll go to Mr. MacNair's."

"The Scotsman?" Sarah came to an abrupt halt. "But we can't. He's not a God-fearing man. And all those Chinese girls... it won't do."

"It will have to do, Mama," Lydia insisted, urging her along. "He's white, and a man, at least. He can't refuse to help us, I know he can't."

Sarah came, but reluctantly. "Your father didn't like him at all. He'd be shocked to know we went there," she said.

Father can't help us now, Lydia thought, but did not say it aloud. They ran across the roughly paved street.

They had gone only a few yards when the sound of running footsteps brought them up short. "Someone's coming," Lydia said. "In here, quick."

She thrust her mother into the deeper shadows of a doorway. They huddled together, watching the way they had come. Already Lydia's cloak was soaked through from the rain and she could feel her mother trembling through her clothes.

Ke Loo's sedan chair materialized out of the rain. This time he came with several attendants, burly-looking coolies wearing, despite the storm, nothing more than loin cloths, their hair in long pigtails down their backs. Two of them, Lydia saw, carried large sacks flung over their shoulders. The procession came to a halt outside the house she and her mother had just quitted.

For a moment Ke Loo leaned from the sedan chair, conferring with the two coolies. Then he disappeared within the curtains, and the two ran stealthily toward the dark house.

Lydia shuddered. They had left not a moment too soon. Ke Loo had come back, clearly intending to take them by force. He had known somehow that Papa was dead. He had guessed the truth, that mother and daughter were without masculine protection. In China, that meant they were at the mercy of a man such as himself.

"We mustn't stay here," she whispered, urging her mother from the doorway. She had seen everything she needed to see, and to remain where they were was to invite discovery. When Ke Loo learned they were gone, he was certain to look for them.

An alley led from the street a few doors down, and in a moment more it had swallowed them up. As they vanished into its gloom, Lydia heard an angry shout from the direction of their house.

Though it was only a few streets to Peter MacNair's house, it seemed to take an eternity to reach there. At any minute Lydia expected to hear the sounds of pursuit. She hurried her mother along as quickly as she could, but Sarah was by now barely able to walk. Lydia was half supporting, half carrying her by the time they arrived, stumbling and staggering through the rain.

Lydia felt a surge of relief when she saw the dim light filtering through a shuttered window. She had been afraid to contemplate the possibility that he might not be there, and there would have been no place else for them to turn.

Of course, they still did not know what kind of welcome to expect, but though she would never have said so to her mother, she could not help being glad that, if they had to flee, circumstances had forced them to come here. It was as if heaven were granting the secret wish that she had made, that the Scotsman would somehow take notice of her, instead of ignoring her as he had done before.

He'll see now that I'm no child, she thought, without at all considering the full import of the idea.

"You wait here," she said, guiding her mother to the shelter of a gateway. "I'll be right back."

She was grateful that her mother was too weak to argue. She was sure it would only alarm Mr. MacNair to find a sick woman on his doorstep, without a moment to be prepared for the event. And if it crossed her mind that this way she would have a moment or two of his undivided attention, she steadfastly refused to recognize that thought as she ran up the path and tapped, rather timidly, at his door.

To her surprise the door swung open almost at once upon what she thought at first to be an empty room, before she realized that whoever had opened it had stepped behind it as he did so. As a result, neither of them could, for the moment, see the other.

"About time you got here," a masculine voice said from behind the door. "Get inside, before I get my death of pneumonia."

Speechless, Lydia stepped obediently into the house. As the door started to swing shut after her, the male voice added, "And get those clothes off right quick. I've had my fill of waiting."

Lydia gave a horrified gasp and whirled about.

"Damnation," Peter MacNair swore, his mouth dropping open in astonishment.

His surprise, however, was nothing compared to Lydia's, for the closing of the door had revealed the handsome Scotsman behind it, and he was as naked as the day he was born!

CHAPTER THREE

Never in her life had Lydia seen a naked man, and the reality was far different from anything that she might have imagined. As if of their own accord, her eyes went to his loins and the turgid member thrusting out.

But however do they manage to conceal it in their trousers? she wondered, and at once went crimson, bringing her glance upward again.

"What the devil are you doing here?" he demanded, more angry than embarrassed.

"I—I've brought my mother," Lydia stammered, unable to meet his eyes either. "We need your help."

He sighed with exasperation. "Of all the—"

"Please, Mr. MacNair," she interrupted him, "would you... could you...." She fluttered a hand in the general direction of his midsection.

"Just a minute." He strode impatiently into the adjoining bedroom. "Did you say your mother's with you?" he called from in there.

"She's just outside. Please, may I bring her in?"

He barked a curt yes. Lydia hurried out, grateful for the cold rush of air on her burning cheeks. By the time she had brought her mother inside, Peter MacNair had donned a silk robe, not unlike the one Ke Loo had worn earlier.

"Good Lord, she looks half drowned," Peter said. "Here, put her on the couch." He helped guide Sarah to the couch. She collapsed upon it, barely conscious.

"It's not that," Lydia said, "It's the fever, cholera I think. I'm sorry to expose you to it this way."

He knelt by the couch, feeling Sarah's temperature and her pulse. "I've been exposed before. You can't travel in this blasted country and not run into it. What's this all about, anyway?"

She told him, as briefly as she could, of her father's death and their fear of the anti-white sentiment among the Chinese.

"You were right to worry about that," he said. "These people hate foreigners at the best of times, and when they get worked up like this, there's no telling what they might do."

"Aren't you afraid?" she asked.

"Of those yellow devils?" He gave a dry laugh. "Not likely. If any of them come here looking for trouble, they'd better have a taste for lead."

As if in response to his challenge, there was a knock at the door. Lydia jumped and gave a little squeal of fright

"Easy," he said, standing.

"Don't answer it, please," she whispered, clutching at his sleeve as he moved toward the door. "It may be Ke Loo."

"The mandarin?" He gave her a startled look. She nodded. "Wait here," he said. He shook off her hand and took up a gun from the table nearby, holding it down at his side as he opened the door.

Lydia could not see who was there, nor hear the brief whispered conversation. She remembered that he had been expecting someone else when she had arrived, probably one of the sing-song girls; she had seen them before, coming in and out of the house.

She blushed again, recalling too the sight of Peter MacNair when she had turned and seen him behind the door. She was certain that if she but closed her eyes she would see him again as clearly as before. Indeed, she was certain she could never see him again without also seeing that same image.

Apparently he had sent away whoever was outside, for he closed the door and turned back to the room.

"Now then," he said, coming back to her, "what's this about

Ke Loo? Why should he be looking for you?"

She told him the rest, watching his face grow grimmer as she spoke. "I'm truly sorry to barge in on you like this," she concluded, "but there was no one else to turn to. In my mother's condition...." Her voice trailed off. Peter's expression offered no encouragement.

"And now what?" he asked gruffly. "What the devil am I supposed to do with you?"

"I—I thought perhaps in a day or so this violence against the whites might settle down again."

"It probably will. But Ke Loo won't. I suppose you're something of a novelty to him. They don't see many white women this far into the interior, certainly none your age. And the Chinese marry very young girls. But I've had some dealings with that mandarin before, and I can tell you one thing, once he's got his mind set on something, he'll never quit till he has his way."

"But surely you'll be leaving here before too long."

"Tomorrow, with any luck, or the next day," he said.

"Couldn't you take us with you then?"

"You think Ke Loo won't be looking for you? He'll have spies watching all along the roads for you—and there's few things more conspicuous than a couple of American women in China. We wouldn't get fifty miles before you'd be spotted, and then it'd be my neck as well as yours. No, thank you. I told you, I'm not afraid of these devils, but I've got no desire to get my throat cut either, especially when it wouldn't do you a damn bit of good."

Lydia sank into a chair, tears beginning to roll down her cheeks. It was all more than she could bear, everything that had happened to her. And now the man that she had been so sure would help them was being utterly cold and unfeeling.

"Here, none of that," he said impatiently. She heard a rattle of china and a moment later he thrust something under her nose.

"Drink this," he ordered.

"Wh-what is it?"

"Rice wine. A bit of Scotch whisky would do better, but

this'll help some. Go on, drink it, it'll do you good. All in one swallow now."

She did as he said, emptying the little porcelain cup in one swallow. The wine had a peculiar, medicinal taste and it burned as it went down, but almost at once she could feel a warm glow radiating from her stomach.

"Thank you," she sniffled.

He turned wordlessly and went to stand at one of the shuttered windows, gazing out into the darkness. For a long moment the only sound was the patter of the rain outside. Then Sarah moved on the couch and moaned softly, bringing Lydia a renewed awareness of their plight.

"What are we going to do?" Lydia asked.

"I think you've got no choice but to spend the night here," he said. "Your mother's in no condition to go anywhere. You do realize that she...." He paused and did not finish what he had been going to say, though Lydia thought she knew: her mother was dying. The cholera was almost always fatal, and Mama had been so weak, from nursing Papa, and from worry. Already her face had that ghastly, fallen-in look.

"You'd better get her out of those wet clothes," Peter said. "I'll get her some blankets. Might as well leave her on the couch."

They made Sarah as comfortable as possible on the couch. Once or twice Peter found her staring at him, though he couldn't be sure, with her fever, whether she was even aware of what she was seeing.

"There's another robe in the bedroom there," he said to Lydia when they were finished. "You're pretty wet yourself, there's no sense in your getting a chill."

He watched her disappear into the bedroom. A mere child, and in a damnable fix. He'd spoken only today to Colonel Wu, who was in charge of the local military, and the colonel had warned him in the plainest terms that it was impossible for him to guarantee anyone's safety just now; his troops were exhausted and jittery from dealing with the cholera, and beginning as well to share the anti-white sentiment affecting the rest of the population. It was this conversation that had convinced MacNair to leave as soon as he could for the coast, where it would be safer.

But though he was confident of getting there on his own, being saddled with two women—or, more likely, one, since the mother looked as if she wouldn't last the night—would slow him down considerably. Worse, there wasn't a chance in hell of transporting even one of them undetected, and if Ke Loo was really determined to get his hands on the little one, he'd be madder than a wet hen. Mad enough, maybe, to have both their throats cut.

At the same time, he couldn't very well go and leave her here, on her own. Sooner or later the Chinese would get around to this house, if they were killing whites. He'd been literally buying time, paying outrageous bribes to those Chinese with whom he'd been in contact, but that couldn't last forever, and his supply of cash was running low.

He was startled by a feeble tugging at his sleeve, and he looked down to find Sarah trying to get his attention.

"You should sleep, Mrs. Holt," he started to say, but she shook her head impatiently and gestured for him to bend closer.

"You must—help my daughter, please," she whispered when he knelt by the couch.

"I'll do my best for both of you," he said.

She shook her head again. "No, don't mind about me, I shall be glad to join my husband—soon, I think—but I want my daughter to live—I beg you...." Her eyes closed, and her hand dropped from his sleeve.

* * * * * * *

It was a relief to be out of her wet clothes. Dressed in the silk robe, Lydia paused to look at the wall of his bedroom.

Some artist, perhaps centuries before, had done a painting on the wall. There was the branch of a plum tree, in full blossom, and a bird on the branch, singing, and there in the background the slightest curved rim of the moon, as if it had just wafted above the horizon. It was little more than a few deft strokes of the brush, in the manner of the Chinese artists, and yet it seemed to capture the scene in all its eloquence. She felt she had only to listen to hear the nightingale's song to the moon, and she almost fancied she could catch the fragrant scent of the pale blossoms.

It was all the more impressive because in every other respect the house, like most of those she had seen in China, was little more than a hovel, with its floor of hard-packed earth and its whitewashed walls.

She was so absorbed in contemplating the scene that she was not aware that Peter MacNair had walked into the room, until he spoke.

"It's lovely, isn't it," he said, coming to stand behind her. "I call it 'night song'."

"Who painted it, do you know?" she asked.

"And why did he paint it here, in this filthy shack, you mean? I'm afraid I don't have the answer to either question, but to me it seems to symbolize China, the beauty and the filth, the elegance and the shabbiness, all inseparable. They see no contradiction. A Scotchman, or an American, living in this hovel, would have put the same time to use building a fence, or an outbuilding, or clearing a field. A Chinaman would paint that, and consider the time well spent."

"You sound as if you love China," she said, surprised.

"I do," he said. "And despise her too. But I can never know her. No man can, least of all an outsider. She's a moonbeam clothed in veils, like one of those crystals that is clear one moment and clouded the next, you know not how."

His voice had gone husky, as if he spoke of a woman with whom he was passionately involved, and for the moment he seemed to have forgotten that she was there.

Of a sudden, Lydia was aware of his closeness, of the vibrant throb of his voice. His scent was in the room, the scent of pipe tobacco and whisky, and something else, too, that she knew instinctively was carnal, though she had never smelled it before.

She felt a strange warmth coursing through her veins, at once thrilling and frightening. It was like being sucked into a vortex, dreading it and yet being drawn irresistibly forward.

Her nerves atingle, she sought distraction, glancing quickly about the room. "And these," she said, picking up one of several jars atop the wooden dresser; she opened it and found it filled with rice powder. "Are these part of the mystery of China too, or is there some more prosaic reason for them?"

He laughed, breaking the spell that had fallen briefly upon them.

"Here, what do you think of this," he said, unscrewing another container and offering it to her. It was perfume. At first she could not quite place it, though it was familiar; then she knew. She had smelled it in the streets when the sedan chairs went by, carrying the singsong girls.

"They're cosmetics," she said, surprised.

"They're worth a fortune back in the States," he said. "American women are just getting interested in this sort of thing, though they're well behind their European cousins."

"Is this what you came to China for?"

"Partly. Though I had hopes of learning some of the Empress's secrets."

"The Dowager Empress? Are these her perfumes and lotions?"

"I'm afraid not," he sighed. "No one's allowed to use her personal blends except herself, nor even know the formulas. I spent weeks in Peking trying to bribe someone into bringing me samples, at least, with no success. These are only the ones used by the prost—professional women throughout the country, but at that they're very good. I'm taking them back as samples. I'll have chemists analyze them, imitate them, and the American women will snatch them up as fast as they're bottled. There's nothing even close to them available now."

She sniffed the perfume again. It was heady, smelling of lotus and the dark green shade of the bamboo forest. She could well believe that women would buy such a scent, if it could be duplicated.

"And the Empress's perfume, it's different from this?"

"There's a secret scent," he said. "I encountered it just once—a serving girl brought a scarf that had been dabbed lightly with it—it's intoxicating. No man could resist it, or the woman wearing it. It's one of the great perfumes, perhaps the greatest. And only one woman in the world wears it."

"But how did you come to be involved in this sort of thing?"

"My father was a chemist in Edinburgh. Among other things, he bottled a scent much favored by the local ladies. When I came to America, I worked for a time at a place where they made cosmetics. I saw how much money they were making for third-rate items. Then one night I had an encounter with a Chinese girl, and the scent she was wearing intrigued me. I asked her about it, and she told me it had come from China. She was unhappy because it was almost gone, and she said there was nothing in America to equal the lotions and powders and scents that were commonplace here. The more I thought about it, the more convinced I became that if I could obtain a variety of these creams and lotions, I could start my own company and make a fortune. I begged and borrowed what money I could and, well, here I am. Now all I've got to do is get back to San Francisco alive."

His last words brought home once again to Lydia the seriousness of her plight. Wearily she pushed her still damp hair back from her face.

"Sorry," he said, seeing the gesture. "Here I am rattling on about creams and scents and powders, and you must be exhausted."

"I'd better go see about Mama," she said, moving as if to go past him.

"She's all right," he said. "She was sleeping when I left her."

He hadn't meant to take her in his arms, but she looked so young and frail and helpless that he instinctively put out a hand. The next moment, without his knowing quite how it had happened, he was holding her to him, her head against his chest.

He felt the warmth of her tears as she began to cry again, noise-lessly.

"It's all right," he comforted her, holding her close.

"I'm so frightened," she said, her words muffled. "I don't want to die."

"I'll see that you don't, no matter what else," he said.

After a moment her tears stopped, but neither of them moved to end their embrace. For the first time, it dawned on him that perhaps she wasn't quite such a child as he had thought. Neither of them wore anything more than the thin silk robes, and through the sleek fabric he could feel the tips of her breasts burning into his chest.

Her breath quickened, and she tilted her face up to look into his. Her lashes were still damp with her recent tears, but already her eyes were smoldering with a desire that transcended fear and grief. The intensity of her passion startled him, at the same moment that it invoked a response in him. He pulled her tighter against him. Her lips parted, perhaps to speak, to protest even, but in the next instant, his had closed over them....

Lydia felt as if she were drowning. She had always thought the term "falling in love" rather a silly one, and yet, suddenly, she felt as if she were doing exactly that. Her knees buckled and if she had not been clinging to him she was sure she would have toppled to the floor. Even so, she had a feeling of sinking downward, swirling, all but swooning.

She seemed to have lost her senses to everything else about her, yet she was acutely aware of everything about him, of every point at which they touched. She could feel the hardness of his member, imprisoned between them, pressing against her belly; the memory of his naked splendor flashed suddenly across her consciousness, like lightning shattering the night, and suddenly it seemed as if all the secrets, all the mysteries, all the childish wonderings and puzzlements, had been made clear to her, and she knew—knew what was to be, and how it would happen, and knew that it would be wonderful.

So that's what it all meant, she thought, and laughed a silent, inward laugh to think what a fool she had been to be afraid, to dread the time when the experience would be hers. She had heard women speak in whispers of a wife's duty as if it were some onerous obligation to submit to a man's caresses, yet she had never known anything so splendid, so thrilling, as this moment.

Peter moaned, taking his mouth from hers and burying it in her hair. "God forgive me," he whispered, more to himself than to her.

Yes, she thought, *forgive us both,* for she knew that he was no more to blame than she was. From the moment of their first meeting she had wanted this, without even knowing what it was that she wanted. Some instinct had drawn her to him, her body longing for his body, for this suffocating sweetness that robbed her of her will. It was almost painful to feel the forbidden pleasure that swept over her.

She felt him tugging at her robe and she moved away from him slightly, letting it drop to the floor about her feet. Wantonly she kicked it away, and moved once more against him, to find that he had shed his robe too. Hotly she pressed naked flesh against naked flesh, whimpering with an almost delirious delight as his hand moved down her back, tracing the curve of her spine, outlining the fullness of her hips, her buttocks, then still lower. She parted her thighs slightly, and felt the last trace of her shame vanish as he touched her there.

At last he bent and swept her up into his arms. Not taking his mouth from hers, he carried her across the room and lowered her to the bed. Though he had carried her with ease, his breath sounded harsh and labored as he lowered himself beside her, and then they were again touching from head to toe. His tongue found its way into her mouth, searching, probing, even as his hands cupped and fondled her throbbing breasts. She moaned softly and writhed against him. How hard his body felt against hers, his manly chest, his muscled limbs—and that pulsating hardness that pressed now against her thighs.

He moved over her, parting her thighs, and she felt the first burning touch at the center of her passion, gentle at first, then probing, insistent....

Her body spasmed involuntarily as she felt a brief, stabbing pain, and she cried out, twisting as if to evade him, but his body held hers pinned to the bed, and the next instant she felt him within her.

What have I done? she thought in panic, the pain having brought her momentarily back to earth, but as he began to move within her a new wave of pleasure swept over her, and she forgot shame and pain and began to move with him, tentatively at first, awkwardly, and then with increasing urgency, panting and gasping now, even as he was. She needed...she wanted...but she did not know what drove them faster and faster, their bodies slapping noisily together.

She felt as if she were soaring upward under a great dark cloud that blotted everything from sight, aching sweetly, their bodies melted into one. Something was driving her, urging her on, something closer...closer...something....

The cloud suddenly exploded in a blinding sunburst of sensation. She seemed to have left the earth, to have surrendered everything to this unbearable ecstasy. She heard distant sobs and realized they were her own.

Slowly she drifted back to earth, becoming once more aware of him as someone separate from herself. He was still moving within her, his breath coming faster and faster. His body gave a violent spasm and he plunged deeply, gasping and shuddering.

She clung to him weakly, blissfully, grateful for the pleasure and the deep sense of relaxation he had given her, and then, almost at once, she was asleep.

Beside her, Peter MacNair lay for hours staring at the ceiling. He felt guilt and remorse for what he had done, notwithstanding the almost unbelievable pleasure she had given him. A mere girl, and he had taken advantage of her innocence and her grief. It was no excuse that she had been eager for the experience, or that he hadn't intended for that to happen until it had been too late to prevent it.

Worse, he couldn't even make amends in the manner that he knew she expected. It was hopeless that he could take her to safety in Shanghai. It was a journey of more than six hundred miles. Ke Loo would certainly be watching the roads, and in his anger he might kill both of them. The mandarin was not a man who liked having his wishes thwarted.

Even in the unlikely event that they were able to evade Ke Loo, there were plenty of other dangers just now. A man traveling alone might stand a chance, but traveling with a woman, a mere girl at that, was hopeless. If it was only a matter of risking his neck, he wouldn't hesitate. He'd risked it often enough in the past. But he didn't want the girl's life on his hands.

Like it or not, there was only one way to be sure of her safety. However much she dreaded and feared Ke Loo, at least she would be safe as his wife. No one would dare attack her then. Surely it was better to be alive in a Chinese palace than dead in a Chinese field?

Yes, he was convinced that for her own sake it would be best if she became Ke Loo's wife. The question was, how to convince her of that? How did one tell a sixteen-year-old American girl, whose father had just died and whose mother would die within a few hours, that she must marry a Chinese prince who terrified her, and live the rest of her life in a foreign land, as little more than a slave?

It was not the sort of problem that made for an easy night's sleep, he thought ruefully, watching the first grey light of dawn make its tentative advance across the ceiling.

CHAPTER FOUR

Lydia woke with a lingering smile on her face, though it quickly vanished as she recalled the events of the past few days.

Mama, she thought, scrambling out of bed. She felt guilty for having forgotten her in the arms of Peter MacNair, though she was grateful for the first good night's sleep she'd had in ages. Her cheeks reddened when she thought of Peter, who was nowhere to be seen. She knew that she should regret what had happened the night before, but how could she regret anything so splendid? How could she regret falling in love? For of that there was no doubt.

She ran into the adjoining room and stopped short, giving a little cry of alarm when she saw the figure of a Chinese peasant leaning over her mother. Was this some angry coolie come to murder them or perhaps an agent of Ke Loo who had traced them here?

The figure straightened and turned toward her, and she saw that it was an old woman, her face like yellowed parchment.

"Who are you?" Lydia demanded, first in English and then, seeing the woman's baffled expression, in Chinese.

"I am the nurse," she explained.

"The nurse—but I don't understand—"

"Gentleman come early, say mistress lady is ill. He pay, I take care."

Lydia felt a wave of relief, mixed with new gratitude. How kind her lover was, and how generous. He had risen early, while she still slept, and arranged for a nurse to care for Mama. Now, no doubt, he was making arrangements for their flight.

She blushed again as she thought of how she might repay him for all his efforts. In the meantime, she ought to do what she could to make ready. Perhaps she could even get some of their things from their house. It was possible that Ke-Loo had given up his search for them and gone on his way. It was her understanding that he had only been stopping here in the city, and that his actual home was farther to the north. He might even now be wending his way northward, with nothing but a memory of thwarted desire.

"How is she?" she asked, coming to the couch.

Sarah moaned just then, and the nurse wet a dirty rag and put it to her lips. "She very bad," she said matter-of-factly. "She will die soon."

"But she mustn't," Lydia cried. "You must keep her alive till we reach Shanghai. The doctors there will be able to help her, I know they will."

The woman gave her a peculiar look, but did not reply. For a moment Lydia stood watching helplessly as the nurse bathed her mother's face. A distant clatter in the street outside reminded her that it was already growing late. Peter would surely be back soon. She must have herself and her mother ready to go when he came.

Someone—Peter, or the nurse—had hung their wet clothes out to dry in the morning sunlight. Lydia brought them in and began to dress hurriedly. She was just finishing when she heard the sound of the front door, and Peter came in.

Her quick smile of greeting faded when she saw the grimness of his expression.

"What is it?" she asked. "Has something happened—oh!"

She saw that he was carrying a purple parasol, which he handed wordlessly to her. She recognized it at once; she had seen it only a few days before.

"It's Mrs. Blaise's," she said. "Does this mean...are they...?" She could not bring herself to say the word.

He nodded. "All three of them."

She shuddered, as though someone had walked over her grave. She thought of Reginald. In a way, he had been responsible for bringing her and Peter together, and now Reginald was dead, and his parents as well, and her own dear father.

"We must get away from this dreadful place," she said aloud, "while there's still time."

"Lydia, I want to talk to you," he said, taking her hand in his.

"Oh, darling, I love you," she cried, "but can't we talk when we're on the road? Will the nurse come with us?"

"Lydia," he said again, but he was interrupted by a commotion from outside, and the chatter of several voices.

"Someone's there," she said in a frightened whisper. "What are we to do? We must hide."

There was no time to hide, however, for a moment later the front door burst open, and Ke Loo came into the house, followed by his servants.

Lydia clapped a hand to her mouth to stifle her scream. She looked wide-eyed from the mandarin to Peter. To her horror, she saw that Peter was not in the least surprised to see the mandarin; his expression was one of infinite sadness.

"You?" she cried. "You brought him here?" Peter nodded.

"Lydia, I must talk to you," he said.

"But how could you? Last night—I thought that you loved me."

"My poor child," he said. "Don't you understand?"

"I understand that you've betrayed me to that—that yellow fiend," she said, pointing. Ke Loo stood just inside the door, smiling, his hands folded serenely in front of him.

"I went to see Colonel Wu first thing this morning," Peter said, speaking rapidly. "He told me that there was no way he could guarantee our safety. Then I went to Ke Loo. I even tried to buy our safety from him, I offered him all the cash I had left, with no success. Don't you know what that parasol means? Why do you think I brought it to you, why do you think he gave it to me? Ke Loo had those people stopped on the road, and killed, in a fit of anger because you'd eluded him. He'd already learned that you were here. He'd have had us killed too if we'd tried to leave. I've saved your life. This way there's no real danger."

"Not for you, at least," she said bitterly.

"I can understand your anger."

Tears threatened, but this time her anger was stronger than her grief, and she fought them back. "No," she said quickly, "No, you cannot. I hate you, Peter MacNair. I shall always hate you. I shall never cease to pray that you will suffer as I am suffering, at the hands of love."

"Lydia, don't, please, this is difficult enough. If, as you say, you loved me...."

She gave a shrill, hysterical laugh. "Yes, yes, I loved you, that was my curse. Well then, let it be yours as well. May you never be free of my love—and may it never cease to cause you pain!"

She did cry then, great heartrending sobs that shook her whole body, while the tears rushed down her cheeks. He put out a hand to comfort her, but she slapped it away.

"Don't touch me, you Judas," she cried.

He made no further move to touch her. For several moments they all waited while she cried into her hands. When her sobs grew somewhat quieter, Peter said, "The nurse will stay here with your mother."

"He can't mean to separate us," Lydia said, turning her red-rimmed eyes to him.

"But you must know that she's dying," he said brutally. "It's impossible for her to travel, and it can't be more than a matter of hours. I promise you, I won't leave myself until she's—until it's over."

"And I've no doubt Ke Loo has promised you safe passage to Shanghai, once you're no longer burdened with two unfortunate women."

"He's promised me that he at least won't try to stop my leaving, though that wasn't my chief concern. He's also agreed to take you to your former house, if you want to collect anything."

"What do you think I might need?" she asked, her voice dripping venom. "A shroud, perhaps?"

At least that made him wince. "Don't, I beg you," he said, averting his eyes.

Lydia turned from him, and catching sight of the couch on which her mother lay, she ran across the room and threw herself over her mother's body. Though she had never been as close to her as she had been to Papa, it was a bitter blow to lose her now as well. It was a cruel fate for her mother, to die with neither husband nor daughter at her side, in a foreign land, in this pitiful way.

Behind her, Ke Loo cleared his throat impatiently.

"I assured him that you would go willingly," Peter said. "It will be far more comfortable for you than being bound, which I'm afraid is the alternative."

She clung to her mother a moment longer. Then, feeling incredibly old, as old even as this ancient land in which she found herself a prisoner, she got slowly to her feet.

"I'm quite ready," she said, squaring her shoulders; she would not give them—especially Peter MacNair—the satisfaction of seeing her cowed and beaten. She was an American, the daughter of the Reverend Joshua Holt; and, notwithstanding her angry remark to her betrayer, she did not intend to die. She meant to survive, somehow, to live to escape. She would return to her own country some day, she swore it, because she had a purpose that would enable her to endure anything, no matter how dreadful.

She wanted revenge! She would never rest until she'd gotten that.

One of Ke Loo's servants brought out a coil of rope and spoke in an undertone to his master.

"Tell him we won't need that," she said, speaking to MacNair though she did not deign to look at him again. "It's not ropes, it's my trust in you that has made me a prisoner."

* * * * * * *

They set out almost at once. A luxurious chair had been

provided for her, borne by four peasants. At first there were two burly coolies who ran alongside the chair as well to prevent any attempted escape. For a short while Lydia sat dry-eyed, seething with anger and the need for revenge. But the chair rocked gently and in the curtained privacy, Lydia gave vent to her anguish, sobbing into the pillows until they were stained with her tears.

It was infamous! This couldn't be happening to her, not in the nineteenth century! Surely even in China there must be some form of authority. If Colonel Wu could do nothing, she'd beg someone else for help, she'd go to the Empress if necessary.

A fresh bout of sobbing assailed her. The Empress of China wasn't going to listen to a mere girl, even if she could get to her. Anyway, it was said that the Dragon Empress hated the foreign devils as much as her subjects did.

Hopeless. She must be a slave to that cruel and terrifying mandarin, to submit to his caresses, and all because she had been betrayed by that monster, Peter MacNair.

She swore aloud, momentarily forgetting her grief in her anger. Over and over she repeated her vow, that someday, somehow, she would see Peter MacNair suffer as she suffered.

At length her tears ran dry and her grief faded to a dull gloom. Despite the horror of her situation, she was only sixteen, and China fascinated her. She found herself becoming interested in her surroundings, watching through the curtains as the great panorama that was China paraded itself before her eyes.

The coolies, mere beasts of burden to those who employed them, jogged quickly along. The peasants stood thigh-deep in water, working their fields with tools as ancient as the land. A water buffalo regarded her cynically, as if sharing with her a grim view of their circumstances. Old women tottered along the road.

Though they paused twice to rest and to make a brief meal of cold rice, she only saw her captor at a distance. She began to wonder if perhaps she had misjudged his intentions. Chinese men frequently had more than one wife, she had heard, the others being called concubines. She had heard of one prince with so many concubines that many of them never did meet him, though they lived all their lives in his palace.

Perhaps that was what fate intended for her. MacNair had said that to Ke Loo she was a novelty; perhaps he had satisfied his curiosity in acquiring her and, that accomplished, had lost interest in her.

Night fell and still they jounced along. A coolie ran before her chair carrying a lantern, its pale light giving her glimpses of a banyan tree, a thicket of bamboo, or the water gleaming darkly in the rice fields.

At last they passed one of the memorial arches that the Chinese raise to honor a virtuous woman or an eminent scholar, and she knew that they were near a town. The coolies seemed to quicken their step. The road led uphill and through the city gates. The streets were crowded still and the bearers shouted for the crowds to make way.

She was weary from the aftermath of the shocks she had suffered and the long day's journey. They carried the chair into the courtyard of an inn and set it down.

She had never been inside a Chinese inn before, for when she had traveled inland with her parents, they had managed to find whites with whom to stay the night.

The courtyard was packed with people sitting at long tables, drinking tea or eating rice. Toward the rear, partially hidden in the shadows, two naked coolies were sluicing themselves with water.

She was taken to a chamber at the end of the yard, protected from the gaze of others by an elaborately carved screen. It was a large, windowless room with an open roof and a floor of trodden earth, its only furnishings a table with two wooden chairs and a pair of wooden pallets covered with filthy matting.

Notwithstanding its filth, she would have sunk wearily onto one of these had not Ke Loo's servant clucked and scolded, preventing her from doing so.

"You wait," he said, in almost his only English. He vanished, to return in a moment with a tied bundle. Untying it, he quickly replaced the dirty matting with clean taken from the bundle, and covered this in turn with silk cloths and pillows, until a luxurious bed had been made.

"Food," the servant said when she stretched out with a weary sigh upon the bed. "You wait."

"I'm too tired to eat anything," she said, closing her eyes. "Just let me sleep, please."

"You wait," he said, going out.

She was asleep almost at once, despite the chatter of voices from the courtyard and the other rooms. In her dreams she was back again in Kansas. She had not been there since she was a child, and it was with a thrill of recognition that she saw again those great, broad plains, stretching as far as the eye could see, and the breeze making rippling waves on the surface of the ripening wheat. The wind soughing through the apple orchard, the scent of fresh-baked bread, lying in the velvet softness of the fresh-sprung grass—how long ago and far away it seemed, as if this alien land had become reality for her, and that was the stuff of fairy tales. Once she had sat listening to her parents make plans, and dreamed dreams of ancient China, of the mysterious East, as now she lay and dreamed of home—a home she might never see again.

Even in her sleep, a single tear escaped her eyes and wound its way down one cheek.

She was awakened by a sharply spoken command. She blinked, and saw Ke Loo standing by the bed. He had shed his embroidered robe and wore black trousers and a matching tunic, and in the dim light of the single lamp his eyes seemed to gleam with a light all their own.

He grinned, and in his grin Lydia saw the end to her last hope, that he might not desire her physically. He motioned for her to remove her clothing.

"Please," she begged, hoping against hope. "I—I'm so tired...."

For an answer he lifted one hand and she saw that he held a whip made of knotted ropes, such as she had sometimes seen used on criminals and slaves. He brought it down loudly upon the scarred surface of the table, the noise making her flinch.

His meaning was clear. Regardless of the lack of ceremony, she was for all intents and purposes his wife now, and the wife's role was to serve her husband. To refuse to do so would be to invite a beating, and far from being shocked, the others in the inn would sympathize with him if they knew the reason for his actions.

Too frightened to do otherwise, she got hastily to her feet and began to fumble with the fastenings of her gown, her fingers numb and clumsy.

As she undressed, Ke Loo watched her with little-concealed lust. She would have liked at least to undress in privacy, but as she watched Ke Loo swished the knotted whip to and fro impatiently, and she was afraid to ask.

Her gown fell to the floor, leaving her in just her shift. Though it had been warm in the room, she now felt an icy cold.

"This too," he ordered, gesturing at her shift.

She obeyed his command numbly, her teeth beginning to chatter. Naked before him, she avoided his gaze. She felt sick with revulsion as she heard him shedding his own clothing.

She wanted to cry out in anguish when he came to her, his naked body bloated and leathery looking. He pushed her back upon the bed, pausing over her to stare down at her bare flesh. She dreaded what was to follow, and at the same time wished that he would get on with it, so that it could be the sooner finished.

A wave of nausea swept over her as he began to run his hands over her, probing, fondling. But would it ever be finished? She was his wife now, his slave, really. How could she ever hope to escape from him, from China?

I must escape from China, she thought at once. How else was she to have revenge on Peter MacNair?

The thought of him brought uninvited memories, in contrast to what was happening to her with this repulsive creature. She remembered the pounding of her pulse, the quickening of her breath when Peter had touched her, there in the same spot where rude hands now sported. Peter's hands had been so skilled, so demanding, and yet at the same time so gentle, urging her on to the heights of passion.

Sick with disgust she stared upward, seeing the starlit sky through the open roof. Fat, soft fingers crawled over her flesh like so many rapacious insects. She would never again know the pleasure that those long, slim fingers had given her, never feel his lips moving, burning a course over her breasts, touching each tingling nipple—how she hated him!

She nearly jumped when these other hands pawed greedily at her breasts, causing a pain she was almost grateful for; it distracted her attention from the horrible wet lips covering hers, the thick, hungry tongue forcing its way into her mouth. She was crushed beneath his weight and felt him forcing himself into her. She moaned in agony, and he laughed softly into her ear, mistaking the sound for one of pleasure.

"Little lotus flower," he called her. The name sickened her. How could he think she was enjoying this nightmare, when he knew that she had fled from him, that she feared and hated him, and had been forced into this position? It was the ultimate cruelty, to credit her with welcoming this merciless pounding as his fat beastly body rose and fell over her.

His hands went beneath her, clawing at the tender flesh of her buttocks, digging into her. She writhed in pain, thrashing to escape his scratching nails, but her movements only fueled his ardor.

"Yes, yes, that is right," he gasped, slobbering on her throat, his breath fetid in her nostrils.

I can't stand a moment more, she thought. *I shall be sick, I shall die.* She rolled from side to side, tossing her head to and fro. She was moaning repeatedly now, in agony and shame, but even her cries seemed to heighten his pleasure.

At last she could stand no more, and opened her mouth to scream, but once again he kissed her, stifling her cries. Finally she felt him stiffen, felt the pain of a powerful, final thrust, and he began to shudder and grunt in the throes of his ecstasy.

He seemed to lie upon her for an eternity before finally getting to his feet. She lay with her eyes closed, as pale as death, while he donned his clothes once more. She expected him to say something, or to come to bid her goodnight, but when the silence had grown peculiarly long she opened her eyes to find that he had dressed and gone.

She began to sob again, almost hysterically this time, muffling her sobs in one of the silken pillows. It was over—but tomorrow would be the same, and before her stretched a long, unbroken line of such tomorrows, for years, perhaps forever!

She cried herself into a stupor, and slept until the stirring in the inn roused her to the dawn, and marked the end of her wedding night.

CHAPTER FIVE

They traveled for more than six weeks, covering what she guessed to be twenty miles or so a day. The scenery grew monotonous, each day the same little rounded hills, the same bamboo groves, the same little farmhouses nestled in the hollows.

Each night was the same, too. Always there was the Chinese inn, one hardly distinguishable from the next, each night the silk-lined bed prepared for her, and then the visit from her husband, to sate his lust.

Repetition had dulled her senses, so that she no longer writhed in agony nor sobbed herself to sleep afterward, but lay passive and numb until he had finished. Once or twice her lack of response had angered him and he had gone so far as to swear at her in Chinese—she hadn't been sure of the words, but their intent was unmistakable. He had even threatened her with the rope whip, but the threat held no terror for her. He could cause her no more pain that way than what he inflicted upon her in his ardor. He could beat her to death, but that would only provide release from her misery.

It seemed as if their journey would never end. Then, soon after they had set out one morning, she became aware of a commotion in the train of bearers and the coolies began to shout to one another in a dialect that she couldn't understand.

Unexpectedly they came to a stop, though they had been traveling less than an hour, and the chair was set down. The sun had not yet penetrated the thick morning mists, and the countryside had an ethereal, otherworldly look. She stepped out from the chair, slowly realizing that they were speaking to her, watching her with excited expressions as if there were some great surprise in store for her. They were calling her attention to something, and she turned, following the direction of their pointing fingers—and gave a gasp of astonishment.

It seemed to rise from the very mist, awesome, frightening, incredibly majestic—the Great Wall of China.

Everything that she'd ever read or heard came rushing back to her—the greatest, the largest structure ever made; a million lives had been forfeit in its building; each stone was stained with bloody tears. It stretched in splendid solitude from the farthest reaches of Asia, up mountains and down dark valleys, as mysterious and terrible as the empire it protected.

She stood for a long time, staring in an awe that penetrated even through her misery. The coolies grew restless, and at length an order came from Ke Loo's chair, and they prepared to set out again.

It was only later in the day that she came to realize, from things she observed and overheard, that Ke Loo had himself arranged for her glimpse of the wall. He had taken them several days' journey out of their way in order that she might view the country's most spectacular sight. It was impossible to guess why. He might have wanted to impress upon her that China was not without her marvels, perhaps to ease her fears at being forced to make her home here.

Whatever his reasons, it gave her cause for reflection. However odious and repulsive Ke Loo might be to her, he was a man, and he was her husband, in deed if not in name. However real her dream of escape might be, it was still only a dream. She would be at Ke Loo's mercy for many years, dependent upon him for her every need—possibly forever. If she meant to escape at all, she must first survive, and in order to do that, she must somehow make the best of the situation.

When Ke Loo came to her room that night, he did not find her clothed, as was usually the case. Instead, she had undressed, and swathed herself in one of the silk cloths used to cover the bed, wrapping it round and round herself, like a sarong. Unlike her full-skirted, high-necked gown, this makeshift garment revealed as much as it concealed, her budding breasts standing out in elegant relief.

The mandarin paused in the middle of the room, staring first in surprise, then in pleasure. She was reclining on the bed, provocatively posed, and she waited, motionless, while he quickly shed his clothes. She was so nervous that her breath came hard, but she managed to smile at him for the first time ever.

He smiled in reply, and she saw his member rise up from the thick tangle of hair at his loins, growing with his delight.

She wanted to shut her eyes to the sight, to block the experience from her mind as she had learned to do in the preceding days, but she resisted the urge. She wanted to live, to survive; she could not do that without Ke Loo's support. She had no weapons, no strength to match his, no means to resist or escape him.

But she had her wiles, and with those, perhaps, she could conquer.

Perhaps she could even live to see Peter MacNair again, and have the satisfaction of seeing him suffer.

Ke Loo came to the bed, crouching over her, tearing hungrily at the cloth covering her body. To his amazement, she slapped at his hand. He stopped, glowering angrily, but his anger turned to bewilderment when he saw that she was smiling seductively at him.

She took his wrist and brought his hand to her breast, moving his hand upon it, but slowly, softly.

"Gently, my lord," she told him in his native tongue.

He smiled again, delighted at her new attitude. No Chinese woman would have dared to instruct a man in lovemaking, nor resist whatever he desired. He fondled her breast gently, as she had indicated.

She lifted her arms about his neck and parted her lips to welcome his. As she felt his weight upon her, she closed her mind to what was happening.

I will live, she thought, feeling his touch, newly tender, upon her thighs.

I will survive.

I will have my revenge.

* * * * * * *

While they were still on their journey, Lydia missed her monthly, and by the time they had arrived at their destination, she was certain that she was with child.

Her feelings were a mass of contradictions. Some motherly instinct within her filled her with joy at the thought of her own child, a darling baby to hold and cuddle. In the wake of losing her parents, she welcomed the hope of someone to love, someone who loved her in return.

But a half-Chinese child? Her feelings recoiled at the thought that Ke Loo was the child's father, and it made her sick in the pit of her stomach to think of the child being conceived with him on one of those nights in the dreadful inns.

A new idea occurred to her: what if Ke Loo weren't the father of the child? What if it were Peter MacNair?

Her immediate reaction was a feeling of relief that the baby would not be of mixed blood, but no sooner had that idea crossed her mind than she was filled with anger at the prospect that she might be carrying the child of the one man she hated most in all the world. She would rather die!

Of course, she really didn't want to die. She had survived so much already. And then she would think of eyes the color of sable, long-lashed and shining; what a lovely child she would be, the daughter of Peter MacNair; and little she would know of her father's perfidy.

Yet another thought sobered her: would Ke Loo welcome a child who looked like Peter MacNair? Surely not. And as for a daughter, she well knew they were not welcomed in China.

During the journey, they had stopped for a rest near a hillside covered with graves and, with her guards and the nurse following her, she had made her way up the hill to a stumpy little tower, cone-shaped and made of rough-hewn stone. It had struck her as quaint and picturesque, and she had thought it some sort of memorial.

There were a number of baskets strewn about on the ground, and on one side of the structure a rope extended from an opening. A sickening odor escaped from the opening, and in an instant she had realized the nauseating truth: it was a baby tower, and the rope was used to gently lower the babies into the deep pit beneath the tower.

It had left her shaken and ill. She was filled with horror at the thought of her child, her very own daughter, suffering so cruel and ignominious a fate.

A boy, then—she would pray for a son. And she must pray too that he was Ke Loo's son; else, his gender notwithstanding, he was little likely to escape the mandarin's displeasure.

No matter who the father, though, no matter what the color of his skin or the shape of his eyes, he would be hers, and she would love him.

And no one would take him from her.

* * * * * * *

It was with such thoughts as these that she arrived in Kalgan, Ke Loo's city. It lay not far from the Great Wall itself, on the route of the caravans that wound across the vast Gobi desert on their way to Peking.

Summer was waning, and the bleak Chinese winter would soon be upon them. The last straggling caravans, laden with goods of every imaginable sort, hurried southward, and soon the desert route would be closed until spring.

At the moment, however, the city was teeming, even by Chinese standards. Everywhere that they had been, Lydia had been an object of great curiosity, but nowhere more so than here. The amah whom Ke Loo had assigned to attend to her told her that no white woman had ever before ventured into this region of China. Here too, Ke Loo was a great lord, and as such great interest attached to his doings. The news that he had brought with him a foreign devil as a bride had somehow preceded them.

"I don't see how," Lydia complained. "We've only just gotten here ourselves, and they've no trains or telegraph, or anything like that."

"Men travel on foot," the amah replied, grinning at the girl's naiveté. "News travels on the wind."

Despite her predicament, Lydia could not help feeling a certain excitement at knowing she would be living in a palace. Like most Chinese palaces, Ke Loo's was in fact a series of separate buildings, joined by numerous gardens and courtyards, the whole contained within a high wall that afforded them quiet and privacy though they were actually in the very heart of the city.

She was to live in a little house of her own, surrounded by a garden with ornamental pools and almond trees. There were only two rooms, a sort of sitting-dining room, and a large bedroom.

"Evidently my lord expects me to do nothing but eat and sleep," Lydia said when she had explored her quarters.

The amah, who shared the house with her, giggled. She found her new charge shockingly outspoken. It was not a woman's place after all, to question such matters.

Lydia's facetious remark, however, proved closer to the mark then she had expected. Immediately upon their arrival, a brief wedding ceremony had been performed, making her Ke Loo's wife in fact as well as in deed, but she considered this of little consequence. What did that matter, in view of the fact that she was really a slave?

From the moment that her condition had been confirmed, however, the mandarin ceased his nocturnal visits to her, though he came every day and studied her briefly, as if weighing her in the balance.

"I wish for a son," he declared at the beginning.

"As if I had any choice in the matter," Lydia complained privately, but she too hoped for a son. She could not bear to think of what might happen if the child were a girl. It would be horrible to have a child for a few minutes, only to have it snatched from her arms and put to death.

At first it had been a great relief not to see Ke Loo except for a few minutes each day, and she was certainly grateful that he had foregone his nightly assaults on her. She reveled in her privacy.

She soon decided, however, that privacy could be a curse as well as a blessing, for excepting the amah and the women servants who came in and out to care for her needs, and who only giggled and averted their eyes when she tried to make conversation with them, she saw no one. Chinese women, especially wives of noblemen, lived in a purdah as complete as that of a princess in a Turkish harem.

Summer became winter, with scarcely a day of autumn, or so it seemed to Lydia. The last caravans had made their noisy way through and a relative serenity settled upon the isolated city. The winds blowing from the desert swept across the garden, leaving a fine sifting of sand on everything. The trees were barren, the earth had turned brown, and the ornamental pools lay as still and black as sheets of polished marble.

She was lonely and bored. She closed her mind to memories of her parents, and the life she had once known. She would not dwell upon such things, nor upon the repugnance she felt for the man who was now her husband. That way lay madness and she could not undo what had been done. She had made up her mind, lying with Ke Loo in one of those inns, that her only hope to survive, and to retain her sanity, was to take each day as it came. The yesterdays were gone, and tomorrow too far away to do her any good.

Still, she longed for conversation in her own language with her own kind of people. She would happily have worked in the palace, but she quickly learned that this was unheard of for the wife of a Chinese prince. The long nails that she had observed on aristocratic Chinese women, often covered with elaborate nail guards, were a visible symbol of their wealth and leisure, for anyone could see at a glance that they did not have to lift a hand in any sort of labor. For her to be seen at household work would cause Ke Loo to lose face, and to a Chinese, losing face was the worst thing that could happen.

"But what do these women do with their time?" Lydia demanded of the amah.

"Time is a luxury," the amah said.

"Well, I can't just sit all day contemplating the mountains," Lydia said, indicating the snow-capped range that could be seen from the garden.

The amah only smiled. She had concluded very quickly that the foreign woman was peculiar. They were, she had been told, a primitive people.

To fill her time, Lydia worked to improve her knowledge of the Chinese language, and even the amah was pleased at how quickly she learned.

Even this left her with time on her hands, however, and she often paced restlessly from one of the palace's many gardens to the next. At the amah's suggestion, she attempted to learn the intricate embroidery with which many of the women entertained themselves, but she soon found that she had no aptitude for such work, and she grew tired of constantly pricking her fingers.

It was while strolling through the gardens that Lydia one day came upon one of the servant women kneeling at a low table. She had spread before her an array of dishes and containers, and she was carefully measuring ingredients from one to another. She might have been preparing a recipe, except that she was far from the kitchen.

To Lydia's further puzzlement, the servant shook one of the rose bushes close at hand, sending a shower of petals to the ground; she then collected the fallen petals putting them into one of the containers. When she saw Lydia, however, she paused in her efforts and made a low obeisance.

"What are you making?" Lydia asked.

Smiling shyly, the woman handed her a small vial. Thinking she was to taste its contents, Lydia raised it to her lips, which earned her a startled look and a giggle.

"No, no, this," the woman said; taking the vial, she brought it to her nose and sniffed deeply, then handed it once again to Lydia.

It was perfume. Lydia was reminded at once of Peter MacNair and the cosmetics he had been collecting to take back to America with him. She knew that Chinese women used a great many such things; even the servant women here in the palace whitened their faces with powder. She had been curious, but this was the first time she had actually seen their manufacture.

She looked down at the table at which the woman was working and saw that various containers held a variety of such items. There was the white face powder, made, she had been told, from rice, and a satiny cream that smelled of almond blossoms, and yet another vial in which she could see flower petals floating.

"Will you teach me to make these?" she asked.

The servant giggled again, until she saw that the foreigner was indeed serious; properly chastened, she nodded in mute compliance.

* * * * * * *

Lydia was grateful at last to have a hobby to occupy her time, and one which would not cause Ke Loo to lose face, for the making of lotions and perfumes was one of the few pastimes practiced by women of the aristocratic class. It was an ancient art, and though there were certain basic procedures and ingredients, each woman had her own secret formulas, which were jealously guarded, and often handed down as treasures from mother to daughter. The royal perfume maker, she was told, was one of the most favored in the Empress's retinue, but one hapless maid had been put to death for merely mentioning the name of one of the secret ingredients.

As her pregnancy advanced, Lydia found herself more and more absorbed in creating her own special scents and creams. The gardens of the palace were filled with myriad blossoms, each of which could be used for a scent, or blended with others in infinite variations.

Her hours were now filled with the scents of almond and myrrh, lemon and tangerine, patchouli and sandalwood. With the first tentative approach of spring came new blossoms and new variations.

And with spring, too, came her child. The warm fragrant breezes of April were wafting through her little house when she felt the first of the pains.

"Send to my husband to say that my time has come," she directed the nurse, putting aside a perfume that she had been blending. "And then fetch the midwife."

For a brief moment she allowed herself the luxury of wishing for her mother. How comforting it would be to have her here now, to hold her hand and listen to her reassuring voice. It was the first time she had thought of her parents in weeks.

"I mustn't dwell on such things," she thought, stubbornly thrusting the thought from her.

* * * * * * *

Her labor was prolonged and severe. It was as if her child well knew what difficult circumstances awaited, and resisted being thrust into so harsh a world.

It was done at last. Lydia lay in a semi-stupor induced by some drug the midwife had given her, and heard the first angry cries. She opened her eyes, willing away the effects of the drug.

"Bring him to me," she said, struggling to lift her head from the pillow.

The midwife and the amah exchanged glances. Lydia's heart skipped a beat.

"What is it?" she asked, fear making her voice shrill. "Is something wrong with him?"

The amah bent over the bed to wipe her brow with a wet cloth. "You must rest," she said.

Lydia slapped her hand away. "No. I want to see my baby. Bring him to me."

The Chinese women looked at one another again. The amah nodded her head. The midwife wrapped the baby in cloth and came to the bed.

Lydia took the child in her arms, her eyes wide with fright as she looked him over. He was Chinese, that was her first thought, seeing the straight black hair, the slightly tilted eyes, squeezed shut now, the mouth wide with his cries.

"Why, there's nothing wrong with him at all," she said, breaking into a grin. "He's as sound as a dollar."

The amah bent and pulled open the cloth wrapping the baby. Lydia glanced down. His hands were balled into fists, his little legs were kicking furiously....

Her heart sank. "A girl," she said. She could hardly credit her eyes. She'd prayed so much, she'd been so certain. "It's a girl."

In the next moment she was overcome by a wave of shame. She had been so long with the Chinese that she had begun to think like them. As if it mattered to her! It was a baby, *her* baby, and she loved it.

As for Ke Loo, she'd make him see, it couldn't matter that much to him. After all, when the peasants put their daughters out to die, it was because they couldn't afford to feed and raise a girl, just to see her go off to work for someone else, but Ke Loo had no worries over money. He could afford a girl child just as well as a boy. She'd make him understand.

She wrapped the blanket around her daughter again, and hugged her close.

My daughter, she thought, *my own child.* For the first time since she had been betrayed by Peter MacNair, she felt joy in her heart, and was glad to be alive.

"I shall call you....," she said aloud, and paused. She had been about to call her Sarah, after her mother; but she couldn't, not a child fathered by Ke Loo, who had left her mother to die.

A gentle breeze brushed her cheek. "I shall call you April," she said, laughing with delight. "April, my child of the spring."

There was a noise in the garden, and Ke Loo came in. Lydia's joy faded as she saw his face; he knew already.

He barked a command and the amah fairly snatched the baby from Lydia's arms, rushing to take it to the father. Ke Loo threw the blanket to the floor, holding the infant up for his inspection.

He swore aloud and shoved the baby back at the amah. "Drown it," he said.

"No," Lydia cried, struggling up from her bed.

Ke Loo ignored her, signaling the amah to carry out his instructions. She started for the garden with the screaming baby.

Lydia staggered after her for a few steps but she was too weak to run, and even should she reach her, the amah had no choice but to obey Ke Loo.

"Stop it," Lydia cried. She looked around and saw the midwife's knife lying on a table near the bed. Without pausing to consider, she snatched it up and held it to her throat.

"Stop it, I say, or I'll kill myself!"

The amah stopped in her tracks, looking from Lydia to Ke Loo. The midwife gasped with horror.

"I mean it," Lydia said, speaking to her husband in Chinese. "If the baby dies, I shall die too."

She had no way of weighing the effect of her threat. Ke Loo had not visited her bed in months, because she was pregnant, and she had no way of knowing whether she was anything more than a novelty to him, whose appeal might already have faded. He glowered angrily at her. The knife point cut into the flesh of her trembling throat.

At last, with a dismissive gesture, Ke Loo swore aloud again. "Give her the child," he barked, turning on his heel and striding angrily from the room.

The Chinese women broke into excited chatter, laughing nervously as they discussed the marvel of a woman defying her husband's direct orders.

Lydia went to the amah and took her daughter in her arms. Almost at once April ceased her shrill screams.

"That's better, my darling," Lydia murmured, holding her close. "You need have no fears. Your mother will take care of everything, wait and see."

And she would take care of everything too, she vowed it. Before, the only thing she had had to live for had been her oath of revenge upon Peter MacNair. Now, however, she had something else that mattered, something that mattered more to her than anything else.

She had her daughter. And her daughter would not grow up a slave, a prisoner in a Chinese harem. She had defied Ke Loo to save the child. She would defy anyone, anything, to ensure her daughter's wellbeing.

"You shall be rich and beautiful," she murmured, touching her daughter's chin with the tip of one gentle finger. "You shall have everything your heart desires, the finest clothes, the finest jewels, the finest perfumes. Your mother swears it."

She strolled into the garden, averting her eyes from the pool in which April had nearly been drowned. Beyond the wall towered the great mountain range of northern China; and there, far, far to the east, lay America.

"Someday," she said, hugging the baby still closer, "somehow, I swear it, we shall go home."

"Home." She repeated the word in a whisper, and felt the sting of tears in her eyes.

Her own land, her own people, so very far away. It would soon be a year since she had been betrayed by Peter MacNair; already it was difficult to recall exactly her parents' faces. She ate and lived and spoke Chinese.

She must see that her daughter spoke English as well as Chinese. She must see that her beloved April grew up knowing who and what she was. It would not do for the child to feel like a foreigner when at last they reached America.

When. She would not say, "if." She would not even let herself

think "if."
    Always, it must be "when."

PART TWO

CHAPTER SIX

"Is this the Forbidden City, Mama?" April asked.

"In English, please, dear," Lydia said, smiling indulgently. "You know you're to speak in English whenever we're alone."

"The amah says English is the language of the foreign devils."

"English is our language," Lydia said emphatically. "And we are Americans, not foreign devils. We are not Chinese."

"Father is Chinese," April said, not so much arguing a point as stating a fact.

"Mother is not. And neither are you," Lydia said in a firm voice.

The bearers jostled the chair in which they were riding. "This is Peking," she answered the earlier question. "The Forbidden City is the name of the Empress's palace."

"And are we going to stay there?" April asked, reverting once more to Chinese.

"Let us hope so," Lydia said wearily, not noticing the change in language. "I can't bear to think of another night in a Chinese inn."

"I like them," April said.

"That's because you've never known what a proper hotel is. Or a proper city."

Outside the curtains, the streets of Peking were a riot of confusion. Peddlers shouted their wares: rice cakes, toys, sweets. Dancers and mimes, water bearers and puppeteers vied for attention and space in the winding roadway. A string of camels wound their way through the crowd, making a pair of carts collide with one another, the coolies cursing angrily.

Notwithstanding her mother's disdain, April was fascinated by it all. Though she was ten years old, she had scarcely been outside her father's palace before this journey; and now here they were, after weeks and weeks of trudging across the land, in Peking itself, the royal city. Any minute now they would actually enter the Tien An Men gate, the Gate of Heavenly Peace, that led to the Imperial Palace. Perhaps she would even meet Tz'u-Hsi, the Dragon Empress, herself—though that seemed unlikely if what Mama said was true, and they really were Americans instead of Chinese. It was said that the Empress hated all foreigners passionately, and spoke of one day ridding her country of them.

Unconsciously, April frowned. It was very difficult to understand. Not even her amah had made it clear to her how she and Mama could be American, when Li Ahn, her baby brother, was Chinese. Nor was there any question that he was Chinese, for the amah had told her that Li Ahn was a distant cousin to the Dowager Empress herself, and that could hardly be true otherwise.

It was for this reason that they had made the long journey to Peking, so that the Empress could meet this new cousin for herself. Of course, Li Ahn was traveling with his own amah, in the chair immediately behind their father's; he would hardly ride with the mere women. Indeed, in the year since he had been born, April had only been permitted to see her brother on one brief occasion, and then she had been, as usual, so terrified by her father's scowling face, she'd scarcely been able to look at the bawling infant before he had been whisked away back to the royal quarters where he lived.

There was a noise from the front of their procession, a beating of gongs and a blaring of trumpets, and Lydia knew that they were entering the gates of the Forbidden City, the Imperial Palace. Looking from between the curtains, she could see the rosy walls and the yellow tiled roofs. She wondered if the ruckus had frightened her son.

Her son; she smiled ruefully to herself. After nearly a year, she had seen little more of the child than April had. Almost from the moment of his birth he had been whisked away to a specially prepared house within the royal compound and given over to the care of a bevy of special nurses.

She supposed that it had been done in part because he was a boy and boy children were treated quite differently from girl children; and no doubt too it had been in part Ke Loo's determination to see that she did not corrupt the boy, as she had April, with foreign influences.

Still, though Lydia's heart had ached for her son, she was certainly glad to have given Ke Loo at last the son he had so coveted. All these years she had lived in dread that he might yet change his mind and take her daughter from her, to put her to death, or to sell her to one of the special houses where they trained young girls to be courtesans and mistresses to wealthy gentlemen.

Her fear had enabled her to welcome Ke Loo to her bed with an ardor that had surprised and delighted him, for she had been convinced that the only hope for her daughter's safety lay in presenting him with a son as soon as possible.

Fate had remained cruel to her, though, for her second child, the much longed-for son, had died within minutes of its birth, and twice after that she had suffered miscarriages in the early stages of her pregnancies. This last time, Ke Loo had ordered her to bed almost from the first.

She had been right in her supposition, however. Since the birth of Li Ahn, Ke Loo had lost interest in April. Indeed, content at last to have a son, he had apparently lost interest in Lydia herself. He had come to her bed only once in the past year, and that had been a desultory event. Though she was greatly relieved, Lydia had long since learned the importance to the Chinese of not losing face, and she had complained long and bitterly to the other women of the palace of her husband's neglect, all the while secretly hoping it would continue. Thus far, she had been lucky.

They had gone through the gate and were now within the fabled Forbidden City itself. Bronze lions guarded marble courtyards filled with dwarf trees and ornamental pools ringed with reeds. Here, as in Kalgan, the palace was in fact a number of individual buildings, some of them immense halls for ceremonial purposes, others tiny cottages in which lived the residents of the palace. The walls and pillars were of a dull red, the curved yellow roofs forming a billowing sea of gold. Rouged faces peered from the windows as their procession passed.

Indeed, except that everything here was multiplied many times over, Lydia soon felt that she might as well be back in Kalgan, for there was little difference in her life.

She and April and the amah had been installed in their own little house in the women's quarters. Li Ahn stayed near his father.

Servants and eunuchs rushed to see to their comfort, but no summons came from the Empress, nor from the Emperor, the youthful puppet in whose name she ruled. This was hardly surprising. They had been invited—commanded, she supposed, though it would be phrased as an invitation to save face—to Peking so that the Empress could look over Li Ahn.

No doubt that meant to determine if his appearance revealed his half-foreign parentage. Ke Loo was a distant cousin of the Empress, and though such a succession was highly improbable, Li Ahn was nonetheless a possible heir to the throne of China. The current Emperor, after all, had been only a nephew of the Dowager Empress.

Lydia had often wondered, as they wound their way across China, what the Empress would do if the boy looked American and not Chinese. Probably, she supposed, put him to death, and his mother and sister as well, rather than embarrass herself.

Lydia made up her mind to keep April close by her side while they were within the palace. She had not survived this long only to lose her life to some old woman's whim.

* * * * * * *

The days passed, however, without incident. Once an unfamiliar Chinese woman came into her apartment. Lydia had been attempting to read from a Chinese scroll, and looked up to find the woman standing just inside the door, staring at her.

"Hello," Lydia said, grateful for a friendly overture.

The woman did not reply, however; she continued to stare at her for a moment longer, as if appraising her. Then, without a word, she turned and left. Lydia puzzled over the peculiar visit for a minute or two, but she could find no explanation for it, or the woman's behavior, and she dismissed it from her mind.

Otherwise, she saw no one but her daughter and the servants. Not even Ke Loo had come to inspect their quarters.

Restless, without even her perfume-making to occupy her time, Lydia strolled one day into one of the gardens, when an uproar broke out nearby. There were shouts and screams, and the sound of breaking pottery.

Later, she learned that a coolie had been leading his diseased water buffalo through the street outside the palace when the beast, going quite mad, had bolted. He had knocked over several stalls, creating a disturbance, and had then fled from his pursuers, straight past the guards and through one of the side gates leading to the Forbidden City.

Frightened to follow, the coolie had stood helplessly outside, watching the beast break several ancient urns before heading for the women's quarters, scattering guards and eunuchs as he went.

Curious as to the cause of the commotion, Lydia went to see what was happening. She came into one of the courtyards at almost the same moment that the bull entered from the opposite end.

The women who had been sitting there, mostly concubines, jumped up, screaming, and attempted to flee; but these were women of the highest caste and their tiny bound feet did not lend themselves to running. As Lydia watched, one of the women fell headlong to the marble paving.

It was a horrible moment. The fallen woman lay directly in

the path the bull would follow on charging forward, and she would surely be crushed beneath those massive hooves.

For a moment the animal had paused in confusion, pawing the ground and tossing his head, searching for an escape from the men pursuing him. Without pausing to consider the danger to herself, Lydia rushed forward and snatched the woman up from the ground.

"Quickly, this way," she said, supporting her and helping her toward one of the little houses.

Catching sight of them, the buffalo snorted and dashed forward again, but by this time the two women had reached the house and dashed inside. In a moment the eunuchs had rushed into the courtyard and, almost as suddenly as it had begun, the incident was over, the bellowing beast being led away in ropes.

To Lydia's amazement, the woman she had rescued fell to her knees, clasping Lydia's hand and kissing it. "You have saved the life of Chan Cho," she said. "Chan Cho will be eternally in your debt."

"Please, it was nothing," Lydia assured her. "No, get up, you mustn't," she insisted when the woman continued to kiss her hand.

Chan Cho got to her feet. Even standing, she did not quite come to Lydia's shoulder, and her face when she turned it up was the face of a doll, of such delicate beauty that it almost took Lydia's breath away.

"How shall I repay you?" Chan Cho asked.

"If you must talk of repaying me," Lydia said with a smile, "let it be by becoming my friend, for I have none here."

Chan Cho smiled too, and the delicate mask became the face of a young and lovely girl. "I too would welcome a friend," she said. "You're the wife of Prince Ke Loo."

"You know me?"

Chan Cho giggled. "The only white woman in the palace," she said. "Everyone speaks of you since you come."

Lydia giggled too, at her own naiveté. She was probably the only white woman who had ever been inside the Forbidden

City. It was doubtful if anyone here was unaware of her presence. She marveled once again at the elaborate courtesy of the Chinese, so subtle that she had actually forgotten what a curiosity she must be to the people in the palace, many of whom did not venture outside the walls for years. It was odd to think that the compound that held the foreign legations—American, English, French and German—was within sight of the Imperial Palace, yet many of the women here had never set eyes on a white woman before she had come.

It was not until afterward that the amah, who was quite awed by the splendor of the palace, informed her that Chan Cho was a person of some note in the palace retinue.

"She is the chief concubine of the Emperor," the amah said, obviously impressed with Lydia's new friendship. "Other women in the palace fear her, for it is said that what she whispers into the Emperor's ear is heard by the Empress as well."

"Which would explain why she was so glad to have a friend," Lydia said. Her years in the palace at Kalgan had taught her that intrigues among the servants were unending. Rivalries, the struggle for favor and for influence, often produced lifelong enmities, and while everyone curried the favor of those whose influence could be useful, there was no telling who might be out of favor tomorrow. Real friendships were almost nonexistent, lest one be disgraced along with those one befriended.

If this were true in a minor palace in an insignificant city, it must be all the more so here in the Imperial Palace in Peking. One so close to the Emperor as Chan Cho must certainly be the object of intense jealousy and hatred, even among the sycophants who most loudly sang her praises.

The preeminence of Chan Cho in the palace was soon revealed. The very day after the incident with the runaway buffalo, Lydia received a summons from the Dragon Empress herself. The servants were all atwitter, and even Lydia could not help feeling apprehensive. Despite ten years as the wife of Ke Loo, she hadn't the faintest idea how one was expected to behave before the Dowager.

"You must kowtow so," the amah told her, prostrating herself on the floor.

April giggled at the sight and, immediately growing serious, asked, "Can I go too?"

"I don't think the old dragon would welcome an uninvited guest," Lydia said. "But never you mind, someday they may bow to us."

"When?" April asked.

"When we're rich and famous—and back in America."

"What's America like?"

Lydia hesitated a moment before answering. It had been so long since she had seen her native land that her own memories were blurred. She could not be certain now what she actually remembered from her childhood and what she had imagined. For the first time, it occurred to her that America would seem foreign to them when they returned. It was an unpleasant thought.

"It's very nice," she said flatly.

She was about to make her way to the meeting with the Empress when a messenger arrived with a small casket, a gift from Chan Cho. Inside was a single strand of grey pearls.

"They're exquisite," Lydia exclaimed, taking them from the box. The pearls were perfectly matched, and quite obviously worth a fortune.

"Chan Cho is the Pearl Concubine," the amah explained. "That is, the number one concubine."

Lydia fastened the pearls about her neck. She had chosen a mauve-colored kimono embroidered with lavender peonies so finely wrought that one could almost feel the dew upon their petals, and the pearls were the perfect complement.

She would have liked to wear yellow, the imperial color, in defiance of the old dragon who ruled China and hated foreigners; or better yet, her old bombazine, that she had been wearing when Peter MacNair had betrayed her so many years ago, but it had long since worn out. Even if she had saved it, it would no longer fit. She had grown taller, and shed the baby fat that had made her appear plump. Her breasts, that had so embarrassed her when they had first started to bud, were full now, but even after the rigors of childbirth, her waist was tiny.

"Oh, Mama, you look beautiful," April said, clapping her hands.

"Very pretty," the amah agreed, without meaning it. The foreign lady, in her opinion, was too tall and too voluptuous to be considered attractive by Chinese standards, and what Chinese woman had ever been born with hair the color of burning gold? There was no understanding men; a fine prince like Ke Loo could have had a proper Chinese wife, after all.

Studying her reflection in the looking glass, Lydia was thinking of her age. She was twenty-seven, and felt older. It was China, she thought, so ancient herself, that made her feel older. She had been sixteen when Ke Loo carried her off; her youth had been wasted in a Chinese palace. It was one more score she would have to settle one day with the man who had betrayed her.

This thought, as it always did, gave her the courage to face what awaited her.

"It will have to do," she said aloud.

She knew that it was important for her husband's sake that she make a good impression upon the Empress, and she had decided to visit him before she went to her appointment with the Empress, to set his mind at ease.

She had never been to his quarters before, though she knew which of the little square bungalows was his. It did not occur to her to have herself announced. Someone was singing as she approached, and the door was standing ajar.

Lydia stopped in the open doorway. Ke Loo was reclining on a divan while a Chinese woman played a lute and sang to him. Something about the woman gave her pause. It was a moment before she remembered: this was the woman who had come mysteriously to stare at her a few days before.

While she stood indecisively in the doorway, the song ended. For a moment Ke Loo remained in silence; then he rose and, bending over his companion, kissed her on the lips. The woman's arms lifted about his neck, and she returned the kiss hotly.

Lydia turned and ran lightly from the scene, grateful that they had remained unaware of her presence. She supposed that it was not at all surprising that her husband should have another woman. Theirs was a loveless marriage, after all, and since the birth of their son he rarely came to her bed, which suited her quite well.

Still, though she was hardly jealous, it could not but make her position more tenuous. What if Ke Loo should decide that he preferred this other woman?

Would he then set her free? It seemed unlikely. There were foreign diplomats close at hand here in Peking. Surely they would not take kindly to the story of an American girl taken against her will and held a virtual prisoner for eleven long years. It could make trouble for the Dragon Empress, and she had not fared well in quarrels with the hated foreigners.

But if Ke Loo no longer desired her, and he would not free her, what other alternatives were there?

* * * * * *

She was taken, not to the most important of the royal receiving rooms, but to the smaller hall in which the Empress received scholars and those who had placed highly in examinations.

When she was shown into the room in which the Dowager Empress waited, Lydia quite forgot herself and dropped a hasty curtsy instead of kowtowing, as she had been taught.

The Empress was a squat and dumpy-looking old lady, who reminded Lydia of old likenesses of Queen Victoria. Still, she was impressive. She wore a robe of mandarin yellow silk, the imperial color, profusely embroidered with her symbol, the phoenix. Her shining black hair had been knotted atop her head and she wore a sable hat encrusted with jewels. Her high, painted Manchu shoes were square.

Lydia lifted her face and found the old woman's ebony eyes

studying her intently. It was like a dash of cold water. It would be hard not to recognize the barely veiled hostility in those eyes. She was reminded that the Empress hated foreigners.

"We are told that you have saved the life of our beloved Chan Cho," the Empress said.

"That's putting it rather grandly, I'm afraid," Lydia said; she had bowed beforehand to show the proper humility expected of her, and thus make a good impression, but despite herself she felt her back stiffening in the face of this obvious disapproval. "It was really nothing."

She saw the Empress's glance go to the strand of grey pearls she was wearing, the gift from Chan Cho. Had Chan Cho committed a faux pas? The Empress looked ever so faintly envious.

"You are a maker of perfumes," the Empress said.

"I've only just begun to learn," Lydia replied. "I've brought this as a gift, though it is unworthy," she added, remembering Chinese manners. She produced a little jade bottle that contained her latest and, she thought, her best perfume.

A servant took the bottle from her and, at the Empress's command, opened it and held it for the Empress to smell. Her face remained expressionless, though Lydia had the impression that the Dragon Empress also found the scent unworthy. Without comment, she ordered the bottle stoppered again.

Consequently, Lydia was surprised when the Empress said, "We shall make you keeper of the royal perfumes."

"I—I'm honored, of course," Lydia said, curtsying again.

For a moment more the old woman's shrewd black eyes were fastened on her. Their unwavering gaze made Lydia uncomfortable. She felt that she had been weighed in the balance and found wanting.

The interview apparently was ended. The Empress barked a command and servants brought her chair, draped in the imperial yellow silk. She was assisted into it and borne out on the shoulders of nearly thirty eunuchs. Another eunuch led Lydia— on foot—back to her own quarters.

CHAPTER SEVEN

Though she had never ceased to find him repugnant, in the years since she had first become Ke Loo's bride, Lydia had gradually ceased to be afraid. No one in his palace would have dared to harm her, and in time it had become apparent that Ke Loo himself meant her no violence, so long as she remained obedient to his wishes. There had even been times, particularly after the birth of Li Ahn, when he had treated her kindly, and he had always been lavish in his gifts.

From the time that she had learned they were to travel to Peking, to the Forbidden City, however, Lydia had found herself uneasy about the physical safety of herself and her children.

The anti-white violence that had been sweeping the country all those years ago had died down, as her father had predicted, only to flare up again intermittently over the years.

It was now on the increase again. In Kalgan, in Ke Loo's palace, they would have had little to fear, but here in Peking they were at the very center of unrest. Nor did Ke Loo's protection count for as much here, for despite his royal connection, he was a rather minor figure in the palace.

The Empress's dislike for foreigners was well known and no doubt shared by many of the residents of the palace, who could be expected to follow her lead. Poison was a common means of disposing of enemies in China. It would be an easy matter for some resentful servant to slip something into their food. For that matter, the bungalows within the walls of the Forbidden City had no locks; anyone might steal into their rooms while they were sleeping. Two swift blows with a dagger would rid the palace of the "foreign devils."

That she had good reason to be afraid was quickly made evident. On the day following her interview with the Empress, Ke Loo came to see her, for the first time since the day of their arrival. She had been seated on a couch and she rose quickly to greet him, but before she could speak a word he struck her sharply across the face.

The blow, and her immediate anger, brought tears to her eyes. "I pray my husband will tell me in what way I have failed to please him," she said, her voice icy.

"Should I be pleased that you have displeased the Empress?" he demanded, his voice going shrill as it always did when he was angry.

"But that's not fair," Lydia cried, too angry to think of being docile. "I've done nothing to offend the old Buddha. She'd made up her mind to dislike me before she ever met me. I saw it in her eyes when I was presented to her. I can't be held accountable for her whims and prejudices."

"The whims of the Empress are the commands of her subjects," Ke Loo said. "You have brought shame on your husband and son."

It was foolish, and dangerous, she knew, to quarrel with her mandarin husband, but the unfairness of his charges was more than she could take calmly.

"What nonsense," she said hotly. "I can't help the color of my skin. Anyway, you knew how the Empress felt about foreigners, why did you bring me here in the first place? Or marry me at all, for that matter? I certainly wanted none of it. And I'll be only too happy to leave, any time I'm allowed to."

"You will not leave," Ke Loo fairly shouted, banging his fist down upon a teakwood table with such force that the porcelain vase standing there fell to the floor and shattered. He whirled about and strode angrily from the room.

His taunt seemed to reverberate through the room when he had gone. Of course, there had never been any question that she was his prisoner, lavish gifts or no lavish gifts.

His words seemed particularly ominous, however, here in the winter palace. She should have held her tongue, after all. If the Empress really had taken a dislike to her, and Ke Loo's anger certainly seemed to confirm that, then she and April most assuredly were in danger. Even if the Empress herself did not order any violence against her, who was to say that some zealous subject might not seek to gain the Empress's favor by disposing of her "enemies?"

Aside from treading cautiously, however, there was little that she could do. Even if a proper display of humility might change the Empress's feelings, and there was no guarantee of that, she was in no position to demand another audience. The Empress saw whom she liked and when it suited her.

The foreign legations were only a short distance away, but it might as well have been a hundred miles. It would be impossible for her and April to leave the palace undetected. Not only the outer gates, but even the inner gates of the palace were guarded. They would not reach the outer wall before Ke Loo had been informed, and she could well imagine his fury at that news. If she had only herself to think of it might be different, but there was April to consider.

For all its luxury and splendor, the Forbidden City was nothing more than a silk-lined prison, from which she could foresee no prospect of escape.

* * * * * * *

In her anxiety, Lydia had all but forgotten that the Empress had named her keeper of the royal perfumes. Chan Cho came for her in the morning, to take her to the place where the cosmetics were stored.

"Will I be allowed to mix the perfumes?" Lydia asked.

Chan Cho shook her head. "That is for the royal perfume maker only," she replied. "But you will learn to make the rest."

They had come to one of the smaller buildings to the rear of the Forbidden City. Inside the building was a miniature warehouse for cosmetics. Shelves held countless jars and bottles of every cream, lotion, pomade and unguent imaginable. In a second room, Lydia saw baskets of flower blossoms, along with vials and jars. This was where the cosmetics were manufactured.

"And these are all for the Empress alone?" Lydia asked.

"It is forbidden for any other to use," Chan Cho replied. "Only the Empress."

"Is this the royal perfume?" Lydia took a scent bottle from one of the shelves. She was remembering the story Peter MacNair had told her years ago, of a serving girl who brought him a scarf that had been scented with the royal perfume.

"Yes," Chan Cho said, her eyes wide with fright. "But every drop is measured. Do not...."

"I only want to smell it," Lydia assured her. She held the stopper to her nose.

MacNair had been right in this one thing, at least: the Empress's perfume was incomparable. It seemed to be blended of a thousand different scents, each touching some familiar chord, though she could not identify any of them. It was incense, and moonlight; it was the lotus, and the almond tree; it was the wind in the reeds that grew beside the pond. It was the very soul of China, and the essence of womanhood.

There was a footstep outside. Chan Cho snatched the bottle from her hand and hastily stoppered it, returning it to the shelf.

A servant came in, bearing a basket of roses, which she carried into the second room.

Lydia listened half-heartedly as Chan Cho explained to her the cataloging of the items stored on the shelves. There were creams to cleanse the skin, and creams to soften the skin, and still others which were said to make the lines disappear from the face; there were rice powders to whiten the face, and dark powders to add shadows to the brows, or about the eye itself; there were rouges, in every shade of red, for the cheeks and the lips.

All the while, as Chan Cho talked, Lydia's thoughts kept returning to the magnificent perfume that was worn by the Empress alone of all the women in the world. She could well believe that it would be worth a fortune to duplicate the formula, as Peter MacNair had once told her. Any woman would be willing to spend a lot of money for such a scent.

But one girl, according to the stories, had been put to death merely for mentioning to an outsider one of the ingredients in the perfume. Lydia had long since learned the Chinese penchant for exaggeration, to them a perfectly acceptable way to heighten the dramatic emphasis of a story, and it was possible that this story too had been dramatized.

Still, only the day before, along with most of the palace's residents, she had gone into one of the large courtyards to witness an execution. The Empress had watched without expression as one of her ministers had been beheaded for some act of thievery. The deed had been done with one stroke of an axe, wielded by a powerful eunuch, while the doves fluttered in the eaves, and the bystanders stood with nicely folded hands.

Under the circumstances, the royal perfume maker was hardly likely to reveal the secret formula.

Lydia did learn, however, to make almost everything else, including a number of other scents designated as "royal" perfumes, but worn by the other women of the palace. Even these, and all the various creams and lotions manufactured for the Empress and her ladies, were of the finest quality, and would be the envy of any Western woman.

The one forbidden scent continued to exercise a fascination for Lydia, however.

* * * * * * *

Lydia was surprised that night by a second visit from her husband, so soon after the last one. She was just preparing for bed when he arrived. His gait was a trifle unsteady, and she guessed that he had been drinking rather heavily, but at least he was in an amorous rather than a violent mood.

April was already asleep behind the screen that separated their sleeping areas. Thinking that she would be safer in her husband's good graces than out of them, Lydia made a pretense of welcoming him to her bed.

It was a pretense she had perfected for her own, and later for her daughter's safety, but it had never ceased to be an ordeal for her. In fairness to Ke Loo, she had come to see that he had many qualities that she could respect. He was a man of strong will and determination and so long as his wishes were obeyed, he was kind and generous. By Chinese standards, he could be called lenient toward his wife. He had even, at her coaching, learned gentleness in his lovemaking.

This night, however, there was nothing gentle about him. She clenched her teeth and credited it to lingering displeasure with her. No doubt he was using sex as a means of punishing her.

She submitted appropriately, though she would not give him the satisfaction of crying out, neither in pain nor in pleasure.

It was thankfully brief. His body pummeled hers for only a short time before she felt the familiar arching of his back and the stiffening of his limbs that announced his finish.

When he was done, he lay for a few moments holding her almost tenderly in his arms, as if reluctant to leave her. It was an unusual gesture for him, and she was on the verge of speaking to him when, with his more customary abruptness, he got up from bed. In another moment, he was gone.

She awakened in the morning to find that the amah who had come with them from Kalgan had been replaced.

"She is gone," was all the new amah, who was surly and unfriendly, would say.

"Did she just run away during the night?" Lydia asked.

"Gone," was the reply.

Lydia puzzled over the news. Perhaps the woman had grown homesick, and had left for home; yet she had shown no sign of such feelings. If anything, she had seemed thrilled and proud to be in the Forbidden City.

At any rate, she thought it her duty to inform her husband of the departure. The woman, after all, had been in his employ. She sent one of the servant women to ask if Ke Loo would spare a moment to see her upon an important matter.

The woman returned with downcast eyes and an alarming announcement.

"Prince Ke Loo is gone," she said.

"Gone?" Lydia's feeling of bewilderment was followed almost at once by one of dread. "I don't understand—what do you mean, gone?"

"Prince Ke Loo departed at dawn. He returns to his own city," the woman said.

"But—but that's impossible, he couldn't have gone, and left his wife and daughter...." Lydia checked herself.

Ke Loo cared nothing for his daughter, and he had long since lost interest in his wife. She had satisfied his requirements by providing him with a son. And there was already another woman who had caught his eye. Had she gone with him, to become his wife?

She thought of Ke Loo's visit the night before. In retrospect, it seemed a farewell visit. If Ke Loo had really returned home, leaving her behind, what was to become of her, and of April? The Dowager Empress would never set them free. They would remain as slaves here, until....

"Until we die," she thought, a cold shiver zigzagging its way down her spine.

Suddenly she seemed to see unfriendly faces everywhere. Of course, she had always been an outsider, and there had always been many who had looked askance at her, but this morning every pair of eyes seemed hostile. The new amah—had the old one returned to Kalgan with Ke Loo, or had she only been replaced because she might have felt some affection, some concern for her charges?

It was a different maid who brought their rice and tea for breakfast. She did not greet them with a bright smile, as the previous girl had done, but kept her eyes sullenly downcast.

Only once did she speak, and that was done so surreptitiously that Lydia was not altogether certain that she hadn't, in her anxiety, imagined it.

As the girl was bending down to set the tray on the table, she leaned close to Lydia. The amah was across the room, her back to them.

"Chan Cho say, eat nothing," the maid whispered.

Before Lydia could speak, or question her, the girl had left the tray and was gliding swiftly, silently from the room, past the amah, who cast a cold and searching look at her.

Lydia stared down at the exquisite bowls set upon the lacquered tray. Her fears had not been groundless, then, the foolish fancies of a frightened woman.

Chan Cho's message was clear enough: someone meant to poison them.

CHAPTER EIGHT

"Mama, I'm hungry."

"Hush, darling," Lydia said. "I'll find us something."

She went into the garden. Earlier, when the amah had gone out for a short while, Lydia had emptied their breakfast bowls behind the low bushes growing outside their window.

They could not go indefinitely, however, without something to eat. And even if they escaped poisoning, would not something else be tried?

Or had Chan Cho exaggerated the danger? Even if Ke Loo had gone without her, surely no one had reason to wish her dead.

As quickly as that thought had come, it vanished. There were many here, including the Empress herself, who hated her for being American.

She looked around. This garden contained nothing but ornamental plants, but in the neighboring courtyard was a plum tree, its branches heavy with fruit.

She made a bowl of the front of her tunic and filled it with plums. She was on her way back to their cottage when she realized that one of the palace's stray cats had found the food she had tossed into the shrubbery earlier.

"Scoot," she cried, running up and stamping her foot to chase the cat away.

She was too late. Even as the cat sidled gracefully away from the bushes, it dropped abruptly to the ground and began to writhe and gag.

Horror-struck, Lydia watched the hapless creature's death

throes, until it lay still, its eyes glassy, its mouth open in a final, pitiful plea.

Trembling with fear, Lydia hid the lifeless body behind the bushes. She shuddered at the necessity of touching the animal, but she could not leave it where it was, to be found and reveal its secret.

She came into the cottage, to see a kimono-clad figure bending over April.

"Oh, don't," she cried, dropping the precious plums on the floor and rushing forward.

It was Chan Cho, however, and not the amah, who was with April. Far from doing her harm, she had been offering her a tea cake neatly wrapped in a silk scarf.

"That is good," Chan Cho said, seeing the spilled plums. "And see, I have brought tea cakes. You did not eat breakfast?"

"No. Thank heaven for your warning," Lydia replied, taking one of the cakes and hungrily biting into it. After a moment, she asked. "But I don't understand. Why should someone want to kill us? And who, do you know?"

Chan Cho lowered her eyes. "Your husband has gone," she said.

"Yes, I know that."

"There is another who loves him. She wishes to be his wife."

"But there's nothing in Chinese law to prevent Ke Loo from having a second wife," Lydia said. "Or divorcing me, for that matter."

"There is no need to divorce dead wife," Chan Cho said matter-of-factly.

"But surely even here in China she can't just get away with murdering someone," Lydia cried.

Chan Cho shrugged; her meaning was clear. Who was there to object, or take action to prevent such a murder? Certainly not the Empress, who would probably consider herself well rid of the problem. And such murder was not, she knew, so reprehensible to the Chinese way of thinking as it would be to the Occidental.

Lydia sank wearily onto the couch. "What are we to do?" she asked.

"You must leave the palace," Chan Cho said.

"Yes, but...."

"Tonight. I will come for you at the midnight hour. Everything will be arranged. Until then, you must pretend to eat and sleep. You must act as in a play. I will come for you when all is dark and still."

"But what of my son?" Lydia asked. "What's to become of him?"

"The son is with his father, and so it must remain. Even if he were here, you could not take him. Ke Loo would never rest until he had his son back."

Lydia recognized the truth of what Chan Cho said. Ke Loo might consider himself well rid of a wife who had ceased to interest him, and a daughter who never had, but he would never relinquish his son.

"Chan Cho, I don't know how to repay you for what you're doing," Lydia said.

"You saved Chan Cho's life. Chan Cho pay for life, with life," she said.

Lydia started to say something more, but Chan Cho put a finger to her lips. There was a noise from the adjoining room, and a moment later the new amah came in, scowling.

Lydia turned to where Chan Cho had been, but she had already disappeared into the garden. Only a distant flutter of silk told which way she had gone.

* * * * * * *

The night had turned cold, and a wind from the north sent little swirls of dust dancing across the courtyards.

Lydia and April, dressed as Chinese peasants in clothes that Chan Cho had sent to them, huddled in the darkness, waiting for Chan Cho.

Lydia had wrapped the grey pearls in a small cloth, and

hidden that inside her tunic. It was all the fortune she had. Most of the gifts Ke Loo had given her over the years had remained behind, in Kalgan.

If only we had them now, Lydia thought. The pearls would no doubt be enough to buy their passage to America, to San Francisco, where her mother's brother had lived. But would she be able to find him, if he was even still alive? It had been so many years. And if not, how was she to provide for herself and her daughter? There was no one else to whom she could turn.

She thought of Peter MacNair, and at once dismissed the idea, angry with herself for even considering a man she hated with all her heart and soul.

Despite herself, he crept back into her thoughts. He had come to China for the purpose of making a fortune from scents and lotions; and he had assured her that those of the Empress were priceless.

"Wait here for Chan Cho," she whispered to April. "If anyone else comes, hide in the garden."

"Where are you going?" April asked, her voice tremulous.

Lydia planted a quick kiss on her forehead. "Don't be frightened," she said. "I'm going to find our fortune."

* * * * * * *

The gardens and courtyards of the Forbidden City lay swathed in ominous shadows. In the branches of the trees, the moon played a game of hide and seek.

Lydia made her way cautiously, fearful of arousing the sleeping inhabitants. She found the building she wanted, and used her key to open the door.

She dared not use a light inside, but she knew exactly where to find the bottle that contained the Empress' personal perfume. She had long been fascinated by it, and more than once had taken it down from the shelf to experience again the intoxicating scent.

She took, too, as many as she could of the various creams

and lotions. With them, she was certain she could find a way of financing her own cosmetics company. If Peter MacNair could make a fortune with what he had obtained in China, how much better might she do with these?

She turned to go, but a movement in the darkness made her squeal with fright. Another of the palace cats slipped past her feet and out the open door.

Lydia sighed with relief; she had nearly dropped the perfume. Her heart pounding, she too slipped out the open door and ran as fast as she could for her own house.

Chan Cho was already there, looking anxious. When she saw what Lydia had brought, her anxiety deepened.

"You mustn't take," she said, shaking her head. "Empress will be furious."

Lydia wrapped the precious cosmetics in a bundle. "She'll be furious anyway," she said. "And we'll need these far more than she. There, I'm ready now." She hoisted the bundle onto her shoulder.

Chan Cho's eyes were wide with fright, but she did not argue further. "Come," she said, leading the way.

Lydia followed, keeping April between them. She saw with dismay that they were going toward the gate that lay farthest away from the foreign legations. If they left by this gate, they would have to make their way clear around the walls of the Forbidden City before they could reach the walled compound of the legations.

"Can't we go the other way?" she asked in a whisper.

"This way. Come," was all Chan Cho said, again putting a finger to her lips.

After a time, she signaled for Lydia and April to wait in the shadows of an arch, while she went forward. A guard came out to challenge her. Lydia watched impatiently as the two conferred. At length the guard disappeared into the darkness, and Chan Cho motioned for them to come forward.

Lydia looked over her shoulder as they went, half expecting the guard to come forward to challenge them as well.

As if reading her thoughts, Chan Cho said, "The guard is a relative of mine."

They neared the outer gate. Once again Chan Cho motioned for them to wait, while she went forward to speak to the guard, and once again the guard conveniently disappeared.

Thank heaven for her many relatives, Lydia thought, hurrying forward with April's hand in her own.

The postern gate stood open and unguarded. They passed through it, and found themselves outside the Forbidden City. Lydia hugged her daughter, a laugh bubbling up in her throat. They had made it! They were free!

A harsh whisper from Chan Cho reminded her, however, that they were not yet safe, merely because they were outside the palace. The Empress's power stretched across the vast country of China, and even if she were glad to be rid of the two of them, she would be furious when she discovered what Lydia had taken with her.

As if to confirm that they were indeed not yet out of danger, she heard the sound of running footsteps in the street. The guards, she wondered, coming to capture them and return them to the palace? Had her theft already been discovered? She held April close, staring in the direction of the footsteps.

A coolie in ragged blue trousers ran toward them. Chan Cho stepped out to intercept him, and spoke briefly. He waited while she came back to where Lydia and April stood trembling.

"This is my cousin," Chan Cho said, indicating the coolie. "He will take you to the home of my aunt. You will be safe there."

"Your aunt? But can't we go to the American embassy," Lydia asked. "That would be safest of all. If he'll only take us to the legation compound, anyone there would take us in."

Even as she spoke, a commotion broke out in the distance, within the walls of the palace they had just quitted. Lydia saw lights flare in the distance, and heard shouting voices.

"Too late," Chan Cho said. "They find you gone."

Lydia stared in the direction of the uproar. How could anyone have found them gone, in the middle of the night? Unless—unless someone had come to their quarters; but there was only one reason for anyone to come at such an hour, in the darkness.

She shivered at the narrowness of their escape. The poison having failed, it had been planned to kill them while they slept. Had it not been for Chan Cho, they would be dead by now. *And might be soon anyway*, she thought frantically.

"Go with my cousin," Chan Cho said, pushing them in his direction.

"You must come with us," Lydia cried. "It won't be safe for you here."

"Chan Cho is safe," she insisted. "Go, quickly."

There was no time to argue. The coolie said something in a dialect she didn't understand, and turned to go, whether they followed him or not. Helplessly, Lydia ran after him, hurrying April along.

She looked back once, meaning to say goodbye, but Chan Cho had already disappeared. The walls of the Forbidden City loomed massive and threatening in the darkness.

"Run, run!" the coolie said, following his own advice.

They raced along the dark, winding streets, in and out of alleyways where she could scarcely distinguish his lithe figure before them. Her lungs burned with the unaccustomed exertion, and once April stumbled and fell to the ground.

"Wait," Lydia cried, stooping to help her to her feet.

"No wait," he called back, scarcely pausing. "Run, hurry!"

She lost all sense of direction. They seemed to run forever, through that dark, mysterious city, and always in the distance she heard the hue and cry that had erupted within the Palace, seeming to echo through her very being.

Ghostly footsteps pursued them in her terrified imagination, and at every turning she expected to find the guards of the Empress waiting to seize them and take them back.

"Mama...I'm tired...," April gasped, stumbling again.

Lydia did not waste breath this time on begging their distant guide to stop. She swept her daughter up in her arms and staggered forward. Her legs felt like leaden weights and her entire body ached. She ran a few yards, and fell against the corner of a building.

It was impossible. She could go no further. Yet if they lost their guide now, they were as good as done for. Two foreigners could hardly find their way through the city of Peking undetected, and there was little doubt that the Empress would scour the city for them.

It was over. She began to cry wearily, surrendering to the despair that had chased her through the torturous streets.

She gave a bleat of terror as a hand touched her shoulder, but it was only Chan Cho's cousin. He had come back for them, after all.

"Just here," he said, taking April from her and flinging the child unceremoniously across his shoulder like a bag of flour. "Hurry, run."

Somehow she found the strength to stumble on, weaving drunkenly. He went around a corner. She followed, and stopped in her tracks, her heart missing a beat.

He had vanished, with April!

Just when she would have screamed aloud, a shadow moved among the other shadows at her side, and she realized he had stepped into the open doorway there.

She stepped through as well, to be swallowed up in a darkness as total as death.

CHAPTER NINE

It was not until later that she came to realize that she had been brought to an opium den. She had heard of these since she had been in China, and her imagination had painted an exotic picture for her, a squalid room where the depraved victims beg for the drug that will give them release.

In fact, under other circumstances, this place might have been described as cheerful. It was homelike and cozy, and clean enough by the prevailing standards. A brightly lit room had been divided into cubicles in which the raised floor had been covered with matting to form a sort of couch.

Though she was not allowed into the den itself, the glimpses that she had into the room were likely to reveal an elderly gentleman reading his newspaper, his pipe by his side, or a group playing chess, while one dandled a baby.

A bead-curtained doorway at the rear led to a narrow hall, off which were the living quarters, but these were in stark contrast to the smoking quarters. Lydia and April were given a room no bigger than a good-sized closet, with a tiny window that opened onto an alleyway. They slept on pallets on the floor, and in the morning Chan Cho's aunt, Ah Wan, brought them cold rice and tea.

It was clear from the first that Ah Wan had not undertaken this dangerous responsibility voluntarily. She was surly and uncommunicative, with a broad face and enormous, masculine hands, and she overpowered her quiet-voiced husband, who seemed ever to be scurrying out of her way.

"You stay here," Ah Wan ordered, indicating their little room. "Must not be seen."

Lydia quickly began to fear that they had exchanged one prison for another, less luxurious one. The room was airless, and grew stifling hot as the day progressed. The only sanitary provisions were a cracked chamber pot, emptied all too infrequently by Ah Wan's husband, and a basin of river water in which to bathe their hands and faces.

Chan Cho had had no opportunity to explain what she had planned beyond this stage in their flight, and Ah Wan gruffly dismissed Lydia's questions on the matter.

There was nothing for it, Lydia thought morosely, but to endure their lot as best they could, and wait until they heard from Chan Cho. It was unthinkable for them to leave on their own, and there was no way for Lydia to know what was going on in the city outside their little room, whether the Empress was still searching for them, or whether Ke Loo had perhaps retraced his steps and was once again in Peking, looking for them also.

"We shall have to wait for Chan Cho," she said when April asked what they were going to do now. "She'll come for us when it's safe, I'm certain of it."

Chan Cho did not come, however. The day passed, and the next, and the next, and still there was no word.

Their room became more oppressive and Ah Wan more curt. Lydia watched the light and the dark follow one another past the little window and wondered if they had jumped from the frying pan into the fire.

At sundown on the fourth day, Ah Wan came to the door of their room.

"Come with me," she said, in a voice that brooked no argument. When April rose too, Ah Wan shook her head vigorously. "Daughter stay. Only you come."

Puzzled, but hopeful that some solution to their dilemma might be forthcoming, Lydia went along with her. Ah Wan led her down some back steps to the street, first giving her a coolie hat to wear. It was already growing dark, and with her head down, the hat would serve to conceal her Western features.

It was the first she had been outside since their flight and even the fetid Peking air smelled sweet and fresh this once. Ah Wan had given her no clue to their destination, and having already learned the futility of trying to obtain information from that source, Lydia followed silently along.

Their route was circuitous, probably to avoid any crowds. They met few passersby, and though each time her pulse quickened, she felt sure there was little likelihood of detection.

With a shock, she realized that Ah Wan had led her to the square outside the Forbidden City itself. When she caught sight of the great red walls, Lydia had a fleeting fear that Ah Wan had led her into a trap, but she as quickly realized that the square was momentarily empty but for a peddler hurrying homeward.

Ah Wan had come to a halt.

"Why have you brought me here?" Lydia asked, bewildered.

Ah Wan pointed. Lydia followed her finger, looking up at a corner of the wall, where a long pole had been set in the ground, with something atop it.

Recognition came in stages. At first she did not comprehend at all. Then, with a thrill of horror, she realized that the object atop the pole was a human head and, a moment later, that the face forever frozen in a grimace of agony and terror was Chan Cho's.

Lydia staggered backward as if she had been struck a blow, and her stomach gave a warning turn. Unable to help herself, she fell against a rough wall and retched violently, all the while aware of Ah Wan's disapproving glower.

At last the nausea passed, to be replaced by a keen-edged grief. The lovely Chan Cho, her only friend in the city, perhaps in the world, had been killed, most certainly for helping her to escape! It was barbarous beyond, belief.

A pair of coolies entered the square from a side street, chatting amiably. Ah Wan tugged at her sleeve.

"Come," she commanded.

Once again Lydia followed her blindly, this time only dimly aware of her surroundings. The night, which had seemed so sweet a few minutes before, had turned cold and frightening.

Lydia's thoughts were racing. Without Chan Cho's help, what was to become of her and April? Even if they could pass undetected through the streets of Peking, she had no idea of the route to take from Ah Wan's opium den to the compound of the foreign legations, without someone to guide them.

Would Ah Wan help her? Lydia stared at the broad figure ahead of her. She seemed to see in the square set of the shoulders and the firm planting of each step an intense dislike.

Few in China had any affection for foreigners, and Ah Wan was assuredly no exception. She had been willing to help them before, at Chan Cho's request, but her aid had clearly been reluctant. Chan Cho was dead now, and it was evident that Ah Wan held her accountable.

Once Ah Wan glanced back at her, and her dark eyes smoldered with resentment. Lydia shivered involuntarily. She had an urge to run away, to take her chances in the dark streets rather than return to that oppressive room that awaited her.

Of course, she could not run away without April. Quite possibly that was why Ah Wan had insisted that April stay behind. But surely if Ah Wan had meant to betray her, she could have done so easily at the Forbidden City. This thought gave her the only comfort she could take in her present circumstances.

As she had done since she had been betrayed into marriage to Ke Loo, Lydia forced herself to think of the present only. They were alive. That was something to be grateful for. And they were in Peking; in Kalgan she had been far distant from any other Westerners, and any hope of escape. Here, somewhere down these twisting streets, were people who would help her, if she could only reach them.

Reaching them, though, was another matter.

* * * * * * *

Back in the cramped room behind the opium den, Lydia listened to snatches of an argument between Ah Wan and her husband. Ah Wan was for putting them out at once, to fend for themselves. The husband argued that they had promised Chan Cho to look after the foreigners; and, he pointed out, the foreign woman had previously saved Chan Cho's life.

"Only to take it away from her again," Ah Wan reminded him.

Their son, whom Lydia now knew was the coolie who had met them at the palace and guided them here, joined in the discussion.

"Let us sell them to the Empress," he suggested. "It is said a reward will be paid."

Ominously, their voices dropped at this point, so that Lydia could not tell what the response was to this idea.

April stirred in her sleep, and instinctively Lydia put a comforting hand on her. Somehow, she would have to persuade them to let her stay, until she could find a safe way of reaching the foreign compound. She put her hand to her throat, and as she did so, her fingers touched the cool surface of a pearl.

Of course, the pearls that Chan Cho had given her. Once again Chan Cho had saved their lives, even though she had lost her own.

She slipped the pearls from her throat. Even in the dim light they looked lustrous and rare. Aside from the cosmetics she had stolen from the Empress, these were all she had of value. She had planned to sell them one at a time to meet their expenses until she had managed to make a living for them.

Making a living, however, would be moot if they were to die here.

She went into the room where the Chinese family was arguing. They stopped, staring in surprise and a palpable resentment when she came in.

"I want to stay here," she said, in their tongue. Ah Wan made a gesture of dismissal. "No, wait," Lydia added quickly, removing the pearls from her pocket. "I can pay for your trouble, with these."

The men jumped to their feet, their eyes wide. Even Ah Wan lost her hostility for a moment, coming forward to snatch the pearls greedily from Lydia's hand.

"Where did you get these?" she demanded.

"They were a gift, from...." Lydia paused. "From my husband," she lied. If they knew that the pearls came from Chan Cho, they might claim them anyway as their property.

Ah Wan's husband leaned forward to examine the pearls closer. He gave Lydia a look that might even have been tinged with respect.

"These pearls are very old," he said. "Very valuable."

"They—they're worth nothing to me if I lose my life," Lydia said. "I will give them to you, if you will let me stay here as long as is necessary."

Their son, the coolie, smiled a trifle too warmly at her. "That will not be necessary," he said. "I will arrange to accompany you to the legation compound."

Lydia met his gaze steadily. What he was suggesting, of course, was the best idea. Once at any of the legations, and she and April would be safe, but she had heard him speaking earlier of the dangers of trying to escort her there.

"That is the one place the Empress's spies will be watching," he had said, not ten minutes before. "Impossible to go there on foot."

Why, she wondered, had he suddenly changed his mind? His smile looked eager, friendly—but she knew that his feelings for her were anything but friendly. His eyes were inscrutable. And it was he who had suggested betraying them to the Empress for a reward.

"No, I don't think it's safe to try to go there just yet," she said finally. "We want to stay here. In return, the pearls are yours."

Ah Wan hesitated a moment longer; but the pearls were worth a fortune, even to the casual eye.

"Agreed," she said curtly, shoving the pearls into a pocket of her tunic as if they were a mere bauble.

Lydia went back to her pallet in the airless room where April slept, innocently unafraid.

She had bought their safety—for the present. Greed had given them a respite. But for how long? Ah Wan and her family were frightened and resentful, and the pearls were now theirs. When would they grow tired of their bargain, and begin to think once more of ridding themselves of their unwelcome guests?

She glanced at the little bundle in which she had wrapped the Empress's perfumes and the creams and lotions she had stolen. Perhaps if she hadn't taken them, the Empress would not be so adamant about finding and punishing them. And, for all she knew, it might have been for nothing.

Perhaps Peter MacNair had been wrong in his assessment of the worth of these items. Perhaps they were less valuable than he'd predicted.

Even if he had been right, that had been many years ago. Anyway, what did she know about such matters? Who was she, to think that she could make her own fortune, start a company, manage a business? A mere woman, who had lived her adult life the prisoner-wife of a Chinese prince. Even men, far more qualified than she in experience and disposition, often failed in such enterprises.

She threw herself wearily upon the pallet, assailed by fears so great as to verge upon despair.

CHAPTER TEN

As the days passed without event, Lydia found herself wondering more and more if she had made the right decision in remaining at Ah Wan's. Perhaps she should have risked walking into a trap. Certainly they were trapped where they were. She waited and watched, praying for some solution to present itself to her.

At last, just when she had begun to fear that their situation was hopeless, an answer came to her prayers.

"American."

"An American."

"The American is coming."

The whispers raced through the opium den like a March wind. No one came to tell Lydia and April, but Lydia heard two of the maids talking in the narrow corridor outside her room.

Braving Ah Wan's displeasure, for the little cubicles were filled and there was a danger that she might be seen, Lydia came into the hall, startling the two whispering maids.

"Wait," she said when they would have scurried away. "What American? Who's coming?"

"The American," one of them said, "From the legation."

"He comes two, maybe three time," the other said.

They did not wait for further questions, but hurried about their business—Ah Wan was a fierce taskmaster.

Lydia slipped back into her room, a barely suppressed excitement trembling within her. An American, here, perhaps within a few feet of where she was standing; and surely no American would refuse to help her.

But what kind of American would be coming here, to this place? Surely only a profligate would be visiting a Chinese opium den. Could she count on the help of such a man?

"What is it, mother?" April asked.

Lydia glanced at her daughter. In the weeks since they had come here, April had grown noticeably thin and her rosy-hued complexion had paled and grown sallow from the lack of sunlight and fresh air. Even her behavior had changed, for though she had always been quiet, she had been active and interested in everything, where now she was listless and disinterested.

It was this hard, critical look at her daughter that made up Lydia's mind. Any American, even a profligate one, would be better than the fear and hopelessness that were their companions here.

"Quickly," Lydia said, swooping up the bundle that held their few possessions. "Come with me."

"But Ah Wan will be angry," April said, surprised.

"To the devil with Ah Wan," Lydia said, shooing April along.

They went into the corridor. Through the curtain of beads they could see the large room with its numerous cubicles, and the Chinese men who occupied them, some sitting, some reclining. A cloud of smoke hung suspended over everything, like an indulgent observer. Attendants moved here and there, lighting pipes, serving tea. Ah Wan was nowhere to be seen.

Nor, Lydia observed morosely, was the American.

What if she had misunderstood, what if he did not arrive for some minutes? Ah Wan would soon discover what they were about, and would send them, by force if necessary, back to their room, would perhaps even lock them in it.

Holding tight to April's hand, Lydia pushed through the beads. Several of the Chinese looked in her direction. Some, those who had been smoking the opium pipes for some time, only smiled languorously. Others, however, were appropriately startled at the sight of a foreign woman in such a place. There was a stirring, emphasized by the lull in conversation rare in

Chinese gatherings.

Lydia ignored the curious looks. She made her way along the row of cubicles, glancing into each one. The inhabitants stared back at her, some with fear, some with open hostility.

He wasn't there. She went around the entire room, with no success; there was no one who could possibly be American.

Her heart sank. Had she somehow misunderstood? It was too late now to undo what she had done. Any number of people had already seen them; by the end of the day, it would be common knowledge that a foreign woman with a child had been seen here. It would not be long before the agents of the Empress came to investigate.

Tears welled up in her eyes. All of her efforts, all of the scheming and the running, the hopes and the terrors, had been for nothing. They were as doomed as if they had stayed in the palace and allowed themselves to be poisoned.

"Where are we going?" April asked, fidgeting under the increasingly unabashed staring of the Chinese, for whom they were objects of considerable curiosity.

Lydia was about to say, "Nowhere," when her eyes fell upon a beaded curtain that cut off a little room to one side.

In an instant she realized that an American coming here would want, above all else, privacy. He would hardly take his pipe in a cubicle surrounded by Chinese, who might very well rob him, or worse, while he was in a stupor. He would want a room to himself.

She started toward the curtained doorway, and knew that she was right when she saw Ah Wan emerge from the room.

"What are you doing?" Ah Wan demanded.

Lydia did not answer, but pushed past her, through the beaded curtain, shoving April in front of her. A man stood inside the room, his back to her. He was dressed in a Western-style suit, a trifle threadbare, and his once blond hair had faded to the color of old ivory.

He had heard the rustle of the beads, but did not turn. She realized he was in the process of taking off his necktie.

"Set it there, on the table," he said, "I can manage it for myself."

"Excuse me, please," Lydia said, in English.

He looked over his shoulder, surprised to hear that language in such a place. His eyes widened when he saw the two of them, and he turned slowly, the half-untied necktie forgotten, hanging at an awkward slant across his lapel.

"What the devil...?" He shook his head as if he thought they were a product of his dreams and might be so dispelled. "Who are you?"

"I'm Lydia Holt," she said, speaking quickly, as she could hear Ah Wan in the next room, shouting for her son and husband. "And this is my daughter. We're Americans. And we very badly need your help."

"Americans? But what are you doing here?" He looked completely bewildered, and she realized from the glazed look of his eyes that he had already had a pipe. He frowned, squinting, at first one and then the other. "Holt? I haven't heard of anyone by that name here in Peking, and I know everybody at the compound. Where do you come from?"

"From inside the palace. I—I'm afraid the Empress is looking for us."

Ah Wan and her men came into the room behind her, pausing as if to block the way. The American stared, trying to weigh the situation and what she had just told him. For a minute Lydia thought she had not penetrated the opium-induced fog in his mind.

"Right," he said suddenly, tightening the knot of his tie again. "I think we'd better go."

The Chinese still blocked their way. There was a tense moment in which it seemed they would not let them go. The American drew a wallet from his pocket and without counting pulled a handful of bills from it, shoving them into Ah Wan's hand. Reluctantly, she stepped aside, and then Lydia and April were being ushered through the other room, where the Chinese customers had abandoned all pretense and were watching events with avid interest.

"I want to thank you," Lydia started to say when they were on the stairs, but he cut her off.

"Save it," he said. "You won't be so thankful if we all get knives in our backs."

They reached the street. A chair was waiting, apparently for him, and without hesitation he shoved her and April into it, at the same time barking commands to the bearers. Another chair appeared as if by magic, and by the time Lydia's bearers had hoisted the first chair onto their shoulders, he was already clambering into the second.

Lydia sank back wearily into the pillows. The curtains protected them from the eyes of the passersby, and she had heard the American direct the bearers to take them as quickly as possible to the legation compound. A few minutes more, and they would be safe.

It occurred to her, for the first time, that she did not even know the name of their rescuer.

"Where are we going?" April asked again.

"Home," Lydia answered, fresh tears brimming in her eyes. "We're going home."

In the chair behind them, Jeremy Bates found himself wondering what on earth he had gotten himself into. Even on opium, he had realized the tension in the den they'd just left, and he had half expected those yellow devils to try to prevent their leaving, or even, as he'd so lightly suggested, to stab them in the back on their way out. He had heard rumors of a woman who'd escaped the palace, someone the old Dragon badly wanted to find, for some reason or another, but he hadn't heard, or grasped, that the woman was an American.

Where the devil had she come from, anyway? He'd been in Peking for the last two years—at least two years too long, in his opinion—and would soon be heading out, for Seattle, and home. He knew everyone in each of the foreign legations, and he had surely met every trader and missionary who'd passed through; after all, they all got to the legation sooner or later.

And he certainly hadn't met this—what had she said her name was, Laura, Leslie, something like that—he certainly hadn't met her before.

He wouldn't be likely to forget if he had. Not that flaming golden hair, nor those eyes that had in one glance cleared the cobwebs from his mind. By God, if she wasn't the most beautiful thing he'd ever seen! And of all the places to find her; talk about flowers blooming in dungheaps.

He was, and would have been the first to admit it, an unlikely candidate to rescue anyone, except perhaps from boredom, for he had an endless supply of chatter. It was his stock in trade, and his entree into many a party from which he might otherwise have been excluded. Westerners in Peking grew lonely and soon bored with one another's company. The right name and proper behavior still counted, of course, but even a seedy guest, whose morals were not all they should be, could be forgiven if he could be counted on to see that the conversation did not lag, nor grow too ponderous.

Peking had been a mistake for him, one of the more significant in a long string of mistakes that, all in all, summed up the course of his life. He had taken the post, sought it urgently, in the belief that it would take him away from his wife, never for a moment dreaming that she would insist on accompanying him. A woman in a wheelchair; who'd ever have thought she'd choose to traipse clear around the world, endure so much, when she could have been entirely comfortable in her mother's home in Seattle? And all for the sake of a husband who wasn't worth it.

Hadn't she herself pointed that out, time and time again, just in case his own appraisal hadn't revealed that truth to him? In that, at least, he knew that he could depend upon his wife's support for his beliefs.

It was hard now to think that he had ever been in love with her. He'd known from the first that he was beneath her station; it hadn't particularly embarrassed him to hear her say so. As to why she would want to marry him, well, he wasn't so much a fool that he thought he had much competition.

When you were in love with someone, a prominently under-slung jaw could manage to be attractive, but there was no use fooling oneself that anyone else would find it so. Cora had always had a stolid sort of personality. Coming as he did, from a large brood of charming ne'er-do-wells, he had found that a welcome change. He didn't mind in the least that others pronounced her a stick.

It would have been different if that grand old name she was so proud of had been combined with money. An heiress, even a plain one, always had a leg up on less fortunate girls. But a hundred little economies, managed with the smoothness of practice, had given him a pretty good idea of the lay of the land. Otherwise, he would probably not have pursued her as ardu-ously as he had, let alone gotten around to proposing marriage.

Well, he'd read somewhere that one of the worst things that could befall a man was to get what he thought he wanted. It had certainly proven true in his case.

At first, even her incessant nagging had seemed charming. It was really incredible how foolish a man in love could be. And even when his fondness for her ways had begun to pale, he had been content enough. The neighborhood saloon occupied rather more of his time, his home rather less, that was all.

Until the fight.

They'd really only had one, though it had occurred to him more than once that the one had never really ended. They were late, arriving at her parents. He was drunk. She was furious.

To this day, he had no idea why he had larruped up the horses just as she had risen to climb down from the buggy. An acci-dent, everyone else said. Poor Cora, her dress caught on the sidewall, dragged along the street for at least a hundred yards, her legs crushed beneath the wheels. Truly a tragic accident.

But he knew, and Cora knew, that for some drunken reason, he had cracked the whip over the horses at the exact moment she had risen.

Why? He had tried for weeks, months, to remember, and

through the years since to forget, with equal lack of success. She, at any rate, didn't want him to forget. She never ceased to remind him of it. It was the end of every quarrel, the point of every conversation. It was cruel, but he often thought that she felt for her affliction all the passion she had always denied him.

There was a shout in the street, jolting him from his grim reverie. He glanced out, and saw that they had entered through the compound gates. The British legation stood in a parkland of seven acres, and on the opposite side were the German and American legations. He had ordered the bearers to carry them to the American legation.

He thought again of the mysterious woman in the chair ahead of his. Something stirred within him, something he had not felt for so long that he could not recognize it, nor put a name to it. He had a sense of dread, of dark foreboding, and yet at the same time, that something else, could it be—was it possible...?

They had reached their destination, the chair was lowered with a jolt, and in the nick of time he was spared the burden of self-examination.

CHAPTER ELEVEN

Their arrival in the small diplomatic community created a sensation. It was a heady experience for Lydia, and she reveled in the sound of American voices speaking her own language. Though it had been more than ten years since her ordeal had begun, she found that manners and styles had not changed that much.

It was more difficult for April. Though Lydia had been adamant about teaching her English and explaining the difference in customs, this was still the girl's first exposure to the Western style of living. She had lived all her life in a Chinese household, and she felt every bit as foreign, Lydia realized, as Lydia herself had when she had first come to China as a girl not much older.

"Never mind, darling," Lydia assured her. "You'll soon get used to it."

Privately, April was not so certain. She had found the transition a jolt. The people, especially the women, were so pale, and their manners so rough, not at all like the elaborate courtesy of even the lower-class Chinese. Nor did she like the clothes. The Western-styled clothes, borrowed from the daughter of one of the French diplomats, that she was now obliged to wear struck her as particularly uncomfortable, with their tightly cinched waists and their voluminous skirts, under which she must wear countless petticoats. How much more comfortable were the simple trousers and tunics or the silk kimonos of the Chinese.

Perhaps most difficult of all had been learning to eat with

silverware. Her mother had often described this process to her, but as there had been no such utensils in the palaces in which they had lived, there had been no opportunity for her to experiment. It really was impossible—how was one to manage rice, after all, with only one fork instead of a pair of chopsticks?

And the meals! A proper Chinese dinner consisted of many different dishes, all served at once, from which the diner ate small quantities of everything. When she had sat down to her first Western meal and had found nothing but a bowl of soup before her, she concluded that this was a poor household indeed, if they could afford nothing more.

For her own part, she would far rather have stayed in the Forbidden City, or returned to Kalgan with her father, though she understood, without knowing the reasons, that this had been impossible.

Well, anyway, her mother was delighted, and for that she was glad. And she was willing, for her mother's sake, to make the effort to fit into this new lifestyle.

But it was an effort.

* * * * * * *

For Lydia, there had been only one really difficult moment.

Jeremy Bates had taken them directly to the American legation and had insisted, almost before there had been time to tell anyone her story, that she make application for a passport.

"These things can take time," he had pointed out. "You'll need papers, and the sooner you get them started, the better."

She met briefly with the American minister, Mr. Conger, who had seconded Bates's suggestion, and turned her over to a pale, sallow-faced clerk who had asked her dozens of questions: her parents' names, her place of birth, her age, and so on. But the most difficult part had been with her name.

"Holt," she answered promptly when the question had been asked.

The pen had paused briefly over the long, official-looking

form he was filling out.

"I'll need your married name," he said, avoiding her gaze.

Lydia felt a slow blush moving upward from her throat. Perhaps the clerk had already heard something of her story; in any event, by the next day it would surely be all through the small compound that she had been forcibly married to a Chinese, who had been April's father.

If she used her maiden name, it would be branding April a bastard. At the same time it was unthinkable that she adopt Ke Loo's name, not only because she despised him and wanted to forget her experiences in China. Though she had been away from her own people for many years, she had a fair idea of the prejudices that influenced their thinking. After all, she shared many of them.

A Chinese name would mark them.

Her hesitation was so lengthy that the clerk cleared his throat. Lydia's thoughts raced backyard. She thought for a moment of Peter MacNair, and though she hated him even more ardently than Ke Loo, she would have willingly used his name, except that it would not fit with the story she had already told.

It came to her out of the blue, just as she was thinking of Peter MacNair and that fateful night she had spent in his arms. The tawdry cottage, the rain-drenched night, and that exquisite painting that had covered one wall....

"Nightsong," she said aloud.

He was so surprised that he lifted his eyes to hers.

"I beg your pardon," he said.

"You asked my married name," she said, smiling trium-phantly. "It's Nightsong. Lydia Nightsong."

"That's a trifle unusual, isn't it?" The pen remained poised above the government form.

"That's the English translation," Lydia said. "And it's no more unusual than many others. I believe Mr. Conger addressed you as Blackstone, didn't he?"

The clerk lowered his eyes and scratched hastily on the paper.

Nightsong. Lydia turned the name over in her mind. Yes, it

was a trifle unusual, but that was all right. So was she, when you got down to it. It would be an easy name for people to remember, when she had made her mark.

* * * * * * *

A week after their arrival, Alice Conger, the minister's wife, threw a party in their honor. Lydia had already met many of the Corps Diplomatique, as they called themselves, and practically all of the wives, but it was exciting to be honored by them all at once. The Russian minister, de Giers, the Frenchman, Pichon, and the German, Baron Von Ketteler, had all complimented her on her bravery, and plied her with questions regarding the Dowager Empress and life within the Forbidden City.

"I'm afraid I saw very little that was really important," was Lydia's stock answer to such questions, "And I only met the Empress once, very briefly."

"Yes, but did she speak of the diplomatic corps at all, or mention any of our governments?" the Frenchman had insisted.

Lydia had shaken her head, smiling sweetly.

She was not really any more comfortable discussing the Forbidden City than she had been living in it. Though Mr. Conger had assured her that she was quite safe where she was, living in his house, she had not yet rid herself of her fear of the Empress's all-pervading influence.

It was hard to accept, having seen it firsthand, that there was any place in China where the Empress could not make her wishes felt. Even though the legation compound was occupied by foreigners, all of the servants were Chinese, as were many of the lesser clerks in the diplomatic offices. A certain Chinese prince, Prince Su, actually had a palace within the compound, and down the street was the Peking Hotel, popular for banquets and dinners.

Surely even here within the walls of the compound, among so many Chinese, however loyal the diplomats considered them, there must be some, perhaps many, who would be willing to carry out the commands of their empress.

Lydia had insisted that April share her bedroom, and she saw to it each night that their doors and windows were locked from within and her stolen hoard of cosmetics safe and untouched. Even so, the slightest sound during the night was enough to rouse her from sleep and leave her staring into the gloom warily for hours.

On this occasion, however, she had promised herself to banish all such thoughts. It was really hard to imagine that she was now approaching thirty, and this was her first grown-up party. She said as much to Claude MacDonald, the handsome Scotsman who was the British minister and her favorite among the diplomats.

"You'll find we have a lot of parties here," he replied, his waxed moustache bobbing. "The ladies are no doubt grateful to you for providing them another excuse, though it hardly seems that they need one. Still, it's a difficult sort of place for women. The entertainments help."

"Look what I've got," Lady MacDonald said, joining them. She was carrying one of the diminutive sleeve dogs, so called because at one time the mandarin princes had made a practice of carrying the animals in their wide sleeves. "Lady Camford brought it for me, as a gift."

"Are you going to eat it?" April asked.

There was a shocked silence. "I don't understand," Lady MacDonald said. "You can't mean, eat the dog?"

"The Chinese do," April answered, somewhat defensively. "It's a great delicacy."

Lady MacDonald's complexion took on a decidedly greenish hue. "How extraordinary," she said, looking down at the small animal in her arms.

"April will have to relearn many aspects of her life," Lydia said quickly. "If you'll excuse us, I think it's time now that she went to bed."

"But I only told the truth," April said as Lydia bustled her away.

"Yes, of course," Lydia said, "but I'm afraid, dear, you'll have to learn that what you know and I know to be the truth, does not necessarily have to be known by everyone else."

"I don't understand." They reached the hallway and came to a stop.

Lydia hesitated; she was not unaware of the difficulties her daughter faced in adjusting to an entirely different lifestyle. Even she had found it more difficult than she had expected.

"We'll be going to America soon," Lydia said, picking her words carefully. "We don't want to seem too different. People will think we're queer, and point fingers at us. We must learn not only to dress and act like Americans, we must *be* Americans— do you understand?"

"But isn't it more important to be yourself?"

"I—" Lydia put a hand to her temple. She had been about to say that she wasn't altogether sure what "herself" was. Was she that sixteen-year-old girl who had traveled the world with her missionary parents, with hardly a home of her own? Or the wife of Ke Loo, who had lived for a decade in a Chinese palace and who had indeed eaten roast dog at banquets? Or was she the woman who had begun to emerge in the last few days, who dressed and looked as neither of those others had looked, and who seemed a stranger to her?

She sighed aloud. "Well, I think this is the wrong time and the wrong place to consider such weighty subjects. Suffice it to say that Westerners do not eat dog, nor approve of its being done. Now, to bed with you. I'll look in on you in a little while."

April gave her a goodnight kiss and went obediently off to bed. Watching her go, it occurred to Lydia that though they might have fled the Forbidden City, and though they might soon return to America, it would be many years before they were truly able to escape China.

She turned to go back to the party, and found Jeremy Bates standing in the doorway, watching her.

"Your daughter's going to have a time of it, you know," he said.

"She's young, and she's bright," Lydia said. "In a year's time, perhaps two, she'll be a young American miss, and China will be only a distant memory."

"Did you find it so easy to forget the past?"

For a moment Lydia's smile turned hard, and there was a glint in her eyes that he thought actually looked dangerous. Not for the first time he found himself thinking that this was a woman of imperious will, who would not rest until she'd gotten whatever it was that she wanted. It was exhilarating, provocative even, and not a little frightening.

"I never forget," she said, in such a way that he knew it was no idle statement. "Never."

He offered her his arm to return to the festivities. "Then I can only hope that your memories of me will be pleasant ones," he said.

"Pleasant, and forever grateful," she said, taking the arm he'd offered. "You've been so very generous. It wasn't necessary, you know, to arrange for my dresses to be made."

"I felt certain you didn't want to continue wearing those Chinese outfits."

"And you've paid for everything since we've been here—it's no use pretending, Mrs. Conger told me so herself. She also let me understand that you're not a wealthy man."

"My wealth is no concern of Mrs. Conger's," he said sharply.

Realizing she had offended him, she gave his arm a squeeze. "Nevertheless, I am grateful," she said.

He stopped so abruptly that he gave her arm a jerk. "Gratitude can be damnably inadequate," he said.

She could not think what reply to make to that, and before she had come up with a suitable one, he had changed the subject.

"Your papers came just a little while ago."

"Our papers?"

Her delighted expression gave his heart a wrench. *If only her face would light up like that over me,* he thought. She would have looked like that at the lowliest clerk who'd happened to tell her the same thing.

"Yes," he said aloud. "It means you can leave any time you like—or at least any time there's a ship. Which is what I really wanted to talk to you about. The *Horizon* will set sail in a month from Hong Kong. I'll be sailing on her. I wondered if you'd like to book passage—the captain's an acquaintance."

"And we could sail with you—how wonderful," she said.

He blushed. "And my wife," he added hastily.

"Then we've all got something to be grateful for," his wife's voice said from nearby. "For a moment there I was afraid I was to be left behind."

Lydia jumped as though she'd been stung. Even though she knew she had done nothing wrong, she could not quite rid herself of a guilty expression as she turned to Cora Bates. She had only met the wheelchair-bound woman once before, and had perceived at once that Mrs. Bates didn't like her. No doubt she had some reason to disapprove of the attention and money that her husband was spending on another woman, but after all, Lydia thought, her guilt turning to resentment, they had done nothing untoward. She had seen Jeremy Bates only a few times since her rescue, and never privately; Cora Bates had nothing to fear.

Cora Bates, however, was afraid. She knew all too well that hungry look in her husband's eyes; knew, because it had once been turned upon her, though that had been long ago.

How like him, she thought bitterly, *to fall in love with a woman simply because she'd given him an opportunity to play hero. But if I'd been a prisoner in a Chinese opium den, he'd have no doubt run for his life.*

"Your husband was just telling me our papers have come through," Lydia said, determined, more for Jeremy's sake than her own, to be pleasant to his wife. "He's invited us to sail with the two of you on the *Horizon.*"

"So I heard." Cora attempted a smile. Her face, unused to the expression, resisted. "It's my understanding, however, that the cabins on the *Horizon* are already booked up."

"I was just explaining to Mrs. Nightsong that the captain is a friend of ours," Jeremy said in a strained voice.

"Of mine, actually," his wife said. "Captain Conners is an old friend of my family's."

"Who I'm sure, as a favor, will manage to find accommodations for Mrs. Nightsong and her daughter."

"I'm sure there'll be other ships," Lydia said, hoping to head off an argument.

"Don't be too certain," Jeremy said. "They're not as frequent as you'd think. But not to worry. If my wife's friend can't find cabins for you, you can take mine, and travel back with my wife, and I'll take the next ship."

"But we couldn't do that," Lydia protested.

Cora Bates glowered at her husband. She had come out to China with him because she had had an irrational fear that if he once left without her, she might never see him again. She had the same conviction now; her husband might leave China on the next ship, but it would not be to join her.

"I'll drop the captain a line," she said aloud. "These things can always be arranged."

Jeremy beamed. "And think how much fun it will be, making the trip back together."

It was late when Lydia went to look in on April. She was surprised, when she opened the bedroom door, to find the room dark; ordinarily they kept a lamp burning low.

Leaving the door ajar, she stepped into the room. As she did so, she became aware of the acrid smell of a just-extinguished lamp.

She came to an abrupt halt. At the exact same moment, something lunged at her out of the darkness. Her sudden stop, however, had caused her attacker to miscalculate. The light from the corridor glinted off the metal of a knife blade, but the blow that might have killed her sliced the air an inch or so beyond her face.

She screamed and threw herself to the side, colliding with a table there and sending it crashing with its contents to the floor. A moment later, she stepped on a broken dish, and fell to the floor herself.

She had a glimpse of her attacker—the familiar tunic and pants of the Chinese coolie were all she could make out in the pale light from the open doorway.

Then he was gone. Not until he had vanished into the corridor did she become aware of the approaching commotion, voices and running footsteps.

"In here, it's Mrs. Nightsong," someone shouted, and "Get a light."

Lydia sat up as a lamp flooded the room with light. Someone had kneeled beside her, and she felt a protective arm about her shoulders. She saw Jeremy Bates's face etched with concern.

"Are you all right?" he asked. Beyond him, she saw a circle of faces from the party, watching her with a mixture of confusion and alarm.

"Yes, yes, I'm fine—but April...?"

"Mama?" April's voice was quavery with fright. She was huddled under the covers on her bed, only her pale face visible.

"Darling, he didn't harm you?" Lydia rushed to seize her daughter in her arms. "I was afraid...."

"I hid under the covers," April said, clinging tightly to her mother's neck. "I thought it was you coming in, till he put out the lamp. That was just before you came in."

"He got away," one of the gentlemen said, returning from pursuit of the attacker. "Did anyone get hurt here?"

"Who was it, anyway?" someone asked. "What'd they want?"

"Some Chinaman, trying to see what he could steal."

Lydia, still comforting April, looked past her daughter and saw Jeremy Bates watching her. She saw that, like her, he did not accept robbery as the motive for the attack.

"You're sure you're all right now," he asked.

"Yes, I—I'm fine," she said, though she was still trembling. She was thinking what a close call they'd had. If she had come in a few minutes later, perhaps the assassin would already have killed April.

That it was an assassin she had little doubt, though she kept her thoughts to herself. This had almost certainly been someone sent from the palace, carrying out the wishes of the Empress.

This time he had failed; and never again while they were in China would she let April out of her sight, unprotected. No one in China would have such an opportunity again to strike at her child.

Would that be enough? What of later, when they were in San Francisco? She had heard that there were thousands of Chinese living in America, many of them still loyal to the homeland and to its Empress.

Would the tentacles of evil reach that far, even across the vast ocean that separated the two lands?

Would she ever be free of China, and the curse of the Dragon?

When she was alone, Lydia searched out the cosmetics and the royal perfume from their hiding place. She clutched them tightly to her bosom. Perhaps with these she could build the empire that would buy her the safety she needed, safety from the talons of the dreaded Empress.

CHAPTER TWELVE

As a girl, Lydia had sailed to China on one of the sleek, swift clipper ships, so called because of the way they clipped off the miles at sea. When they set sail from Hong Kong for San Francisco and Seattle, it was on one of the newer, square-rigged ships that, Jeremy informed her, were now replacing the clippers on the China trade.

"They're slower, but they carry more cargo," he explained, while they stood at the rail watching Hong Kong island slip below the horizon.

Lydia sighed. "Everything has changed," she said. "I'm afraid we'll feel like strangers in a strange land."

"What you need," Jeremy said, "is someone at your side, someone to take care of things."

"Someone like you?" she asked, smiling.

He blushed. "It would give me a great deal of pleasure to take care of you, Lydia."

She laid a hand on his. "Jeremy, we mustn't forget that you have a wife."

"My wife is a hopeless cripple."

"All the more reason," she said; seeing his glum look, she added, "Besides, you've already done so much for us."

"I've done nothing," he said petulantly.

"Nothing?" She gave a little laugh. "Our passage on this ship, the clothes on our backs, even the trunks they're packed in—I don't know how I shall ever repay you."

He looked directly at her then, his eyes seeking and holding hers. It was her turn to blush. Cora Bates would spend the journey confined to her suite, hindered by her infirmity from moving about the ship. No such infirmity hindered her husband, however; he was free to walk about at will, even along the corridor to the adjoining rooms he had managed to obtain for Lydia and April.

She was not so naive that she did not realize how badly he wanted to visit her cabin, nor for what purpose. And she supposed in fairness that she owed Jeremy the reward he desired. After all, without him they would not be here at all, and at any rate, he wanted nothing more than others had taken, with less right.

Still, she held back from committing herself, just as she now pried her gaze from his and looked down once more at the rolling waves beneath them. It was not only that she felt no such desire for him; she was fond of him, and grateful, and she had had much practice at pretending an eagerness she did not feel.

It was his wife. Cora might be confined to her cabin, but she managed to make her presence felt wherever they were. Even now, Lydia almost thought she could feel those dark, unfriendly eyes boring into her. So real was the sensation that she actually looked over her shoulder, to find not Cora but her friend, the captain's wife, staring at the two of them.

Watching them, for Cora? It was certainly not beyond the realm of possibility, and it emphasized once again for her that they were not free to do as they wished.

"Good afternoon, Mrs. Nightsong, Mr. Bates," Mrs. Conners greeted them, coming forward along the deck. "I hope I'm not intruding."

"Not at all," Jeremy said, "we were saying farewell to Hong Kong."

"Is she still in sight?" Mrs. Conners asked.

"Yes," Jeremy said; at the same moment, Lydia said "No." They laughed, a trifle uneasily. Mrs. Conners's face remained expressionless.

"Actually, we were discussing how much the world has changed in the last few years," Lydia said. "I'm afraid I shall feel like a newborn babe in San Francisco."

"I shouldn't worry too much," Mrs. Conners replied. "Some things never change at all, I'm afraid."

April interrupted them at that moment, returning from her exploration of the ship. Here, on an American-owned ship, Lydia had felt safe from any Chinese assailants. Jeremy had made inquiries for her before they had sailed; there were only two Chinese members of the crew, and both had been hands on the ship for several years.

"It's so big," April cried, running up. Until the last few days, her knowledge of sailing vessels had been limited to the junks that traveled up and down the rivers of China.

"Be careful you don't get lost," Lydia said.

"There's nothing to worry about," Mrs. Conners said. "My husband is aware of everything on his ship."

Lydia flashed her a sweet smile. "Then I shall rest more easily in my bed," she said, taking April's hand. "Come along, darling. I want to rest for a while before dinner. Good day, Mrs. Conners, Mr. Bates."

Though she was able on this one occasion to simply walk away, however, the problem of her relationship with Jeremy was not easily dismissed. The close confinement of the ship threw them together almost constantly, while Cora's condition effectively removed her from the scene. The trip from Hong Kong to San Francisco was more than six thousand miles, and they would be at sea nearly a month.

She had already observed that Jeremy drank heavily, and she could not forget that she had met him in an opium den. It puzzled her, because he did not impress her as a weak-willed man. She knew that his marriage was an unhappy one, but though an outsider might have assumed that he was in the habit of unburdening himself to her, in fact he scarcely ever spoke of his wife. Her presence between them was enough.

Indeed, Jeremy rarely spoke of his feelings at all. Once she commented upon the increase in his drinking since they had set sail.

"I drink to dull the keen edge of frustration," he replied sharply.

"Are you so unhappy?" she asked gently.

He fixed baleful eyes upon her. "It's enough that you know the reason for my unhappiness," he said. "Let us not discuss its depth."

* * * * * * *

There was a cocoon-like quality to life aboard ship. As the days passed and life in China fell gradually behind them, not yet replaced by life in America, Lydia felt as if she were drifting. It was deceptively pleasant to forget the hardships of the past and ignore the challenges yet to be faced.

In such a mood, it would have been easy to have surrendered to the desire that was ever present in Jeremy's eyes. It would cost her little, and give him so much happiness.

She could not forget other eyes, however, for it seemed to her that they were watched constantly. Mrs. Conners was both the captain's wife and a good friend of Cora's, while Cora's condition was such that it garnered instant sympathy among the other women aboard. Strolling about the deck with Jeremy, Lydia observed that the other women passengers frequently glanced sideways at them. Whispered conversations halted abruptly when they passed.

It was evident within a few days of their sailing that they had become an object of shipboard gossip, and not of the friendliest sort.

Until now she had been too much occupied with other matters to seek out casual friendships among the other ladies. She began to try to strike up conversations with those she met, only to have her advances snubbed.

It rankled to think that she should be blamed when she had done nothing wrong. After all, what had she done but save her own and her daughter's lives? She was not to blame if Jeremy had fallen in love with her. If any of them would only voice their suspicions to her directly, she would have gladly answered them—but what answer could one make to a veiled look?

* * * * * * *

They had been at sea a week when Jeremy failed to show up one evening at dinner. Lydia had not seen him the entire afternoon, and she began to worry.

After dinner, she started back to their cabin with April, but as they neared the suite that she knew to be occupied by Jeremy and his wife, Lydia found her footsteps slowing.

She knew that Jeremy's bedroom was separate from his wife's, though she had never been inside the suite. Supposing he were sick? She did not for a moment imagine that Cora's presence would be a comfort at such a time, and at any rate, the sea had been growing rougher, and she understood that Cora had taken to her bed.

Surely she owed it to Jeremy at least to inquire after him?

"You go along to the cabin," she told April. "I'll be there in a moment."

"Is Mr. Bates sick?" April asked. Her own feelings toward Jeremy Bates were even more ambivalent than her mother's, though they had never discussed the matter. She knew that it was Jeremy who had rescued them and made it possible for them to be making their present voyage. Still, there was something about the man that she didn't like. He had a way of looking at them, especially at her mother, which did not quite seem to fit with his words.

"That's what I want to find out," Lydia answered. "Go on, now."

She waited until she had seen April let herself into the small cabin adjoining her own before she tapped lightly at Jeremy's door. There was no answer, and when he did not respond to her second knock either, she tried the door.

It was unlocked. She opened it, and looked inside. The cabin was dark. The curtains had been drawn across the portholes, and the door that connected to his wife's sitting room, and thence to her bedroom, was securely closed.

The dim light, however, did not conceal an acrid scent with which she had become all too familiar not so long ago. Jeremy had been smoking opium.

She let herself into the room and closed the door behind her, lest some passerby recognize the odor as well. She thought that Jeremy was asleep on his bed, but when she came closer he spoke, the unexpected sound of his voice making her jump.

"I was thinking of you," he said.

"Then you might have let me know that you were all right," she said, coming to stand by the bed. "I've been worried about you."

"I'm glad to hear that," he said. After a moment, he said, "You know what I've been doing?"

"Yes." She could not give him her approval, but at the same time it did not seem her right to disapprove either. She made her voice noncommittal.

For a time he said nothing. She half suspected that he was dreaming his pipe dreams again, and wondered if she should go, when he said, "It's a most peculiar sensation. You feel the master of everything, time, space, the universe, only you've no desire to act upon it, it's enough only to *feel*, if you know what I mean."

"I'm not sure." She was sorry now that she had come in, but it was awkward to go. He was lying on the bed, and had made no attempt even to sit up. The chair was too distant to sit in when he was speaking in such a low voice, and she hardly wanted to sit on the bed beside him. She was left to stand, all the while acutely aware of the proximity of his wife. For all she knew, Cora might be just on the other side of that door behind her. What would she think if she came into her husband's bedroom and found Lydia there?

Suddenly he turned away from her and gave a low moan. It was such a pained sound that she immediately thought that she had been mistaken, and he was ill after all.

"Are you all right?" she asked. She put her hand on his forehead, feeling for a fever. His brow felt damp, but cool.

He caught her hand in his, clenching it so tightly that it made her wince.

"Don't you know how I'm suffering?" he said.

"Jeremy...."

"I must have you." He turned his head to look at her. His eyes in the gloom were wide, and filled with a pain so intense that it was all but palpable.

She was ashamed of the little thrill of vanity that it gave her, to be desired with such desperation. She had been so long the victim of others that it was a shock to realize that she too wielded power of a sort. At the same time, there was something else, something so faint that she scarcely recognized it for what it was—a feeling of scorn, of repugnance, almost, that anyone should be so enslaved by passion.

She made no move away when he freed her wrist. He began to fumble with the bodice of her dress.

"Your wife...."

"The door's bolted."

He bared her breasts, and knelt on the bed to bury his face in them, sucking at their tips with the fervor of a hungry baby. Lydia cradled his head in her hands, staring at the spot where his hair had thinned to show his scalp.

He began to paw at her skirt with such frenzy that she was afraid he would tear it.

"Wait," she said, freeing herself from him and standing to shed her gown.

"Don't leave me." His whisper was sibilant with urgency.

"Someday," she said, smiling ruefully into the gloom, "you may regret those words."

"No, never."

She came into his arms. She was inexplicably relieved that he had not undressed, but only tugged his trousers downward.

It was a shock to her to discover that, for all his wanting and waiting, the member pressing against her thigh was not hard at all, but flaccid. She lay in an embarrassed passivity while he fumbled between them.

"Christ Almighty," he swore, burying his face in her hair.

"Wait," she murmured, reaching down.

Though she had slept with Ke Loo scores of times over the years, she had never been called upon to play an active role in such matters. It seemed peculiar to her that, as familiar as she was with the ritual, this was the first time she had ever held a man's penis in her hand.

At first she did not know quite what to do, but her instincts served her well, and she soon felt him begin to stiffen. When at last he entered where he had so long desired to go, it was she who guided him. She felt peculiarly old, as though she, who had led the most sheltered of lives, was a woman of the world, and he an inexperienced youth. That allowed her to feel a merciful tenderness toward him.

She felt little else, however. On those occasions when she had relived in her memory that fateful night with Peter MacNair, it never ceased to amaze her to think with what passion, with what ecstasy, she had responded to him.

Not once in all those many times with Ke Loo had she felt even the slightest stirring of pleasure or passion. The initial pain and humiliation had eventually faded into a sort of numbness; there had been times when she had closed her mind to the act so completely that she had hardly been aware that it was happening.

Whatever feelings Peter MacNair had roused in her had long since died. She knew with certainty that she would never again be capable of responding to the act of lovemaking, or deriving any physical pleasure from it. Yet it did give her a sort of pleasure to repay in this one furtive, sweaty act Jeremy's kindness and generosity to her.

She clung to him, returning his kisses and arching her back as she had learned to do beneath her husband, meeting his thrusts. Having overcome his body's initial reluctance, he rode her now with a mindless abandon, their bellies making little slapping sounds as they came together. He murmured incessantly into her ear, jumbled phrases and silly, tender endearments.

He finished so abruptly that she was still moving beneath him when she suddenly realized he had reached his completion. He sank heavily upon her, kissing her neck and whispering over and over that he loved her.

It was at that unfortunate moment that she heard the creak of a door, and realized in a horrible flash of memory that the door from the corridor into Jeremy's cabin had been left unlocked. She stared in dismay over his shoulder, to see Mrs. Conners, the captain's wife, standing frozen in the doorway.

CHAPTER THIRTEEN

"Look, someone's taken our chairs."

Lydia, pausing in the doorway to the dining salon, looked and saw that April was correct: not only were their chairs missing, but their usual places for breakfast were not even set.

"Mrs. Nightsong." Lydia turned to see the dining steward approaching, his smile fixed, his eyes cool.

"There seems to be a slight problem," she said, uncomfortably aware of eyes turned in their direction, and a distinct lull in conversation.

"Yes. We've run into some difficulties." He hesitated briefly, his smile growing even more condescending. "A seating problem. The captain has asked if you would mind taking your meals in your cabin for the rest of the voyage?"

"In my...I don't understand. What sort of problem?"

"We've run a little short...." The steward gestured toward the empty places.

"But there were chairs enough before today," Lydia said, angry and hurt. "Why, there are chairs all about this ship, surely two could be found for us."

The steward sniffed, his smile vanishing. "I wouldn't know about that, I'm sure," he said. "If you'd like to speak to the captain when he comes in—or perhaps Mrs. Conners?"

Lydia glanced in Mrs. Conners's direction to find the woman's eyes fixed on her, gleaming in malicious triumph. Lydia felt her cheeks burn as she recalled the previous night's incident, when Mrs. Conners had discovered her with Jeremy.

"I came to inquire after your health," she had said, her voice frigid. "But your condition is all too apparent."

With that she had gone, leaving the two of them to wonder what action she would take.

"I doubt she'll tell my wife," Jeremy had said. "Cora's finding the voyage hard as it is. Her friends won't want to make her feel worse."

Lydia had been on the verge of snapping at him that that was little comfort to her, but she had held her tongue. Jeremy, after all, was not alone to blame. She had acted of her own free will.

Now, seeing that Jeremy was not in evidence, and Mrs. Conners and her friends looking so smug, Lydia decided that it was just as well to face the results of her actions.

"Mrs. Nightsong?" The steward was waiting, watching her with ill-concealed disfavor. "If you'd like to speak to Mrs. Conners...?"

"That won't be necessary," Lydia said curtly. "Come along, April."

"Shall I send breakfast to your cabin?" the steward asked as they started out.

"Yes, immediately," Lydia said without pausing.

When the breakfast had been delivered to the cabin, however, she found herself little able to eat it. The fault was not in the food, for as if to compensate them for the humiliation this was easily the most splendid breakfast they had been served since the ship set sail, and April ate with gusto.

Lydia, however, paced the cabin restlessly, only vaguely aware of the increased tossing of the ship as the sea grew steadily rougher. She was experiencing an inner storm to equal the one rising outside.

It was unfair, after all that she had suffered, that now, just when her life was at last on the mend, she should find herself embroiled in this ugly situation. She had lived in China as an oddity, an object of curiosity, disapproval and resentment. Through all those long, lonely years, she had dreamed of living once more among her own people, of being accepted, of establishing friendships with women like herself—and now, on a ship filled with the sort of Americans she had dreamed of getting to know, she found herself as much an object of scorn and derision as she had been before.

Perhaps, she thought bitterly, there were no women like herself; after all, who else had grown up as she had, who could possibly understand the experiences that had shaped and influenced her?

"Am I always to be an outsider?" she asked herself, and felt the sting of tears in her eyes as the probable answer came back to her.

* * * * * * *

She stayed to her cabin throughout the day; ordinarily, she would have allowed April at least to go out—surely Mrs. Conners and her friends had no quarrel with her—but as the day progressed, the bobbing and pitching of the ship grew so severe as to make negotiating the decks actually dangerous.

By lunchtime the question had become moot, as both of them had begun to feel queasy from the constant motion. Lunch, as bountiful and as wonderfully prepared as the breakfast had been, was brought to them promptly at noontime, but neither was able to eat more than a few bites.

Jeremy, Lydia noted resentfully, paid no visits. Lydia wondered if he were relieving his embarrassment by indulging in more opium; he might even be waiting for her to come to him as she had the day before.

It will be a long wait, she promised herself.

* * * * * * *

By dinner, she and April were both abed, and Lydia declined the elaborate spread that the captain sent them. The sky had grown dark long before its accustomed time, and the ship was now tossing so violently that it was an effort even to cross the room to tell the steward to take the dinner away.

"We've hit a squall," the steward informed her. "The captain has asked all passengers to stay in their quarters except in genuine necessity."

"Tell the captain I'll be only too happy to comply," she replied, clinging to the doorjamb.

She had fallen into an uneasy slumber when, an hour or so later, the ship rolled to its port side with such violence that it threatened to capsize. Lydia was thrown from her bed amid the crashing of innumerable objects being flung about.

"Mama," April called from the adjoining cabin.

Lydia fell against the wall as the ship, after what seemed an eternity, righted itself, only to pitch violently in the other direction.

"I'm all right," Lydia called back, shouting because the night was filled with a tumultuous uproar, screaming and shouting and breaking things. "Stay where you are."

She managed to get to her feet and, clinging to the cabin's fastened-down furnishings, made her way to April's cabin. She found April seated on the floor, clinging in fright to the railing of her bunk.

"Are we going to sink?" April asked, her eyes wide.

"Of course not," Lydia said, with a confidence she didn't feel. "Here, put this on." She gave April one of the life vests that were in each cabin for emergency. "If there's any real danger, the captain will warn us."

There was a pounding on the door of the other cabin. "Lydia," Jeremy called.

"In here," she called back, but the noise drowned out her voice.

"Lydia!"

He came in anyway. She heard him call her from the adjoining cabin, and a moment later he appeared in the doorway.

"You're all right, then," he said, seeing the two of them. "I was frightened when you didn't answer."

"Yes, we're all right for the moment. How bad is it, do you

think?" she asked.

"Just a squall," he said, swaying back and forth with the ship's movement. "The captain's asked all the men to give a hand till we weather it out. Just wanted to look in on you first."

Lydia had gotten to her feet, and now she saw that his eyes were dilated and his voice had a thick-muffled sound that she had come to recognize.

"Jeremy, you've been indulging your vice," she cried. "You mustn't go up on deck."

"Nonsense," he said, laughing. "With the captain calling for every available man, you think I'm going to cower in my cabin like a blasted pantywaist? I'm all right, I tell you."

"Jeremy...."

She caught at his arm, but he kissed her hotly and briefly, like a man going into battle, and before she could stop him, he was gone, giving a drunken whoop of laughter as the ship's roll sent him colliding into the wall.

She knew enough of the effects of opium to know that he was in far less than full control of himself; it was not only his balance, it was his judgment that was affected.

The captain must be told. In such a situation, Jeremy was a danger not only to himself but to the others on the ship, who might be suddenly dependent upon his actions for their lives.

"Stay here," she told her daughter. "Hold on to that railing here. I'll be right back."

There wasn't time to don a hat and coat; she flung one of the heavy woolen blankets over her as she ran through the cabin.

Jeremy, staggering as he ran, was just disappearing up the stairs that led to the main deck. Lydia called his name, but the noise here was even greater and her voice was lost in the uproar.

There were others running to and fro in the corridor, and several women were screaming hysterically. Lydia saw a steward and tugged at his sleeve, trying to explain, but he did not even listen.

"Back to your cabin, ma'am, please," he shouted, and was gone before she could get a word out.

She ran for the stairs. The door above was open, and a violent gust of wind threw sheets of water into her face, almost toppling her back down the stairs. Clinging tightly to the handrail, she pulled herself upward.

Nothing had prepared her for the condition of the deck. As she reached the open door, the ship once more tilted to starboard, until the deck lay almost in the water, the angry waves crashing over the railing. A wind of hurricane force snatched the blanket she had thrown about herself and sent it whirling and flapping into the night, and in an instant she was soaked to the skin, her hair hanging plastered across her face. She saw a deck chair smashed to splinters by the force of one giant wave.

A flash of lightening illuminated the scene with a ghastly blue-white glare, and there was Jeremy, clinging to a railing. The ship had begun to right itself, and as she watched, Jeremy let go his hold, and attempted to run for the steps that led to the bridge.

In the same instant, another giant wave came thundering across the deck, just as the light vanished.

"Jeremy!" she screamed, but the roar of the wind and the pounding of the waves made a whisper of her cry.

The lightning flashed again. The deck was empty!

* * * * * * *

"Jeremy!" She would have run forward but someone grabbed her from behind, forcing her back into the comparative shelter of the stairwell.

"Good God, woman, you can't go out there!" It was the steward she'd spoken to a moment before. "You're supposed to be in your cabin."

"Mr. Bates, he's out there!" She shouted at the top of her lungs to make herself heard. "He's been hurt...."

"There's no one there." He held her despite her struggles to break free. "Look."

She did, and saw the empty deck, and the broken railing

where something or someone had crashed through.

"He's been swept overboard. We've got to save him!" she cried. "Tell the captain!"

"Are you daft, woman?" The steward shook her till her head threatened to snap off. "If he is overboard, there's no saving him now, not in this. Go below, in the name of heaven. Don't you see I've got more important things to do than argue with a hysterical woman? We can't risk a whole shipload of passengers for one man. Think of the others. Think of your own daughter."

He slammed her back against the wall, knocking the breath out of her. For several long seconds Lydia stared horror-stricken into his face.

He was right, of course. If Jeremy had been swept into that churning, thunderous sea, there was no hope of finding him, let alone saving him.

She thought of Chan Cho. Chan Cho too had come to her aid, and had paid for it with her life. Now Jeremy was dead. Perhaps if he had never met her, he would still be alive.

"Are you all right now?"

She brought herself back from the abyss of self-doubt and blame. The ship was still being tossed, the storm was still raging, and this man had far more important things that he should be doing than trying to calm her.

"Yes, I'm all right now," she said, pushing her wet hair back from her face. "You needn't worry about me. I'll go back to my cabin."

"You're sure?" He eyed her with concern; it both touched and frightened her.

"Quite sure," she said, turning to the stairs, but she paused. "Only I think someone had better inform the captain that Mr. Bates has been washed overboard."

"I'll take care of it," he said, adding, "if he really is missing."

"He's gone," she said with finality.

And I am still alive, she thought, descending the stairs, *and there is still my daughter, and our future before us.*

Weeping and wringing her hands would accomplish nothing.

Like her parents, like Chan Cho—like the Lydia who had come to China so many years before—Jeremy was dead. But the living must go on, and each day's challenge was more important than anything that had already gone.

"Steward?" She paused once more to look back. He was still watching her.

"Yes?"

"Someone had better inform Mrs. Bates, too."

CHAPTER FOURTEEN

By dawn the ship had passed through the worst of the storm, though it was midday of the following day before the sea was again calm.

Jeremy was confirmed as lost at sea. To her own surprise, Lydia found herself thinking of the bitter, chair-bound woman who had been his wife. Had Cora known through those years of clinging to a loveless marriage that sooner or later some storm had been certain to take him from her? Did she grieve now, for herself, or for him?

That, Lydia found herself thinking, was a question she could well ask herself. Was the sense of loss she felt solely a selfish one? It was true that his death made the future once again more difficult for her, without the knowledge that she could count on Jeremy's support and assistance. He had done so much.

Yet she had been fond of him. They had known one another too briefly, and she was too steeped in the isolation of the past decade of her life, for her to have come to understand the demons that drove him. Since the death of her parents, who had been loving if strict, she had been deprived of any affection other than her daughter's, and she had welcomed Jeremy's show of love. At the same time, she had a suspicion that his ill-fated passion for her owed as much to his unhappy marriage as it did to her charms.

If he had not been married to Cora Bates, but had been a carefree, unattached bachelor, or a widower, would he have fallen so readily in love with Lydia Nightsong? Had it been Cora who was swept overboard, would she have taken with her Jeremy's urgent need for another woman?

She had an unnerving idea that perhaps she had been wrong in accepting at face value Jeremy's reading of his marriage; perhaps after all it really was Cora, and not her, with whom he had been truly in love, without even knowing it himself. That might have been the true core of the bitterness that so poisoned his spirit, driving him to drink and to opium, and ultimately to his death.

It was not a pleasant thought, for it made Cora something of a victim, and herself something less than admirable.

It was with such thoughts as these that she made up her mind that she must go to see the widow. She felt she owed Cora that much, and in truth her condolences might be less hypocritical than most, for she at least shared to some degree in the loss. She had lost the only friend she had in the world.

"Should I come with you?" April asked when Lydia was ready to go.

"No, I think not," Lydia answered. She hesitated, wishing she could think of a sensible reason to give. "I think the fewer visitors just now, the better," she finished lamely.

April nodded understandingly. In fact, she understood the situation better than her mother would have guessed. She was still young, but she had grown up in a Chinese palace, and though she had been sheltered from the eyes of the outside world, such a palace was a hotbed of gossip at the best of times. Without knowing the mechanics involved, she nonetheless had a fair idea of the relationships that existed between men and women.

April's love for her mother ran true and deep, but it had been undeniably tarnished of late. She had been frightened in the palace in Peking, but before that, in her father's palace at Kalgan, she had been happy enough. Of course it had been exciting, at least at first, to make their escape, but she had never quite understood her mother's leaving Ke Loo, who was her husband, and taking up instead with Mr. Bates, who was another woman's husband.

She did not know what "taking up" actually entailed, it was only a phrase she had overheard some other women on the ship use in reference to Mother and Mr. Bates, but she had an intuitive understanding of the flushed, embarrassed manner that her mother had when she returned that night from Mr. Bates's cabin. The fact that they had the following day been asked to take their meals in their rooms had somehow underscored her impression.

April sighed; once, an eternity ago in Kalgan, she had sat in her own little garden and complained to her amah that nothing ever happened in her life. She could certainly no longer make that complaint.

* * * * * * *

It was Mrs. Bourne, another of the passengers, who admitted Lydia to Cora's suite. All of the women passengers were there, clustered around Cora's wheelchair. Lydia saw that, without exception, the looks they gave her were unfriendly. Mrs. Conners, was particularly hostile.

With the others surrounding her, it was a moment before Cora learned who had come in. Lydia saw someone lean down to say something, and like the last snow before the spring sun, the women seemed to melt back away from the chair, until she and Cora faced one another across the cabin.

"I—I've come to offer my condolences," Lydia said, angry with herself for stammering.

"Your condolences?" Cora flung her chair forward, nearly crushing Mrs. Bourne's slippered foot. "You've come to offer your condolences?"

"Yes." Lydia felt her sympathy begin to wither within her. She had learned when hurt to withdraw into a sort of hardness that had heretofore shielded her from what was meant to wound, and she found herself instinctively retreating into such a shell now, though at the same time she could see the others responding unfavorably to it. *Impertinent,* she read in their eyes, and, *cold.*

"We've both suffered a loss," she added. "Your husband was a kind man, and brave."

"And generous," Cora added.

"Yes, certainly generous," Lydia agreed. "Had it not been for him—"

"You would not be here before me," Cora finished, for her, "wearing a dress purchased by my husband, sailing on a ship at my husband's expense, your purse no doubt stuffed with money given you by my husband—here, to offer your condolences—" she managed to give the word an obscene sound "—to my husband's widow. Tell me, Mrs. whatever your name is—"

"Nightsong," Lydia said quietly but firmly. She knew that she should be humble, that she should lower her eyes and respect the widow's grief, but her own pride was at stake now, and foolishly or not she met Cora's gaze without flinching. "It's Mrs. Nightsong."

"How do you account for my husband's generosity?" Cora went on without pausing. "Was he only an over-giving man, do you think? Or were his many gifts to you not gifts at all, but payment for services rendered?"

There was a lengthy silence. Lydia felt her face burning and was aware that all eyes in the room were upon her. She wished with all her heart that she could deny Cora's charge, could tell her, tell them all, that she had not been Jeremy's mistress. But, however reluctantly, she had yielded to his desires not thirty feet from where she was standing now, and though the recollection filled her with shame, she would not now betray the memory of a man who had been so kind to her as Jeremy had, by denying him.

"Whatever services I rendered to your husband," she said coldly, "were only those he was unable to obtain from his wife."

There was a shocked gasp from one of the other women.

"You dare to mock me for being crippled?" Cora demanded.

"It is more than your legs that has failed you," Lydia said. "And more than that, far more, that your husband was forced to seek elsewhere."

"Get out." She said it quietly at first, and then again, her voice rising to a shriek. "Get out, damn you, you hussy, get out!"

Lydia turned to go, but at the door she paused. She had come to say one thing, and she would say it now, no matter if it fell on deaf ears.

"I am sorry, truly sorry," she said without looking back. "I know, as these others may not, how much you've lost, and how long it has pained you."

With that she left, to a babble of voices that began almost as soon as the door was closed. She did not linger to listen to them. She had a fair idea what their subject would be, and their tone.

She had no sooner arrived back at her own cabin, than there was a knock at the door. Thinking it was one of the women come to berate her, Lydia threw the door open with a defiant gesture, only to find herself facing the captain himself.

"Captain Conners," she greeted him, staring in surprise.

"May I come in?" he asked.

Lydia recovered her manners, opening the door wide. "Of course," she said. "This is an unexpected pleasure."

"I'm afraid my visit isn't altogether pleasant," he said, pausing just inside the cabin. "I've come to make a request of you."

He hesitated for a moment. She had a premonition of what he had come to ask, and her heart sank. "What is it that you want?" she asked.

"I think for the peace of mind of everyone concerned, it might be best if you and your daughter confined yourselves to your quarters for the remainder of our journey."

"To our quarters...?"

"Of course your meals will be brought to you, and anything else you might desire, within reason. And if any of the other ladies should want to visit with you, there's no reason why they can't."

"You know perfectly well they wouldn't," Lydia said, embarrassed and growing angry. "They're your wife's friends, and Mrs. Bates's."

"Exactly," he said, managing an awkward smile. "Which

quite explains my problem. The ladies have threatened a veritable revolt, and under the circumstances—Mrs. Bates losing her husband as she just did—well, I don't see how I could refuse."

"And if I refuse? If I don't confine myself to my cabin?"

Captain Conners's smile faded, and his eyes grew dark. "I must remind you, Mrs. NIghtsong, that this is my ship, and those aboard her subject to my command."

"Meaning, I suppose, that you'll have me tied to my bed if I don't cooperate?"

"Mrs. Nightsong, we have just been through a dangerous storm, and a tragic loss. No captain likes to lose a man at sea, and it is harder when that man's wife is aboard as well, especially so when she is a cripple, like poor Mrs. Bates. It is not my wish to punish you for your sins, though sin it certainly was to consort with another woman's husband. But surely you must see that your presence among the others is, shall we say, unwelcome. I should think it would be more comfortable for all concerned—including you and your daughter—if you were to keep to yourselves. This trip will not last forever, and when we have reached San Francisco, you may do what you like. But until then, I'm afraid you must do as I ask."

He did not wait for a reply, but gave her a curt nod, and left her. For a long moment Lydia stared after him, her anger fading into shame and a deep sense of misery.

If only she'd never set foot on this damnable ship. Better to have waited for another sailing, better even, perhaps, to have remained in China.

She had an urge to cry, and was on the verge of doing so when she turned and saw April watching her from the door that connected their rooms.

"Are you all right, Mama?" April asked.

Lydia swallowed hard, fighting back tears. "Yes, dear, I'm fine, thank you," she replied, even managing a wan imitation of a smile. "The captain and I were just talking, and we've decided, after that dreadful storm, and Mr. Bates' accident, that it would be safer if you stayed to your cabin for the rest of the trip, and I'll stay with you, to keep you company. It'll be just the two of us again, the way it was before. Won't that be nice?"

"It sounds wonderful," April said, coming to hug her mother enthusiastically.

It was only later, with the door closed and her mother's muffled sobbing only barely audible, that April sat on the edge of her bed, morosely staring into space.

She was angry with Captain Conners for having accused her mother of sinning and, in a way less clear to her, angry with her mother as well. It had been an effort not to burst into the room while they were having their conversation, and beg them both not to talk that way. It had horrified her when Mama had spoken of being tied to her bed, a threat that had seemed to her entirely real, and she had held her breath until it had been clear that this wasn't going to happen. But it didn't take away the feeling that they were being punished.

Yet, though she had at least a vague inkling of what had existed between her mother and Mr. Bates, it did not seem to her now that it was for this that they were being punished; after all, she was being punished too, and she had scarcely known Mr. Bates.

She had an idea that it was something far more fundamental than that; perhaps they were being punished for leaving Ke Loo—or even for leaving China.

Yes, the more she thought of it, the more reasonable that seemed. China had been their home, for all of her life, at least. And she was Chinese, her amah had insisted upon that.

Suddenly she understood. That was why the Dragon Empress had been angry with them, that was why they had had to flee, and hide in that dreadful place where the men smoked pipes all the time. Of course—and it followed that it wasn't really the captain who was punishing them; it was the Empress herself, showing her anger. And they could never escape from her. Wasn't she called the Celestial Empress? And didn't she rule the world, as the amah had told her often enough? Why then, they would be punished forever, just as they were being punished now, unless...unless, of course, they did as the Empress wished, and returned to what they were, and where they belonged.

April knelt by her bed, the polished wood of the floor hard beneath her knees. She prayed, not to the incomprehensible god that her mother had spoken of to her, nor to the gods of China, where wisdom was honored more than saintliness. She prayed to a woman she'd never met, to the Dowager Empress of China, begging her forgiveness, and her patience, for her mother, and for herself.

"I will return," she promised silently. "I will remain your subject, and one day I will come back to your China—to our China," she corrected herself.

It seemed to her, having prayed, that a burden had been lifted from her, and she went to bed with a lighter heart and an easier conscience.

Her mother, she knew, really wasn't Chinese; even at her young age, April had observed the difference in their appearance, and even if she hadn't, she had heard it mentioned in whispers by others.

Her mother looked like the others aboard the ship, and in the legations in Peking. *Not like me,* April thought, for she could see that she looked different. She looked like her father, and her brother, and all the others in the palace.

She looked Chinese; and, convinced that that was the answer she had been struggling toward as long as she could remember, April slept with a new peace in her heart.

CHAPTER FIFTEEN

"Mother, I can't find my yellow ribbon."

"I've packed it in the trunk already." Lydia paused and looked around the cabin, snatching up a handkerchief and cramming it into the nearly bursting trunk.

It was hopeless. How on earth did anyone ever manage to put everything away, with any hope of finding things again? It was the sort of thing she'd had no need to know in China, and hadn't learned as a girl.

"Oh, look, you nearly forgot this," April cried, running up with Lydia's locket in her hand.

The simple trinket never failed to gave Lydia's heart a pang. It was the only thing she'd managed to hold on to for all these years, the only souvenir of the past.

She snapped the locket open. Her father's faded likeness glowered up at her as if silently admonishing her for some error of neglect or omission. For a moment it seemed as if she could close her eyes and hear his gruff voice again, or feel his firm hand on her shoulder.

Oh, Papa, she thought, succumbing for an instant to that despair that had threatened to engulf her since Jeremy's drowning, *if only you were here to tell me what to do.*

In a matter of minutes they would be disembarking in San Francisco, with none but the vaguest idea of how to proceed. She had nothing but the name of her mother's brother, Richard Whitley, and a faint memory of someone she'd met years before, and whom she hadn't much cared for.

Her memory of the city was even fainter; they had sailed from here when she had been a child of eight. She remembered an eerie sea of ships' masts seemingly growing from the ground. Papa had explained that hundreds of ships had been abandoned during the California gold rush, their crews deserting them in the mad scramble to reach the gold fields and the fortune they were sure awaited them. In time the silt deposited in the bay had filled in and then buried the ships, extending the land outward, and reforming the bay. One of the ships, she remembered, had even functioned as a department store, The City of Paris.

She had observed, as the *Horizon* neared the waterfront, that the forest of masts was gone. Buildings had sprouted on the new land, extending the city down to the water's edge. The abandoned ships were already forgotten beneath the very roots of the city.

She'd written to Richard Whitley before they had left China, to explain that she was his niece and on her way to San Francisco, and had explained as well the deaths of her parents from cholera. The rest of her story she had thought it best to relate in person; it was too fantastic to attempt to tell in a single letter.

Whether he had ever gotten her letter or not she couldn't tell, however. There had been no reply and no time for a second letter to inquire after the first. She could not suppose that he would welcome the arrival of a long-forgotten niece, with a daughter, for whom he must assume responsibility—and yet, what else could she do? There was no one else to whom she could conceivably turn.

Jeremy had promised to make inquiries for her and lend her the cash to tide her over until her uncle could be found, but Jeremy was gone. Though she had already done so countless times already, Lydia opened her reticule and looked at the paltry sum of money remaining there. Jeremy had slipped some money into her hand just before they had boarded the ship in Hong Kong, explaining that she would need the cash for gratuities on the journey, and this was what was left of it. Even knowing little about San Francisco, she felt certain this would not go far. And there wouldn't have been even this much left if they hadn't spent the last weeks confined to their cabins.

It had been a miserable journey. The weather had grown warmer and warmer, the air in the little rooms more and more stifling, until she had looked back upon the interlude in the opium den with envy.

Lydia snapped the locket shut, and slipped it about her neck. Well, whatever awaited them in San Francisco, it would be better than passing their days in these cramped quarters. Only today, knowing that they were inside the bay and approaching the docks, had she ventured above deck, and then only briefly. She had no more wish to rub elbows with Mrs. Conners and her cronies than they with her.

What a relief it would be to set foot on land and put this entire voyage behind her. She closed the trunk and was about to lock it, when there was a rapping at the door. Without waiting for a reply, the captain came into the cabin, accompanied by his wife and Cora Bates. A steward followed behind.

"Sorry to intrude," the captain greeted her, looking slightly embarrassed at being there. "As you know, Mrs. Nightsong, we'll be docking in a short while."

"So I understand," Lydia replied. "Surely you haven't come for a farewell party?"

"We've come," Cora snapped impatiently, "to deprive you of your ill-gotten gains."

"Then I'm afraid you've wasted a trip," Lydia said coldly, "I've gained nothing from this journey but bitter experience. See for yourself, if you like—there is our trunk."

"A trunk purchased by my misguided husband," Cora said. "Which would make it my trunk rather than yours, I should say."

Lydia was stunned; in her wildest imagination she had not dreamed of such a turn of events. "Why, it is mine," she said, reddening. "Jeremy may have purchased it, that's true, but it was a gift. You've no right—"

"I have every right. Here are the receipts," Cora said, brandishing a sheaf of papers. "For the trunk, for the clothing that is presumably packed within it—here, for dressmaking, for bonnets, shoes, a parasol even. Items purchased by my late husband, with our money. They are mine, I tell you, every last stick and button, and you shall not leave this ship with any of them."

"Well, yes, Jeremy did pay for all those things," Lydia agreed, flustered.

"And gave you money as well!"

"Yes, that's true too, but that was a loan, and as for the rest, why they were gifts, most of them, or also loans, which I had every intention of repaying."

"Have you any proof of what you say?" the captain asked. "Something in writing—a letter, perhaps, or some agreement between yourself and Mr. Bates?"

"But of course I haven't—who would have expected—Mr. Bates hadn't planned on being swept overboard," Lydia stammered.

There was a lengthy silence. The two women regarded her venomously. The steward's professional manner concealed perfectly whatever he might have been thinking of this singular confrontation. Only the captain looked ill at ease, but Lydia knew better than to hope for an ally in him, especially with his wife at hand as well.

"Surely," Lydia said, "you can't mean to strip us of everything? I'm a woman alone in the world, with a child to care for. You're speaking of the very clothes on our backs."

"I don't think we need to go quite that far," Mrs. Conners spoke for the first time since entering the cabin. "We don't want to be needlessly cruel, after all. But we could hardly permit you to rob a woman recently widowed of things that ought rightfully to be hers."

"But—are we to be put ashore with nothing more than what we're wearing?" Lydia was aghast—a strange city, a woman with a young girl—how would they survive? It was infamous.

Even Ke Loo had shown more kindness than this.

She turned to the captain. "Surely, Captain Conners, you can't permit this to happen?"

He avoided her pleading gaze. "I'm afraid, Mrs. Nightsong, that Mrs. Bates has the documentation to support her claim. Unless you have other evidence...." He shrugged helplessly.

Lydia felt the sting of tears in her eyes and fought them back. That much satisfaction, at least, she would deny them.

"I see," was all she said.

"I must go now, we'll be docking soon," the captain said. He nodded to the steward. "You'll see that Mrs. Bates' property is returned to her, and that Mrs. Nightsong and her daughter are put ashore."

"Aye aye, sir." Lydia thought she saw a glimmer of sympathy in the steward's eyes, but it was too little and too late to do her any good.

"I'll say farewell, then, Mrs. Nightsong," the captain said, "And wish you luck in your further ventures. Come, my dear."

"Perhaps we should stay...," his wife suggested.

"That won't be necessary," the captain said with an edge to his voice. "The steward will see to things here, and I think Mrs. Nightsong may wish a few minutes to herself."

He ushered the two women out, both of them wearing triumphant expressions.

"I'm sorry, Mrs. Nightsong," the steward said when they had gone. He had brought their meals to them in the weeks since they had been confined, and had formed his own opinion of the ravishingly beautiful woman with the soft and gentle manners, almost like a Chinese girl he visited whenever he was in Hong Kong.

"That's quite all right," she said, turning away because she could no longer prevent the tears from spilling down her cheeks. "You must obey orders."

April dashed in from the adjoining room. "Look, I found my other stocking," she cried, holding it aloft. She saw the steward, and came to an abrupt stop. "Oh. Hello," she said. She'd come to understand that visits from the steward as often as not meant some new trouble for them.

"Give the stocking to the gentleman, dear," Lydia said.

He took it with an obviously embarrassed air, and put it in the trunk, hastily locking it. "I'm told to take everything except what you're wearing," he said. "But if there are any personal articles...."

"Let them have it all," Lydia said bitterly, and then thought better of it. "No, wait—there are my cosmetics, in this little bag here—they're my own, I assure you, Mr. Bates had nothing to do with them. If you like, I can take the matter up with the captain...."

"No need to," the steward said. "Your word's good enough for me, whether it is for anyone else or not."

"Thank you." Lydia clutched the bag of cosmetics to her breast and breathed a sigh of relief. She had gone through too much for these—indeed might never be entirely free of danger from them—to surrender them now to the selfish cruelty of Cora Bates.

These, and her own wits, were all she had left on which to build a future for herself and April. Just as she'd fought for their lives, their freedom, so she would fight for their future.

This was as close as she had ever come to total defeat. She felt a shudder go through the ship, and knew that they were docking. In a matter of minutes they would be ashore in San Francisco; but the arrival that she had looked forward to with such eagerness now loomed before her as yet another ordeal that she must somehow overcome, and more than at any other time, she felt her own helplessness.

* * * * * *

"Where are we going now?" April asked a short while later.

"I'm not sure," Lydia said, looking about her in confusion. At least, she thought, there was something to be said for arriving with nothing more than what they were wearing: it had taken no more than a minute or two to pass through the customs. Less than half an hour before, the steward had accompanied them down the gangplank from the ship, leaving them on the dock with a final farewell and a sympathetic nod; and now, here they were, on the street outside, with all the confusion of traffic and milling crowds about them.

A hackney cab approached, the driver leaning out to ask if she needed a lift. Lydia shook her head, and with her hand on April's shoulder, began to move along through the throng.

The truth was, she had no idea where to go. The hour was already late, afternoon slipping away into evening. She had her uncle's address, but how to get there, or if it really was still his address, or whether he would welcome them, or close the door in their faces—these questions swam round and round in her mind, until her head seemed to be spinning.

"Mama, I'm hungry," April said when they had walked several blocks.

Nearby a street vendor offered freshly cooked shrimp and crab meat. Lydia purchased a little packet of the shrimp and gave them to April, though her own mouth watered at the tempting aroma. From the vendor she got directions to Richard Whitley's address. It seemed a considerable distance, particularly for what might be a wasted trip, but there was nothing else to do. They set out in the direction he had indicated.

They were soon lost. It had been too many years since Lydia had to find her way about a city. It was one thing to be carried in a sedan chair through the streets of a Chinese city, but quite another to be walking about San Francisco. Everything seemed foreign to her; even the goods in the shop windows were unfamiliar, and she saw that the styles she'd found so chic in Peking were in fact several seasons outdated.

At length, Lydia paused in confusion. Had the vendor told her six blocks and then left? Or was it right? Fatigue and hunger had blurred her memory of the directions. She could not even mentally retrace their steps back to the docks.

"What are we going to do?" April asked. Though she made

an effort to sound unafraid, her voice was tremulous.

Lydia looked around. It was growing dark already. If they did not find the address soon, they would make matters worse by arriving in the middle of the night, which would hardly make them any more welcome. If only they had enough money to afford a hotel room for the night, they could at least arrive fresh in the morning.

She shook her head, angrily scolding herself for wasting precious minutes on wishful thinking. "This way, I think," she said aloud, starting off to the right.

An eerie stillness seemed to have settled upon the city. She was used to the East, where the streets teemed with traffic, with passersby and carts and animals and the lavish processions of mandarins.

With the arrival of darkness, everyone seemed to have vanished from San Francisco's streets. Lamps were lighted in windows and in the distance an occasional voice could be heard, but on this street they were the only people out. It was the supper hour, too early for the city's social events to have begun, too late for shoppers and merchants.

Lydia was grateful to hear the clip clop of horses' hooves approaching, until they had come nearly abreast of them, and an unfamiliar voice whistled and called, "Where you going, sister?"

She looked and saw three ruffians in a cart riding slowly alongside of them, leering. Even at a distance they showed signs of intoxication.

"Pay no attention to them," Lydia said, hurrying April along a little faster. Not too far ahead was the lighted entrance to a restaurant. Lydia found herself hoping that someone might emerge from within.

"Hey, wait there," one of the men called. To Lydia's dismay, one of the three leaped down from the cart just behind them, while a minute later, the cart having hurried ahead, his companion clambered down in front of them. Lydia came to an anxious halt, glancing from the man blocking their path to the one grinning at her from behind.

"Gentlemen, please," she began, meaning to plead with them to be allowed to pass; her plea was cut off by a chorus of harsh laughter.

"Gentlemen? Did you hear that, Reb, the lady called us gentlemen," the one behind her yelled.

Reb, the one remaining in the cart, joined in the boisterous laughter.

"That's sure an improvement anyway," the one in front said, still laughing, though his laugh was filled with menace. "Say, you had no call to go and be so stuck up on us just a minute ago. We were just being friendly like, you know, looking for a little fun. What about your girlfriend here, she looks awful young to me. Don't she speak any English?"

In a flash of insight, Lydia realized that the three had taken them for streetwalkers. She could see that it was an easy mistake to make—the two of them, unescorted, with no bags, on this rather shabby-looking street after dark.

"I'm afraid you've made a mistake," Lydia said, managing a somewhat uneasy smile. "This is my daughter, and we've only just—"

The man's laughter vanished. "Your daughter?" He took a step closer, squinting at April. "Why, this here's a Chink. You got a Chink daughter?"

The one behind swore aloud and strode forward, seizing April's shoulder and spinning her around. "Let me see," he said, peering at April's face, contorted now with fear. "Be damned if you ain't right, Joe. Looky here, Reb, the lady's got a Chink kid, you know what that means, don't you, it means she's got herself a Chink lover too."

He suddenly seized Lydia's wrist in a fierce grip. "How about it, honey, your old man a yellow face, is he? How come a pretty woman like you'd wanna take a Chinaman for a sweetie when you could have lots of white men instead?"

"Like us," Reb shouted from the cart

"Mama...," April cried, her voice breaking into a frightened sob.

"It's all right, darling, they aren't going to hurt us," Lydia said with a calm she was far from feeling. At this close range she could smell the liquor on the man's fetid breath.

"That's right," the one called Joe said, his voice suddenly husky. "We don't mean to hurt nobody none, so long as we don't have no trouble. We just want to teach your mama here a little lesson."

"Yeah," said the one holding Lydia's wrist, jerking her toward him until his face was in front of hers, his red-rimmed eyes ablaze with violence and lust. "We want to show her the difference between a pigtailed Chinaman and a proper white man."

"Yeah, a gentleman, like us," Reb called from the cart. "Let's go, come on, dump 'em in here and let's scoot."

"No, please," Lydia pleaded, trying to free her hand, but the man holding her was too strong. To her horror, she saw the other one sweep April up in his arms. April gave a shriek of terror.

"Not my daughter," Lydia cried. "I beg you, let my daughter go!"

"We'll let you both go, all right," her captor said, shoving Lydia toward the cart with such force that she would have fallen had he not held her arm so tightly, "soon's we've had our fun with you, and taught you a lesson or two. We don't cotton to no Chink lovers around here, like you oughta know, Miss Stuck-Up."

Too frightened even to scream, Lydia could only struggle in silence with her assailant, but her struggle was futile. Seizing her in a drunken embrace, he carried her toward the cart where Reb waited, grinning stupidly.

CHAPTER SIXTEEN

Overwhelmed by the horror of their situation, Lydia was unaware that the fray had been joined till she heard her captor give a grunt of pain.

"Let them go, you vermin," a man's voice cried. In the next instant, the man holding Lydia did just that, so unexpectedly that she fell to the sidewalk.

Dazed, she looked up, to see an elegantly dressed gentleman laying about him with a silver-headed walking stick. Though outnumbered and smaller in stature than any one of the three ruffians, he was also sober, and filled with the sort of righteous anger that knows no fear.

"You scum," he swore, turning his attention to the man carrying April, and pummeling him about the head and shoulders with such fury that April too was dropped unceremoniously on the ground. "You filthy swine."

"Ow, ouch," Joe cried, trying to ward off the blows with his hands and getting a loud crack on the knuckles for his efforts. "You fancy pants, I ought to—"

"Damnation," Reb swore from the cart. "Come on, let's get out of here, 'fore someone else hears the racket and gets in it." Without waiting, he larruped up the horses.

His companions evidently agreed with his assessment. In another moment they were clambering aboard the already moving cart, which quickly vanished into the darkness. Lydia could hear one of them swearing loudly until his voice too had faded on the night air.

She got up and ran to where April was gingerly dusting herself off. "Are you all right, darling?" Lydia asked, hugging her daughter to her.

"I—I think so," April said.

"I'm afraid you ought to be a bit more careful about your prospective customers, Miss," the elegantly dressed stranger was saying. Lydia turned, and he caught sight of her face for the first time. "Oh, I am sorry, I thought—but you don't look like the sort to be...."

"Parading my wares on the street?" Lydia finished for him, giving him a crooked smile.

He blushed in confusion. "This neighborhood does have a reputation," he stammered. "A woman alone, at night—a man would probably think...." Again he paused, embarrassed. It occurred to Lydia to wonder what a man of his obvious means and breeding was doing in such a neighborhood, but she did not ask the question aloud. After all, the man had just rescued them from a pretty nasty situation.

Instead, she said, "We've only just arrived from China. We were looking for a place to spend the night and I'm afraid we got lost."

He glanced around, grateful for a discreet escape from an awkward topic. "And now they've stolen your bags," he said.

"My—" Lydia caught herself in time. "Our bags—oh, good heavens, so they have." This was no time, she thought, to try to explain why it was that, having just arrived from China, they had no luggage with them—nothing but the small reticule that had fallen to the ground in the struggle, which she now retrieved, and the carryall that held the cosmetics. Like her statement that they had been looking for a place to spend the night, it was not quite a lie—and certainly simpler than the truth.

"And your money?" the stranger asked. "I suppose they got that too?"

She opened the reticule and jingled the few coins inside. "Oh, dear, this is all I have left," she said.

"But have you no family, no friends in the city?"

"We—I have an uncle. We meant to see him tomorrow—but there's no need to trouble yourself, really, I'm only grateful that you came along when you did. It was very brave of you to take on three such brutes singlehandedly."

"Only cowards would have assaulted defenseless women," he said. "And as for troubling myself, I assure you, it's no trouble at all. Now, I've got an idea, there's a little hotel just a few blocks from here, run by an acquaintance of mine. It's not the grandest, but I'm sure he can find rooms for your maid and yourself, if you'll let me take you there."

Lydia saw April's look of surprise; she silenced her daughter's objection with a sharp glance and a quick shake of her head, though it gave her a pang to see the hurt that spread quickly over her daughter's face. Well, never mind that, they'd already gotten into trouble once by admitting they were mother and daughter, and for all she knew, this gentleman might find the fact no less disturbing than those three oafs who had very nearly abducted them. For the moment it was surely better to let their benefactor's mistake stand. Later, she would make April see the wisdom of her logic.

"That's very kind of you, Mr...?"

"Hanover, Walter Hanover, at your service." He doffed his hat and made a little bow from the waist.

"I'm Lydia Nightsong, and this is—April," she said, with only the slightest hesitation; she had been about to say, "my maid," but at the last minute the lie had refused to come to her lips. "But we can't impose upon you this way. As you've seen, I haven't even enough money on me to pay for a room...."

"Nonsense." He brushed aside her objections with a grandiloquent gesture. "It's my civic duty, to make up for your unfortunate introduction to our fair city. More than that it will give me great pleasure. Come with me."

So adamant was Mr. Hanover that Lydia and April found themselves being ushered along the street without further ado.

Not that Lydia had any great objections to accepting the gentleman's kindness, and any qualms of conscience that she experienced were quickly dismissed. Certainly they needed someplace to spend the night, and without someone's assistance they would have ended up in a park somewhere, if they were lucky—or, she thought with a shudder, at the mercy of scavengers like the three from whom they'd just been rescued.

Mr. Hanover saw and misinterpreted the shudder. "Yes, it does get cool here in the evenings," he said. "Not to fear, we're almost there now, just around this corner—ah, here we are."

The hotel was small and unpretentious, but it looked clean and comfortable. Lydia and April waited on a horsehair sofa while Mr. Hanover spoke for some minutes with the manager. At length he rejoined them, the manager trailing after him.

"There, it's all settled," Mr. Hanover said, with a self-satisfied look on his face, "My friend, Mr. Gray, will see you to your rooms, and you're to let him know if there's anything at all you need—I've explained that you were set upon and all your things stolen."

"I don't know how I could repay you for your kindness," Lydia said.

"There is one thing," he said. "I take it that you haven't had your dinner yet, and I myself was just on my way to dine when our paths crossed. Perhaps you'd do me the honor of dining with me?"

"Why, I'd love to, but my—April hasn't eaten yet either," Lydia replied.

"That's no problem. I'm sure Mr. Gray would be happy to send something up to her room."

"It would be a pleasure," Mr. Gray assured them.

Lydia hesitated. She knew that it was unfair to leave April alone in a strange hotel room on their first night in this strange new country; still, it could be no more difficult than a number of other places they had stayed of late. And she did owe Mr. Hanover something for his bravery and his generosity. A dinner seemed a harmless enough way to repay him.

"In that case," she said aloud, "if you'll give me a few minutes to freshen up, I'll be right down."

To her surprise, April was less understanding.

"But I don't want to eat by myself in my room," she protested when they were alone in their rooms, which were small and modestly furnished, with an air of slightly worn gentility. "It's just like being locked in our cabins on the ship all over again."

"Darling, we weren't exactly locked in our rooms on the ship," Lydia said. "The captain merely asked if we would confine ourselves to them for the remainder of the voyage."

"It's the same thing, isn't it? Anyway, how can you go out with Mr. Hanover? You know nothing about him."

"Why, I know he's a gentleman, a man I should say of some means. And he's certainly been kind to us, which speaks well for him."

April looked down at the floor. "What if he has a wife?" she asked in a sullen voice.

Lydia was taken aback, not only that her daughter should have thought of that question, but that she herself had not.

"Well, and what if he has?" Lydia replied, a trifle too adamantly. "There's no harm in a man's having dinner with a woman."

"Mrs. Bates thought so," April said.

"Mrs. Bates was a bitch," Lydia said quickly and sharply; at once she regretted speaking so impulsively. "However, I give you my word, the very first thing I shall find out about Mr. Hanover's is his marital status."

April looked up then, her expression less sullen than anxious. "Will he be spending the night with you?" she asked.

"Of course not." It was Lydia's turn to avert her eyes. It gave her a stab of shame that her daughter should even consider such a thing, particularly as the same question had crossed her mind; it had occurred to her that Mr. Hanover might expect just such a reward for his efforts. Of course she had anticipated denying him, but she had not failed to realize that doing so might result in their being put on the streets again.

She was grateful for the tap at the door that indicated the arrival of April's dinner. A young man in a braided uniform wheeled in a table laden with rolls and butter, half a roast chicken nesting on a bed of salad, and a bowl of fresh fruit.

For a moment, Lydia wanted more than anything else to remain where she was and share the repast. It was unfair, really; she no more wanted to go to dinner with a strange gentleman than April wanted to eat dinner alone, but what could she do? Fate had conspired against her, it seemed, since her childhood. Life had been an unending battle, in which her only weapons had been her wits and her physical beauty.

Briefly she allowed herself the luxury of feeling monstrously sorry for herself. Then, however, her common sense reasserted itself, and she thrust aside her unhappy reflections. It was no use pretending they weren't in a scrape, because they were, and certainly an hour or so in the company of Mr. Hanover—an innocent hour or so, she promised herself firmly—would be less unpleasant than spending the night huddled in some doorway.

"I must go now," she said aloud, sternly, for she knew that to reveal her reluctance to go would only encourage April's reluctance as well. "Straight to bed when you've eaten, and never you worry, I'll be home before you've started dreaming."

* * * * * * *

She found Mr. Hanover waiting for her in the hotel's small dining room. Apart from another couple, who appeared to be newlyweds, they had the room to themselves.

Lydia rather regretted that discovery, for it lent a romantic atmosphere to the meeting. The other couple spent the time holding hands across the table, and smiling into one another's eyes. It made Lydia feel foolish to continue the stiff, quite formal manner she had decided to adopt with her companion, and almost despite herself she began to relax.

And Mr. Hanover was a pleasant companion, however unromantic a figure he might cut. He was of modest stature, not quite as tall as she was. His dark hair was flecked with grey at the temples, and she suspected that without the neatly trimmed moustache that he wore, his face would appear almost womanish.

He was friendly, however, and his company was easy to enjoy. It was a peculiar experience to sit like this and bask in the admiration of a charming gentlemen. Never had Ke Loo displayed anything but lust or possessiveness toward her, and Jeremy had been such a hangdog, tortured soul. There had been lust in his manner toward her too, but never this warm and easy sort of give and take. It occurred to her with some surprise that this was what she had always heard referred to as "flirtation."

How peculiar, to think that she, a woman who had been told she was beautiful, had nearly reached the age of thirty without experiencing a flirtation.

"Lovely," Walter Hanover said, interrupting her reverie.

"What?" she asked.

"Your smile just then—what a rare and lovely sight it was. It makes a man wish he could see it more often."

"What nonsense," Lydia replied, blushing slightly. "Why, I've been smiling at you since I came down."

"Indeed you have," he said. "So charmingly that one was quite tempted to pretend the smiles were real, until you smiled unconsciously, and made lies of the others—I might add," he said quickly, seeing her frown, "most delightful lies they were."

"I don't know whether to be flattered or offended."

"Flattered, I assure you, Miss Nightsong—or is it Mrs. Nightsong?"

It gave her a start to realize how completely she'd forgotten the question of marriage. She had promised April to find out at once whether or not Mr. Hanover was married, yet it hadn't even crossed her mind until now.

"It's Miss Nightsong," she replied.

"It's hard to imagine so lovely a creature remaining unwed," he said.

"I've been in China since I was a girl. There are few Westerners in China. Missionaries, nuns, a few diplomats, some merchants—most either married or unsuitable. And what of you, Mr. Hanover? You've made no mention of your wife or family."

"I'm a widower. My wife died many years ago, and since then my daughter and I have lived with my mother. I'm forty-three years old, in good health, and rather comfortable financially."

"You make it sound like an inventory of your assets," she said with a laugh.

"Perhaps I meant it so."

"And did you never consider remarrying?"

His answer was rather slow in coming, making her feel that her question had been unwise. "I never had," he said.

Like a bather who, having stepped unhesitatingly into the stream, is frightened to discover its chill and the force of its current, she perceived that she had gone too far, too recklessly. It had been such a pleasure to savor being a woman, to bask in the warmth of this intelligent, cultured gentleman's attraction to her, that she had all but forgotten the difficulties of her situation.

She was married. However much it may have been against her will, however odious that marriage or her husband may have been to her, she was still the wife of a mandarin prince. She had a daughter, half Chinese, and she knew enough about the denizens of her native land to know that being half Chinese was not acceptable in polite society.

They—all those shadows hovering just beyond Walter Hanover's elegantly clad shoulders—would give her nothing, and resent what little she might take. They, who were sheltered, untainted, unstained, they who had no secrets to guard, who could cross conversational brooks without a thought for their footing, they would never permit her such a prize.

And even if they would, he would not. For a fleeting instant, she imagined how his face would change if she were to tell him the truth—of her marriage, of her daughter, or her real circumstances.

"You're smiling again," he said.

"And does it charm you so?" she asked.

He studied her, trying to read her face. "I don't know," he said. "It was so—I don't know how to describe it, amused, and yet sad too."

"You're very perceptive," she said, folding her napkin and putting it alongside her plate. "And now I must go, I'm afraid. It's been a strenuous day, and I left poor April all alone. I'm sure she won't close her eyes until I return."

"You're very solicitous of your maid, aren't you?" he said, coming quickly around to hold her chair. "At least for San Francisco."

"For San Francisco? Are the standards quite different here?"

"Well, she is Chinese. I'm surprised you didn't have some difficulty bringing her into the state."

"Oh? And why is that?"

"Hasn't anyone mentioned the Chinese Exclusion Act? It's tough for Chinese to get in now, unless they're smuggled in."

"What makes you certain we weren't smuggled in?" Lydia asked, more annoyed at the conversation than she cared to show; nor could she tell him that there had been no difficulty over April because April had traveled as her daughter, and she was an American citizen.

Hanover laughed. "I do admire a woman with a sense of humor," he said.

"Tell me, Mr. Hanover," Lydia said. "What was the purpose of the—what did you call it? The Exclusion Act?"

"Just what it says, to keep Chinese from pouring into the state the way they had been. It wasn't such a problem at first, while the railroads were being built; it was the railroad barons who started bringing them in, actually, cheap labor, you understand. Later, they flooded the job market. Employers found out they could hire a Chink to do twice as much work for half the money. It got so that they had all the available jobs, led to some riots, even. White men didn't like it, as you can well imagine."

"But surely it seems unfair to blame the Chinese, doesn't it? They sound more like victims than villains."

They had strolled from the dining room into the hotel's small lobby, empty now but for a clerk reading behind the desk, who gave them no more than a cursory glance before going back to his novel.

Hanover gave another laugh, this one sounding a bit patronizing, and patted her hand. "You feel as you do, my dear, because you've just come from China, and after so many years there it's natural to have a certain sympathy for these people. You'll see it all differently when you've been here a while. In the meantime, if you'll permit me to offer a bit of friendly advice, it won't do to stand up for the Chinese too much, not if you mean to get along in San Francisco society. There are a great many people here who aren't fond of yellow faces."

"Perhaps I've no intention of getting along in San Francisco society, as you put it."

"Now I have offended you by speaking so bluntly," he said, looking properly abashed. "Let us not quarrel, please, certainly not over anything so inconsequential as a Chinese servant. It's still early. Won't you come for a stroll?"

She gave him a stiff smile; she felt suddenly weary and old, for she had a glimpse of her life stretching before her, a barren plain peopled with endless lies and deceits, excuses and pretenses. There was desire too, for she was not such a fool as to think that other men would not look at her as this one did, as Jeremy had, and Ke Loo, and before him Peter MacNair; even that foolish boy, what had his name been—Reginald, yes, that was it; but of love she saw nothing; of happiness, not a trace.

"I'm afraid," she said, "that for me it's quite late already."

CHAPTER SEVENTEEN

San Francisco was, Lydia thought, an incredible city, built as ancient Rome had been, on a series of hills, so that it seemed always to tower above you.

It could hardly have been more unlike Peking. In place of sedan chairs and rickshaws, here were elegant carriages of the most modern design and, even more mind-boggling, train cars that rode tracks right up the steepest of the hillsides.

They, of course, rode no train cars, nor carriages. Fortified with new directions from a passing policeman, she and April had set off again in the morning to find Richard Whitley.

"Will you leave an address for Mr. Hanover?" the clerk had asked when they were leaving the hotel.

"That won't be necessary," Lydia had replied, giving the impression, without actually saying so, that Hanover already knew where to find her.

"Won't Mr. Hanover be angry to find us gone?" April asked.

"Probably," Lydia replied, not without a note of sadness. Walter Hanover had been very kind, and very generous—too much so for her to feel at ease continuing a pretense with him. Better to let him wonder about the peculiar woman with her Chinese maid. This way, at least, he could remember her fondly, and perhaps even wish her well when he thought of her.

And we need all the good wishes we can get, she thought grimly as they trudged up one of the steep inclines. She had balked at adding breakfast to the bill to be paid by their benefactor, and had instead purchased two apples from a vendor, which had been their breakfast and lunch.

That had been hours earlier, however. It was mid afternoon now, and a numb sort of weariness had long since overtaken them.

They found, at last, the address that she had for her uncle, only to find that he had not lived there in several years. A new address, and new directions, had sent them on, only to have the results repeated—Richard Whitley had moved from this location too.

They were on their way now to a third location, and in the process of going from one to the next, they had managed to traverse much of the city proper—a good way, Lydia supposed, to see a strange city, but a tiring one.

April's face was streaked with dirt, for the city was like Peking in that respect, at least. "It can't be much further, dear," Lydia said.

"What if he's not here either?" April asked wearily.

"Why, then, we'll just have to...."

"Mama, look!"

April's unexpected shout so surprised Lydia that at first, though she followed the direction of her daughter's pointing finger, Lydia could see nothing out of the ordinary.

"I don't see...."

"The laundry sign."

Lydia saw it then, a sign in Chinese characters advertising a laundry.

"Yes, dear, there are a great many Chinese here in America, and many of them operate laundries, I've been told. It's nothing out of the ordinary."

"But look, all along the street—there's a bakery, and a market—and look, a tea shop." April who a moment before had appeared so weary that she could hardly put one foot in front of the other, was now fairly dancing up and down with excitement.

Lydia too was looking along the street, at the many shops of a Chinese nature, and the familiar characters on signboards and in windows. It came to her finally; she had heard of such settlements, in New York City and here in San Francisco, though she had all but forgotten the knowledge.

"It's Chinatown," she said in a voice little more than a whisper.

It was peculiar, though she would not sort it out in her mind for many weeks; San Francisco, and America, had seemed to her strange and unfamiliar. The land that should have been home to her had filled her with dread, and she had felt every inch a foreigner.

Here, though, in the city's Chinese community, she had for the first time a sense of familiarity, as if she had come home. The high-pitched babble of voices carried on the wind, the ducks hanging featherless in the window of a market, perhaps more than anything else the scents wafting from the open shops—almond and soy, jasmine and ginger—filled her with a welcome glow of recognition.

For the first time since their arrival, her spirits lifted, and she began to experience that optimism, that hope that had sustained her through all the long years of her marriage-of-imprisonment.

She knew, without any idea how she knew, that this time they would find Richard Whitley. As surely as if the fates had written it out for her—in Chinese characters—she was certain that he would live here, in Chinatown; because this, of course, was where *they* would live. Americans, as she had always perceived them, but in the setting that was now comfortable to them.

Nor did her instinct fail her, for this time they did indeed find her Uncle Richard, though she was not entirely sure afterward if this had been good luck, or bad.

The address turned out to be that of a tailor shop. At first, when she had come in through the front door that set a bell to jangling, she had feared another disappointment, for there was a wizened little Chinese man sitting behind a battered machine, sewing up a pair of trousers. He paused in sewing, glancing first at her, then April, and back to her.

"I help, yes?" he said.

"We're looking for a Mr. Richard Whitley," Lydia said. "Is

he here?"

Before the man could answer, there was a shout from the rear of the shop, behind a doorway hung with a filthy, tattered curtain.

"Why the devil have you stopped sewing, you yellow scum, d'ya think I pay you to chatter with your goddam slanty-eyed relatives?"

The curtain was ripped aside. "Answer me, you filthy son-of-a—" He stopped when he saw the two women. "Why didn't you tell me we had customers?" he demanded, giving Lydia and April an obsequious smile. Even from across the room, he stank of whiskey and unwashed clothing, and he hadn't shaved in several days.

"Afternoon, ladies," he greeted them. "If you're looking for fine tailoring, you've come to the right place, though there's few enough with taste to know the difference. What can I do to please you?" This last was said with an unmistakable glint in his red-rimmed eyes, which so frightened Lydia that had there been any place else for them to turn she would have seized April's hand and fled the place there and then. As it was, however, there was no one and nowhere else. Here they were, and they would have to make the best of it

"Are you Richard Whitley?" she asked.

His smile faded and the eyes narrowed. "Why do you ask?" he demanded.

"I'm Lydia Nightsong," she said. "Lydia Holt, as you knew me, Sarah Holt's daughter. I wrote to you before, from China—I don't know if you got my letter."

He studied her for a moment, his eyes raking her up and down; she was not unmindful of the way that his gaze lingered at her bosom.

"I got a letter," he said, abruptly turning his attention to the man at the sewing machine. "Goddam you, you yellow bastard, what are you sitting there staring at? I pay you to sew, don't I, not to sit and stare."

The little man bent over his machine and began to work on

the trousers again. Richard Whitley turned back to Lydia.

"What do you want?" he asked.

"I—we need a place to stay," Lydia said, stammering, for this was a far different reunion than she had hoped for. "I'm afraid we've nowhere else to go."

"Does this look like a palace?" he asked, with a sweeping gesture that took in the filthy, disordered shop. "A grand hotel, anybody welcome to flop down and make themselves to home? Come one, come all, huh?"

Lydia felt a sudden stinging behind her eyes. She was so weary, they had come so far—until now, she had not even realized how much she had counted on the welcome of this unremembered uncle. She could not prevent a tear spilling from her eye and running down her cheek.

"I'm sorry, I—I realize this must be an imposition for you," she stammered.

"An imposition? That ain't the half of it, a damned nuisance is more like it. Here, you'd better come back here, I don't want you scaring off any real customers with that blubbering."

He held aside the curtain for them to enter the rear of the shop. Ushering a frightened and weary April before her, Lydia entered a dim, dusty hall that led past a cubicle intended apparently as a dressing room for the shop's customers. At the end of it was a kitchen, with a mound of dirty dishes, some of them green with mould, cluttering the table.

"Who's this?" Richard asked, gesturing with his thumb toward April.

"My daughter," Lydia said. "I mentioned her in my letter."

"You didn't mention she was a Chink," he said accusingly.

"She is my daughter, Mis—Uncle Richard," Lydia said sharply. "Her father was Chinese, through no choice of mine, I assure you, but that makes her no less my daughter. She is your sister's grandchild, and your grandniece—that is, if you are Richard Whitley."

She almost hoped that he would say he was not. If only she'd known what waited for them at the end of their journey! It might have been better to have waited at the hotel for Walter Hanover to return, as they had agreed last night that he would do. What if she had to prostitute herself and live a lie so far as April was concerned? At least he had been kind and generous. She might even have risked flinging herself on his mercy, for surely he could be counted on to have more of that gentle quality than the man before her. It was hard to imagine that they could look forward to much kindness from this man, even if he was her uncle.

"Yeah, that's me all right, more's the pity," he replied. "I suppose that means you're expecting all kinds of charity from me, just because I happened to have the same parents as my sister—and no great shakes they were as parents, if you want to know the truth. They never gave me a thing."

Lydia cast a baleful eye about the room. It revealed a poverty not only of means but of the spirit as well. She wondered that this man and her mother could have flown from the same nest, though she dimly remembered that brother and sister had not been close. Her mother had never lived like this, not even in their travels through the poorest, the most undeveloped regions. "Elbow grease," she used to say, "is cheap."

An idea came to Lydia all at once, and she spoke before she even paused to weigh it.

"It needn't be charity," she said.

"I don't know what else you could call it."

"My daughter and I could work. We could cook for you, and clean house. We could even help you in the shop. There must be odd jobs that need doing."

Richard's eyes narrowed as he considered her suggestion. He looked around the room as she had done, his gaze coming back to Lydia and her daughter. It gave Lydia an uneasy feeling to see those cruel, unfeeling eyes resting upon April's slim shoulders, and she was relieved when they turned back to her.

"This place could use some sprucing up, I suppose," he said. "Can you sew?"

"Yes," she lied without hesitation.

"That Chinaman in there ain't worth the powder it'd take to blow him to pieces. All right," he said, bobbing his chin in a decisive gesture. "That's the way it'll be, then, you'll stay here, sure enough, but I'll expect you to earn your keep, and I don't take no sass from anybody."

"We're very grateful for your generosity," Lydia said, with only the faintest hint of sarcasm, which he failed to detect.

"Well, just see as you remain grateful. And you can start right now, too. I could use some grub, and somebody ought to clean up these dishes." He paused, glancing around again as if searching for something.

"Didn't bring anything with you, did you?" he asked. "Like, say, some pipe?"

"Pipe?"

"Opium. I hear tell it's cheap there."

"No, we have nothing except what we're wearing," Lydia assured him.

"No luggage, either, huh?" His eyes narrowed again. "Didn't get run out of town, did you? Not that it matters, exactly, so long as you keep the work done, and the law doesn't come bothering me."

He started out of the room, but at the curtained doorway he paused and looked back. "And another thing," he added, "I don't want nobody around here thinking I got any Chinks for relatives, it makes the slanty-eyes all uppity if they think one of them's attached to you like that. You tell folks she's an orphan, or something like that, you hear?"

With that he went out. A moment later they heard him swearing at the old man in the shop.

Lydia looked around again, at the filth and the squalor. A flight of stairs led up from one corner to what she presumed were bedrooms above. A single window, its glass so dirty as to allow only the haziest of light to filter through, revealed a brick wall but a few feet away, while a back door stood open on a litter-strewn alleyway.

It was worse, if possible, than the opium den in which they

had hidden from the Dragon Empress. It seemed to Lydia that her whole life had been a succession of prisons, each one smaller, more confining than the one before. She longed to stand free in the sunshine, to fill her lungs with clean fresh air, and to savor the luxury of some corner of the earth that was hers alone.

Her gaze went to her daughter, and she found April's eyes upon her; they were sad, and a little frightened, but there was something more in them that gave Lydia pause. They seemed to be accusing her.

Lydia glanced away. "Well," she said, with all the scant cheer she could muster, "here we are, home, at last."

PART THREE

CHAPTER EIGHTEEN

"Where are you going?"

April paused half in, half out of the door. "Just out," she said, not turning to look at her great-uncle.

"Out where?" Richard came heavily across the kitchen, the smell of stale liquor preceding him. April had to make an effort not to wrinkle her nose. "And how come you never call me Uncle Richard?"

"You're my mother's uncle, aren't you? I can't call you Great-uncle Richard, can I? It's so unwieldy." She had no choice, now that he was standing beside her, but to give him a sideways glance. She found his eyes devouring her hungrily, with the same bestial greed as that with which he consumed the meals prepared for him. She could not say whether he frightened or disgusted her more.

He put out a hand, taking hold of her arm just above the elbow; the touch made her skin crawl.

"You ain't getting fresh with me, are you?" he asked. "There's ways of bringing people down when they get too snooty for their own good, you know."

She tried to free her arm. "Let me go," she said, unable to break his grip.

"You wouldn't be sneaking off to see some fellow, now would you?" he asked, turning her forcibly toward him.

"No," was all she said. She was too frightened now to quite trust her voice. She had begun to tremble, despite her efforts not to.

He felt her shaking, and it seemed to please him. A cruel grin broke across his face.

"So you're afraid, are you," he said. "That suits me fine, I like to see a female's eyes looking scared. Shows she's got the proper respect for a man."

She said nothing. She seemed unable now to remove her eyes from his. Staring at her, holding her trembling arms in his hands, Richard was aware, not for the first time, of her burgeoning womanhood.

She was, he calculated, about thirteen or so, but she had begun early, the way Chinese women did. Anyway, there was no harm in breaking them in young, as he saw it.

This was San Francisco. When he'd come here thirty-five years before, the gold rush had been in full uproar, and not even the vigilante committees that had sprung up from time to time had entirely managed to tame the city's wild ways.

Which suited him just fine. He liked satisfying his appetites when and where, and he didn't much care whether it suited anyone else or not.

He'd taught them younger than this one what the hole was for. And he had a mind too that if he didn't get busy at it soon, someone else might beat him to it.

That was a prospect that rankled. After he'd been so good to them, taking them in the way he did, providing a home for them and all, it wouldn't be fair for someone else to cop the prize. No sir, he'd just about better get cracking.

"Now then, where'd you say you were going?" he asked.

"I've got studies." April could hardly take her eyes off his. In China she had seen animals mesmerized by snakes before they were killed. He was like that, only without the reptiles' cold elegance.

Her answer was one that never failed to annoy him, so much so that his lust abated a little.

"Studies," he said, spitting the word out scornfully. "I never heard of a girl learning to think like a man. What you ought to be studying is how to keep a man happy, that's all the learning a woman needs anyway."

"Hadn't you better be going, dear?" Lydia said, coming in behind him. "Kim Lee will be waiting." He hadn't even heard her come into the room. Her voice startled him so that he let go his hold on the girl.

"I was just leaving," April said. Before he could recover, she had spun away from him, out the door. He watched the swish of her skirt as she disappeared down the alley, his jaw working in frustration.

* * * * * * *

Once safely away, April let out the breath she had been holding for she didn't know how long.

She was always terrified by that man, dreading those moments, avoiding, to the best of her abilities, when she must come into contact with him. She had at least a vague understanding of the burning she saw in his eyes when he looked at her, and so far she had managed to escape being alone with him for more than a minute or so at a time. She was lucky that her mother had come in when she had just now. It had been a mistake, going out through the kitchen instead of the shop, where she could count on her mother's presence. She must learn from it, so as not to make the same mistake again.

She sighed as she came out of the alley onto Grant Avenue, the heart of the city's Chinatown. It was only here that she felt at home. As a girl she had often slipped out of her father's palace in Kalgan and explored that city's teeming streets, and though this paled in comparison, it was still more familiar to her than anything else the city had to offer.

She strolled along slowly, not minding the cacophony of noise nor the throngs that occasionally jostled her, nor even noticing the frequent glances she occasioned, especially from young men. Already she gave promise of ravishing beauty. She had inherited the tawny skin of her father's ancestors and, in striking contrast, her mother's eyes, faded to a pale, soft green.

Her hair hung long and straight to her waist, and her body was already blossoming into a ripe fullness.

She had wanted to go to a public school. She wanted to be like other youngsters, and she had hoped to make friends. But a public school meant being registered and her mother had been afraid that someone would learn she was not merely an orphan child whom Lydia had taken under her wing. They had arranged instead for lessons with an elderly man who resided in the rear of a local bakery. He taught reading, writing and arithmetic and, so long as April's progress in those subjects remained satisfactory, he told her tales of old China.

April loved those stories best of all—of Yang Kuei-fei, the "Precious Consort" for whom a kingdom was lost, by the man who later strangled her; of Genghis Khan, whose throne was a saddle and whose hordes crushed the early city of Peking beneath their horses' hooves; of Kublai Kahn, whose court so thrilled the traveler, Marco Polo.

Though they were ancient history, the China that she had known was little changed from the China of which her tutor spoke. She felt that she could close her eyes and see it all happening. Sometimes the old man spoke of the fierce battles of the past, and it seemed to her that she could hear the blood-curdling cries of the Mongols as they charged down upon the Chinese, and the horrible screams of the wounded and the dying; the smell of blood and death filled her nostrils, and she could all but feel the rough hands of a warrior as she was seized and thrown bodily across the back of a sweating horse, a prize of war for some valiant chieftain.

Or again, she was not a peasant, but the Precious Consort herself, and the cries were not cries of agony, but those cries of strangely pained pleasure that she had heard sometimes from the houses of the concubines, and whose meaning stirred and troubled her even now.

Heaven and earth will pass away, but our love will endure, she thought, remembering one of the stories.

"What have you learned?" her mother asked each day, and

April would tell her of the other lessons, of new tricks to be performed with numbers, of new words learned, but of these stories she said nothing. What would her mother know of a love that would endure forever?

She had reached the bakery, walking slowly, savoring every sight and sound and smell. Someone brushed against her coming out the door as she went in, and the touch left a funny tingling on her skin, so that she almost expected sparks to fly from her fingers when she lifted her hand. She held it up, but there was nothing.

"You are late," her tutor said when she passed through to the room in the rear. He was tiny and shriveled, like the dried figs that they sold next door, and nearly as brown, but his eyes were the eyes of a young girl, deep and liquid.

The old man understood her well. He saw that she was lonely and unhappy, and he had lived long enough to know that this was dangerous, for it left one vulnerable. He ached, not for the hurts she had known, for these had scarcely bruised her youthful spirit, but for the hurt she was yet to know, and that was written indelibly in the pale green of her eyes, foreshadowed in the heart-wrenching shyness of her smile, so slow to move across her face.

But what could he do? He was hired to give her lessons, and the idea had come to him, as he had gradually discovered her deep love for the land she had left behind, that he might give her other lessons as well. He told her stories not only to entertain her, but so that she might learn from them—perhaps not now, but as the curtain of her life lifted, she might understand better the drama being enacted for her, and of which she must be a part.

It was not much, but he was old enough to know that there is little anyway that one can teach another that is of real value, for one's weaknesses will reveal themselves in their own time, and one's real strengths, no one can guess, and other than these, little matters. But it did not stop him from aching for her.

"I would like to hear the story of the five jade pieces," she said, seating herself at the battered little table.

He smiled, and put their work tablet on the table before her.

"Here are your sums for today," he said. "And this time, do as the tailor does, who measures twice, that he need sew only once."

* * * * * * *

"I'm nothing but a poor tailor," Richard Whitley was saying just then. "It don't seem fair to rob a poor man what has worked as hard as I have."

"That may be so," the man behind the desk said. "But your parents' will couldn't be clearer. Half the money for you—which you got long ago—"

"I was robbed of that by a pair of card sharpies, and I tell you, if ever I lay my hands on either one of them, they'll die knowing it."

"—and the other half for your sister."

"Well, she's dead, ain't she, it can't do her no good no matter what."

"The will states very clearly," the lawyer went on, paying little mind to the interruptions, "if she dies before claiming her share, it passes on to her children, if any."

"What if she hadn't got any?" Richard asked.

"But she has," the lawyer said. He was bored and impatient. He didn't much like Whitley, but the man did have a nose for easy cash; and, he was fair with those who helped him get his hands on it.

"Say," Richard said, his eyes narrowing suspiciously, "You wouldn't think of telling her about this would you?"

"Ethically I can't repeat what I discuss with a client."

"Ethically!" Richard showed his respect for that consideration by spitting noisily on the floor. The lawyer frowned in the direction of the spot.

"What if her child died before she claimed the money?" Richard asked, instinctively lowering his voice, though there was no one else about.

"Then it would pass to *her* children."

"What makes you think she's got any?" Richard asked slowly. So far as he knew, April's parentage was a closely guarded secret, and if the lawyer knew something, he was going to know how. He didn't much like the man, but he'd consulted him before, and he knew him well enough to know that he was shrewd and greedy—which was exactly the kind he liked to do business with.

"So far as I know, she hasn't," the lawyer said.

"What happens to the money then?"

"If your sister's child died without any heirs, the money would revert to you."

Richard got up, pushing his chair back noisily, leaving an ugly scratch in the wood of the floor.

"That's what I wanted to know," he said.

CHAPTER NINETEEN

It had been a relief for Lydia to hear the sharp slam of the door as Richard went out, just a moment or so after April. It did occur to her that he might try to follow April, but she comforted herself that there was little danger in broad daylight. Anyway, April had become so enamored of the Chinatown settlement that by now she knew it like the back of her hand. Richard would have a hard time trying to follow April if she didn't want to be followed. There were scores of shops she could dart into where she was known and where she would be safe.

Lydia quickly put aside the coat she had been sewing and got to her feet, stretching wearily. She had been working since before dawn, sewing clothes for herself and April in the hours before the shop opened, a break to prepare breakfast for Richard and April, then back to the machine, sewing for the shop this time. Later, there would be supper to prepare, and the cleaning to do.

Of course, if she did not insist on April's lessons, April would have more time to help with the work; that, however, would mean her being in the house more of the time, and as it was Lydia's nerves were stretched taut every minute that her daughter and her uncle were both in at the same time. April's understanding of Richard's desire might be vague, but Lydia's was not.

Indeed, it frequently seemed to her as if they had only traded one prison and one set of dangers for another.

Nor did it make it easier to consider what a trivial malice

was Richard Whitley's. At least the Dragon Empress of China, who had been evil and a threat to her, had about her a sinister grandeur. Lydia had lived long enough in China to know that there can be a certain honor in being bested by an adversary of consequence. It seemed almost more than she could bear to think of the dangers they had escaped, only to find themselves now at the mercy of so low and squalid a man.

It was only when April and Richard were both out of the house that she felt free to leave herself. Lydia hurried out to do some shopping. Since arriving at her uncle's, she had been acting both as housekeeper and as assistant in his tailoring shop, meaning that she did virtually all the work, since he had dismissed the old Chinese man who had been there when she arrived.

It was endless, exhausting work, for which he paid her little, in addition to their room and board. Try though she might, Lydia had been able to save almost nothing. Her dream of establishing her own cosmetics company still seemed as far beyond her reach as it had ever been. At her current rate of saving, it would take her an entire lifetime and then some to accumulate any sizable amount.

Lydia walked quickly along the street. It had been more than a year since they had arrived from China, and though she had since gotten used to the different pace of life here, like April, she found herself more comfortable in Chinatown. It was still hard for Lydia to recognize the country that she had grown up in as a little girl.

The railroads, she had gradually learned, were responsible for a great part of the change. Rail lines now connected San Francisco with the rest of the country. A small handful of men, however, controlled the railroads, and they were often portrayed in the popular press as a giant, malevolent octopus, an image which seemed pretty much in keeping with their actions. They abused the land and set their freight rates to punish or to bribe those whom they wanted to influence.

In addition to the railroads, the new telephones tied the once isolated west coast to the population centers of the east, though Lydia found the idea of speaking to someone whose face she couldn't see quite unattractive.

There was one difference between China and San Francisco that Lydia could be grateful for. Women here were no longer content to be decorative but helpless. They were to be found working in many different jobs now, as clerks and secretaries, teachers, journalists, even as telegraph operators; and women were active in sports as well.

She could not help thinking that the Chinese costume of loose trousers and simple tunic would have far better suited this modern woman of America than the current fashion of fitted bodice, narrow skirt, and clumsy bustle. Still, there was no denying that women here had more freedom and power than they did elsewhere, no doubt due in part to the freedom they'd had in the gold rush days.

It was the perfect place, she had thought often, for a woman to go into business for herself—if only she had the money to start up operations. She had managed to save the cosmetics, though she knew that the perfume was beginning to fade a little with the passing of time; but she was no closer to producing them than she had been a year ago.

Her errands over, Lydia hurried back to the shop. It was still half an hour before April was due to return from her lessons, but she was always afraid that something would bring her home early, and result in her being alone in the house with Richard.

The shop and the house seemed empty, but Richard's hat was on the rack in the corridor, indicating that he was about somewhere. Not wanting to announce her presence, and thus invite his attention to herself, Lydia stole up the stairs.

Her room, and April's, were empty. Reassured that April was still with her tutor, Lydia started quietly for the stairs, intending to return to the shop and resume her work.

The door to Richard's room, however, had swung open a few inches, giving her as she passed by a glimpse of the badly scarred dresser against the wall. In its mirror, she caught sight of her uncle, lying on his back across his iron-posted bed. At first she thought that he was weeping, and she paused, inclined to offer him her sympathy if some misfortune had befallen him.

A second glance informed her that it was not a handkerchief, as she had supposed, that Richard had buried his face in. She could not at first recognize the scrap of cloth, though there was something oddly familiar about it.

Richard moved just then, holding the cloth out at arm's length to contemplate it more fully, then once more clasping it to his face.

Lydia gave a shocked gasp. He was holding a pair of April's pantaloons, the very pair that had disappeared mysteriously from the laundry a few days before. She felt a shudder of disgust go through her.

Her sharp intake of breath reached Richard's ears. He shot up in the bed, his eyes snapping around to meet hers. Lydia felt a wave of scarlet wash over her cheeks and she tried to jump back from the slightly open door, but it was too late; he had seen her at once.

With a speed that belied his dissolute appearance, he leaped from the bed and crossed the room in three long strides, flinging the door wide.

"Spying on me, are you?" he demanded angrily.

He still carried the silken garment in his hand, and the sight of her daughter's intimate apparel in his coarse fingers gave rise to such anger that Lydia forgot her embarrassment.

"How dare you soil my daughter's clothing with your filthy desires?" she demanded. "She's little more than a child, and you...you...."

She could not find words odious enough to express her opinion of him, and her tirade ended in an angry sputter.

Far from being intimidated by her anger, however, he only laughed and shook the garment in her face. "People who spy ought to expect to see things they don't like," he said, "And as for her being a child, she's woman enough, and right there's the evidence, plain as day."

Lydia made a grab at the fabric, but he snatched it away from her. "Give me those," she demanded.

"Not likely, I kind of fancy them for a souvenir," he replied. His smile vanished suddenly, and his eyes narrowed as he looked down at her. She was breathing heavily, her breasts rising and falling with a rapid rhythm.

"Come down to it," he said, in a husky voice. "You ain't a child either, Madam."

She felt the pricking of fear. "What do you mean?" she demanded, still trying to brazen it out.

"I've got an idea, now. You want me to let your daughter alone, maybe you ought to do something to distract me a little, if you know what I mean."

"You're disgusting." She tried to turn away, but to her dismay he reached out and took a firm hold of her arm. He leaned toward her, his rank smell preceding him.

"Look at it from my point of view, now," he said. "Living with the two of you here, like I am, out of the goodness of my own heart, I can't bring no lady friends in, now can I? And it ain't no good for a man to go too long without certain things, it's bad for his outlook. So, since it's you who's to blame, in a manner of speaking, seems to me like you ought to be willing to make it up to me."

"You're out of your mind," she replied. "Let go of me. I'd sooner die."

Anger fell like a shadow over his face. "You didn't die from whatever Chink gave you the kid," he said. "If you ain't too good for a Chinaman, you damn well ain't too good for a decent white man, that's how I see it."

Lydia opened her mouth to scream, but he clapped a dirty hand over it, stifling her cry.

"Oh, no you don't, my fine lady," he said, dragging her into the room. With one foot he kicked the door shut. The window, closed as well, faced the empty alley. "No one would hear you if you did anyway."

She tried to flail at him with her hands, but to no avail; for all his dissolute appearance, his strength was awesome. In horror she felt the front of her gown being ripped open. A rough hand pawed at her exposed breasts, rubbing and squeezing them cruelly.

The hand was removed from her mouth and again Lydia tried to cry out, but this time it was his mouth that silenced her. His thick lips covered hers, his breath foul in her mouth. While she struggled, she felt herself dragged around, and a moment later she was flung across his bed, the springs creaking mightily.

She cried to kick her attacker, but her skirts impeded her. Richard gave a laugh, and there was a ripping sound as he tore her skirt aside. She felt cold air on her bare thighs, and then his pawing hands were upon her, tearing at her tender flesh. Lydia squirmed helplessly, trying to turn away from him, but to no avail.

"You wouldn't fight so hard if it was some blasted Chinaman, I'll wager," he said.

In fact, she was fighting less hard with each passing moment, for her strength was failing her fast. The struggle was weakening her, and realization of her helplessness in the face of his assault was robbing her of the will to fight. Rough hands seized her ankles, yanking her legs apart, and the shreds of her gown were ripped away.

She felt the weight of his body upon hers, his odor filling her nostrils, his legs shoving hers wider apart; then the piercing shaft of agony between her thighs, rending her flesh.

Lydia gave a gasp of pain as he tore into her. She was close to fainting as the pain seared deep into her belly. He gave a grunt, like some barnyard animal.

"Not so high and mighty now, are you, my sweet niece," he said, laughing coarsely.

She tried to beat at his shoulders with her fists, but she was weak from the shock of being attacked by this loathsome creature, and her blows were as faint as the fluttering of a sparrow's wings. He laughed again and, seizing her wrists, held them above her head while his body continued to pummel hers, their naked flesh coming together with sharp, slapping sounds.

The scene was mercifully brief. His movements grew quicker and more erratic, his breathing rasped louder in her ear, and at last she felt the stiffening of his body that warned of his climax. He moaned loudly, thrusting to the hilt within her, and seconds later collapsed heavily upon her.

She lay battered and defeated, barely conscious, as he stirred and lifted himself from her. She was too ashamed to open her eyes, or even to bring her legs together to hide herself from his sight—what did it matter if he saw what he had just violated so brutally?

He got up finally, nonchalantly tucking himself back into his trousers.

"In the future," he said, "I think we'll just figure this as another of your duties. Only the next time, I don't want so much of a hassle."

He went out of the room and disappeared down the stairs, whistling to himself. Lydia lay for several minutes, too numb to move. At last she stirred herself, but with the renewed activity came a wave of revulsion and horror at what had happened.

Worse, she knew that his threat was not an idle one. In the future she would be at the mercy of his cruel lust—unless she could find a way for her and April to fend for themselves.

Finally she had an idea—a slim one, perhaps, and far from what she had dreamed of; but anything that allowed them to escape from here was worth grasping for.

CHAPTER TWENTY

Later, in her own room, Lydia bathed and applied a healing salve to the wound that Richard had left on her thigh.

She heard the sound of April's footsteps on the stairs, and quickly donned a robe. She could not hide, however, a bruise where Richard had seized her wrist in his brutal grip.

"You've hurt yourself," April said when she saw it.

"Nothing serious," Lydia assured her. "I hit my hand on the sewing machine."

She had made up her mind not to tell April what had happened. It would only frighten her, and there was nothing to be gained. April already went to great lengths to avoid Richard, and she herself would be even more vigilant to see that the two of them were not alone together. Other than that, the best thing she could do was to find a way to remove them from this house.

She had only one resource, the cosmetics she had brought from China. It had been her intention to work until she had saved enough money to start a business of her own, but as things stood, that would take her years, and she now saw that it was impossible to wait so long.

Even if she couldn't start her own business, however, the cosmetics were still worth money. They were of the finest quality, certain to please any woman if they could be duplicated. And the cosmetic industry was booming. She had already looked into that. There was a firm right here in San Francisco, PM Cosmetics, which was very successful. She had sampled some of their products, and despite their large sales, they were decidedly inferior to what she could offer.

Very well then, what was to prevent her from selling her cosmetics to another company, such as PM Cosmetics? Their chemists ought to be able to duplicate what she'd brought from China. Perhaps they would even be willing to manufacture and distribute a separate line for her. And if not, surely they would be willing to pay her some sort of commission for the products. In time, she should be able to make enough to start her own firm, and even if she didn't, she should make enough to live on, without having to remain here at Richard's mercy.

She waited until the following day, until April had gone for her lessons as usual. Then, carrying a bag containing the cosmetic samples, she stole from the shop without bothering to ask Richard's permission.

They had spoken very little since yesterday's incident, and then, to her surprise, Richard had shown something astonishingly akin to contrition.

"You're not limping from that tiny scratch, are you?" he had asked, watching her descend the stairs earlier.

She had given him a look of utter contempt. "Your concern comes rather late, don't you think?" she asked.

"Now there's no use in holding a man responsible for what he does when a woman's got him all roused up," Richard said, his expression very hangdog. "I've been living a bachelor life for a long while, you know. It's hard on a man when all of a sudden he's got a couple of attractive wenches under his nose. Sooner or later he's bound to do something about it."

"My daughter is little more than a child," she replied. For a brief moment his abashed look had caused a twinge of sympathy for him, but she saw the quick flicker of denial in his eyes at her last remark.

"Keep your hands off her," Lydia said, lowering her voice to a warning level.

Richard's expression changed to his more familiar belligerent one. "Maybe I've got something riper to lay my hands on," he said. "Maybe there's somebody old enough to appreciate something good when they get it, even if they do kick up a ruckus."

He had not, however, attempted to lay his hands on her then. For that at least she was grateful. Indeed, in a perverse way, she even found herself grateful that he had reverted to his usual unpleasant character, for she found that brief glimpse of someone gentler oddly unsettling. So few people had shown her kindness in her life that she found herself susceptible to even the slightest touch of it. It would be easy to be deceived into staying as they were, but that was a folly that she would only end up paying for in time.

* * * * * * *

It was a cold day, a thick fog rolling in from the bay though it was early afternoon. The offices of PM Cosmetics were located in the heart of the downtown business district. It was still strange to Lydia, after years in China, to find herself surrounded by the towering buildings of concrete and steel; at the same time she found it strangely exhilarating. One could sense the pulse of the business world in the very structures themselves, brutally thrusting themselves into the yielding heavens. Yet the heavens were not conquered, for on a day like this, one could watch the sky reach down with tendrils of gentle mist that embraced and enveloped the turrets, until those cold, hard lines had been softened into something gentle and pliant and lay hidden behind gentle folds of fog.

Lydia was pleased to find a woman sitting behind the elegant desk in the reception room. There were still few women working in the business world and it spoke well for PM Cosmetics that their hiring practices were so progressive. Surely such a company would not shy away from negotiating a business deal with a woman, either.

"Can I help you?" the receptionist asked.

"I'd like to see someone in charge," Lydia replied.

"May I ask what about?" The girl was polite, but little more. Lydia had anticipated such a problem. After all, she hardly looked like someone an important executive would be eager to see. Not only was she a woman, but her dress, although the best of the two she owned, was shabby.

"I have some cosmetic preparations that I think may be of interest to the firm," Lydia explained.

The receptionist gave her a disparaging smile, as if this were a familiar scene.

"I'm sorry," she said, shuffling the papers on her desk and dismissing Lydia, "but all of our products are created for us by our own chemists, based on formulas brought back from the Far East."

This problem too Lydia had anticipated, and the girl had given her the perfect opening. "If your products are based on Eastern formulas," she said, opening her bag and taking out the vial that contained the precious perfume of the Dragon Empress, "I'm sure someone will find this interesting."

She dabbed a small amount of the perfume on the corner of her handkerchief and handed it across the desk. The receptionist took it with a doubtful look.

"I'm afraid you don't understand," she said. "So many people want to sell us their ideas, but my orders...."

"Please," Lydia interrupted her gently, "if you'll only take that to someone in charge, I promise you, you won't get into trouble."

For a moment the girl hesitated. Then, still reluctant, she lifted the handkerchief to her nose and sniffed. Her eyes widened perceptibly.

"Why, this is—it's wonderful," she said, staring at the scrap of cloth as if she were holding a handful of precious gems.

"You see," Lydia began, "it's...," but before she could finish, someone spoke from the office beyond.

"Miss Adams," a masculine voice called. "Could you come here, please?"

"Wait here," the receptionist said to Lydia. "I am going to show this to someone, someone important."

"Thank you," Lydia replied.

Miss Adams, her aloofness completely vanished, flashed her a quick smile, and hurried to answer the summons. Lydia watched her disappear through a door with frosted glass and a stenciled name that she couldn't make out. Warning herself not to get her hopes too high, Lydia seated herself in one of the wooden chairs along the far wall.

She did not have long to wait. Miss Adams was back almost at once, without the handkerchief, but with her eyes sparkling.

"Come with me, please," she said.

She stepped aside to allow Lydia to precede her into the office. As she did so, Miss Adams said, "This is the lady I just told you about, Miss...," she hesitated.

"Miss Nightsong," Lydia said, "and I'm so glad you were willing to see me. I take it you find my perfume interesting."

Miss Adams had gone out again, closing the door after her. The office into which Lydia had been ushered was furnished in an elegantly masculine manner, with one entire wall of books behind glass doors, and another of tall windows looking down upon Market Street below. There were leather-covered chairs with enormous wings and a fireplace in which a small fire was burning to ward off the day's chill.

Before the windows was a massive desk of carved oak. The man seated behind it had turned in his chair toward the light and was holding the scented handkerchief to his nose. With the light behind him, glaring after the dim reception room, and the cloth to his face, it was difficult to make out his features immediately.

"Interesting is hardly the word," he said. "Breathtaking, I'd say. Even more of a surprise to me, though, is how you happen to be in possession of a sample of the perfume worn by only one woman in the world, and she the Empress of China."

Lydia gave a gasp. "But how could you know that?" she asked. "No white man has ever been privileged to know that scent."

"One has," he said, putting the cloth aside and turning back to her, at the same moment rising from the chair, so that she got her first good look at him. "A servant girl once brought me a scarf scented with this perfume, and I would recognize it anywhere. I wish you'd tell me how you happen to come by it, though, Miss—Nightsong, was it? A peculiar name."

Lydia was struck speechless. His first words had rung a bell far back in her mind, but it was not until her eyes fell upon his face that full realization struck her with the force of a blow.

"You," was all she was finally able to say.

He stared uncomprehendingly. "I don't understand," he said. "Do you know me?"

So transfixed was Lydia that she could not reply, nor was she even aware of a tap at the office door, until Miss Adams opened it and stuck her head into the room.

"The gentleman from New York is here now, Mr. MacNair," she said, and vanished again.

CHAPTER TWENTY-ONE

For a dizzying moment the room seemed to swim about her. Lydia stared in disbelief at the man before her.

Peter MacNair. Through all these years since he had betrayed her to the mandarin, Ke Loo, this man's face had remained etched in acid upon her heart. She had dreamed so long of one day confronting him again, had relished the images of the satisfaction she would have, the scorn she would heap upon him, the shame she would bring him to feel, that she could now scarcely comprehend that the long-awaited moment was upon her.

Miss Adams had gone. They were alone, in a silence that might have lasted a second, or an eternity.

"Do I know you?" he asked, his eyes puzzled, mildly interested. Her lace handkerchief looked incongruous, forgotten in his huge, powerful-looking hand.

The question was like a dash of cold water. He had changed little. There were tiny lines at the corners of his eyes, the suggestion of furrows on his brow, the merest dusting of grey at his temples; that was all. She would have known him anywhere: the eyes the color of sable, the hair that scarcely looked to have been combed since she saw it spilled on a pillow next to hers, the sensual mouth, the purposeful, arrogant way of moving, as he did now, toward her.

"Don't," she murmured, holding up a hand as if to ward him off.

"Are you all right?"

Finally she began to understand. Of course, she had been a

mere child then, sixteen years old, and surely quite a different sight than the woman she was now; and why should he have remembered anyway? No doubt she was but one of many whose trust and love he had betrayed.

It was perhaps the most galling thing of all, that after all her years of hate and bitterness, when they should finally once again meet face to face, he did not even know who she was.

She waited, watching, and saw when the first faint glimmer of comprehension began to show in his eyes. His mouth fell open.

"It can't be," he murmured, astonishment spreading across his face. "No—not that little girl...?"

"Did you think you'd disposed of me forever?" she asked.

"It *is* you." He grinned, and to her horror it was the same grin as before, with the flashing of the eyes, and the dazzling glint of teeth, that had so set a young girl's heart to racing. She hated it, and hated him for it, because even now, as if in memory, her heart beat faster.

"You've changed so," he said.

"I have *been* changed," she said.

"Lydia—yes, that's it."

There were so many things she wanted to say. She wanted to strike out at him, physically as well as verbally; she wanted to fling her contempt in his face, she wanted to unfurl before him the banner of her suffering.

Yet she did nothing. She stood frozen, with a strangely pounding heart and a roaring in her ears that drowned out everything else, but mysteriously let her hear his words, and even the quick intake of his breath.

Dear God, she prayed, *give me a way to hurt him, lend me the power to make him weep, as I have wept, and ache, as I have ached.*

The prayer remained unanswered. He came to her. She might have been dreaming, for as if it were another woman entirely and she only a bystander, she seemed to see him take her in his arms. For an instant, the woman's arms lifted, as if she would put them about his massive shoulders, and her trembling lips parted.

"No!" She slapped out at him with her hand, as if to strike him, but he moved back, staring in surprise.

"Stay away from me, you—you monster," Lydia cried. She was furious, with him for what he had done all those years ago, and with herself for not fulfilling her dreams of vengeance.

Tears stinging her eyes, she turned and dashed from the room, past a startled Miss Adams, who called after her. Lydia did not pause, but fled along the corridor and down the stairs, blindly pushing past a startled trio waiting in the vestibule.

She ran out of the building and straight into the arms of an astonished gentleman, who grabbed her and prevented her from falling down, as she would otherwise have done.

"Miss Nightsong," a remembered voice said. "What's wrong, are you in trouble?"

Recovering her balance, Lydia looked at the man holding her arms to steady her. For a moment, seeing him through a veil of tears, she could not place him.

"I hope you're not being assaulted again," he said, looking angrily past her at three gentlemen in the lobby, who were still staring after her in an unfriendly manner.

"Mr. Hanover," Lydia cried.

"If those cads...."

"No, please," she said, tugging at his sleeve. "It was nothing to do with them—but I must get away from here, at once. If I could find a hackney...."

"There's no need for that," he said. "My carriage is waiting right here. Please, permit me."

"Oh, yes, thank you," she said gratefully. She let him hurry her to the carriage. A footman, seeing his master approach, leaped down to open the door for them.

Looking back over her shoulder, Lydia saw Peter MacNair emerge from the stairwell, pausing to look about for her.

"Oh, hurry," she exclaimed, hastily entering the waiting carriage.

Obediently Walter Hanover leaped into the cab after her and barked an order for the driver to start up at once. The footman had to scramble to avoid being left behind. As the coach sped away, Lydia looked back and saw a frustrated Peter MacNair standing at the curb, staring after them.

Until now, Lydia had been so concerned with escaping Peter MacNair that the other details of the event had had little impact. Having successfully gotten away, however, she now became fully aware of what had happened.

"Walter Hanover," she said again, sinking back against the cushions and turning her attention to her companion.

"Well, I'm grateful to see you still remember my name," he said, smiling.

"Oh, I could never forget anyone as kind as you were to us when we first arrived."

"You certainly managed to forget our last luncheon appointment," he said, but without bitterness.

Lydia had the grace to lower her lashes. "I'm sorry about that," she said. "Something came up, and I had no way of contacting you. Do forgive me, please."

"I will," he said, adding, "but only if I may collect my raincheck now. Will you have lunch with me?"

"Why—yes, of course," Lydia said, hesitating no more than a few seconds.

So much had happened so quickly—meeting Peter MacNair again, after so long a time, and then once more running into Walter Hanover.

"We seem fated to meet, don't we?" she said, speaking as much to herself as to him.

"Yes," he said. "Apparently when you're in trouble. Do you want to tell me what the difficulty was back there, or isn't it any of my business?"

"It was nothing, really," she said, sighing. "I ran into someone I'd once quarreled with."

"Rather violently, it would seem," he said, but he took her hand and patted it gently. "Never mind, you needn't tell me about it if you don't want. Are you all right now?"

"Yes, thank you. You're very kind." She gave him a smile. Inside, her emotions were seething. How incredible it had been to find herself so nonplussed at being confronted with the man she'd waited so long to meet again. She could hardly fathom the nature of her reaction to him. Had she really burst into tears, like some heart-struck schoolgirl? Where were the oaths, the curses she'd meant to rain upon him?

Of course, it had been a shock. PM Cosmetics—whoever would have dreamed that the initials would stand for Peter MacNair? Yet it was perfectly logical. After all, he had been in China for the express purpose of gathering cosmetic samples with which to start just such a business, and he had told her at the time that he came from San Francisco. She ought to have been prepared for the discovery.

It left her, however, with no place to turn. She hadn't the money to found her own company, and she certainly was not going to go into business with Peter MacNair, however desperate her situation.

Which left her exactly where she had been earlier, trapped in that hateful house with Richard Whitley, and not a chance of escape. Somewhere, there had to be a solution, an answer to her dilemma.

"Here you are," Walter Hanover said beside her.

Lydia started; she had been so absorbed in her own thoughts that she had almost forgotten the man who twice now had come to her rescue.

"What...?"

"The restaurant." He indicated the open window of the carriage. She looked, and saw that they had arrived at the Palace Hotel, which had the most fashionable restaurant in the city.

"But I'm not really dressed for anything so fine," she said, embarrassed to remember suddenly her shabby dress and the badly scuffed shoes that were all she had to wear.

"What nonsense, you'll be the envy of every dowager in the place—and I the envy of every man."

The footman had come around to open the door. He gave Lydia his hand, helping her down. She turned to flash a genuinely warm smile at Walter. It had occurred to her that perhaps she was not quite as trapped as she had just thought. There might, after all, be an answer to her prayers. It took no great prescience to see that Walter was a man of considerable means and any fool could see how enchanted he was with her.

He interrupted her thoughts to ask, "And your little Chinese maid, is she still with you?"

Lydia paused for a few seconds before answering. Now, she knew, was the right time to tell him the truth. If he was shocked to know that she had a daughter of mixed blood, well, she would most likely never see him again. On the other hand, he might well applaud her honesty, and she might still benefit from the attention of a man who was both wealthy and interested in her.

"To tell you the truth, April is actually," she began, but before she could finish, an altercation had begun almost directly in front of them. An elderly Oriental couple, dressed quite well, had wandered inside the hotel, clearly for no other purpose than to have a look. The hotel's doorman, however, had turned from seeing some guests into a carriage and, spying the couple, had descended upon them in anger.

"Get out, you yellow devils," he ordered. Seizing the man by the collar of his obviously expensive suit, he propelled him violently from the premises, the frightened wife running after them with little cries of alarm. As Lydia and Walter watched, the man was thrown bodily into the street. The doorman went back to his post, wiping his hands together as if they had been soiled. Lydia saw the wife bend down to help her husband to his feet.

"How dreadful," Lydia murmured.

"You mustn't mind," Walter said, taking her elbow and ushering her forward. "They shouldn't have shown such effrontery. I told you before, and I'm sure you've since discovered for yourself, Orientals are not often well looked upon here in San Francisco. But never mind about that, what were you saying before?"

"About April," she said. "My maid. You were right, she has found it a bit difficult here."

"Not leaving you, is she? Yellow-skinned or not, good maids are hard to come by these days, I can tell you that."

"No, no, she's not leaving," Lydia said. "I wouldn't think of letting her go. She means the world to me."

"I understand."

"No," she said again, giving him a warm smile, "I doubt if you could ever understand the relationship between us. She's like a daughter to me."

He laughed, but there was a warning edge to his voice. "I can certainly admire your affection and concern for someone who is beneath you," he said, "but you must be careful making statements such as that. There are many people who wouldn't understand. What if someone were to take you literally? Can you imagine how people would react if they thought you had a daughter of Chinese blood?"

"Do you mean I'd be thrown out of here, like that unfortunate couple a moment ago?" she asked.

"Exactly—and I'd probably give them a hand," he said, laughing again to show he meant no offense.

"Then I promise I will tell no one that she's my daughter."

They went into the restaurant, laughing gaily together.

CHAPTER TWENTY-TWO

"David's home!"

Peter MacNair's youngest son, Efrem, ran to greet him with the news as soon as Peter had entered the front door of the Nob Hill mansion he now called home.

"He is, is he?" Peter answered, catching the eight-year-old up in his arms. He swung him around playfully before handing him into the arms of Mrs. Steinmetz, the thick-set, dour nurse, who had followed her charge into the hall. "And where do you suppose he's to be found at this moment?"

"They're in the billiards room," Mrs. Steinmetz answered for Efrem. Her tone expressed an unwavering disapproval. The lax splendor of San Francisco's nouveaux riches grated upon her Teutonic sensibilities.

"Mama told him you'd deal with him when you got home," Efrem added, eyes shining at the prospect.

"That's enough, Efrem." Lorna MacNair's voice had the sting of a birch switch. She had come out of the library, the spectacles which were never worn outside the family circle balanced rather precariously on her nose. She was tall and thin, lovely in an austere way, though stiffness was becoming rigidity as she neared forty.

"Mrs. Steinmetz," she said, "I've told you not to let the boy run in the hall. He might fall and hurt himself."

"He got away from me, Mrs. MacNair," the nurse answered.

"Then you must watch him more carefully."

"Yes, ma'am, like a hawk."

"Or an American eagle," Peter suggested. Mrs. Steinmetz, failing to see any humor in the remark, gave him a blank look.

"Exactly," she said, taking her charge off. Efrem squirmed in her arms and waved to his father.

Lorna turned a taut cheek to her husband for a kiss. "As you've heard already, your eldest has been sent home somewhat unexpectedly," she said.

"Trouble again?" Peter asked; when she nodded, he asked, "What was it this time, another girl?"

She flashed a quick, hostile look, as if expecting him to be amused, and ready to quarrel with him about it. Seeing him looking properly annoyed, she softened her features slightly, though she was never entirely without a suggestion of a scowl.

"Playing cards," she said. "Several of his schoolmates complained that he'd taken every cent of their money."

"Was he cheating?"

The scowl deepened. "That's hardly the point, is it? Young gentlemen are not expected to be card sharps. This is Nob Hill, not some delta riverboat, and he is the heir to the largest cosmetics firm west of Chicago—a position for which he remains woefully unprepared."

"A position," Peter replied, "which he seems to want not at all."

"It's not a question of what one wants," Lorna said. "One has responsibilities."

He looked about to argue; changing his mind, he said, "I'll speak to him."

"I told him you would," she said.

She watched her husband go along the immense hall, with its simulated heraldic shields and its enormous carved wood chandeliers. It was a corridor that dwarfed many men, but not him. The sight of him, with his long-legged stride and his splendid body, broad in the shoulders and childishly slim in the hips, stirred sensual urges within her. Despite the coldness of her manner, her husband never failed to rouse desire within her, a desire she was often at pains to keep concealed. Only occasionally had it burned beyond her control, and she never failed to hate herself afterward. She would blush with shame at the memory of how she had writhed and clawed and cried aloud, like a common whore, like a woman enslaved by her husband's sexuality.

It happened rarely, and it disgusted her. She would have preferred to hate him without reservation. She knew that he had bought her with his pounding loins and the hard, rippling muscles of his back, exchanging them for her father's silver wealth. She knew that he was beneath her, and she seethed with scorn for him, gnawing at herself with jealousy when he turned to other women, as he so often did, because she knew they were beneath her too, and that she should be glad to be spared his caresses, his searing kisses that went where decent men's lips ought not to go.

Worst of all, the knife that twisted ceaselessly in her stomach was to look into his eyes and to see that he knew the power his body gave him over her.

She had waited for his looks and vigor to fade with the years, as other men's had who were younger than he, for then she would at last ascend to mastery—but they had not, and each time she discovered her hunger for him anew, it both thrilled and hurt her.

She watched, unmoving, until he had disappeared into the billiards room, and for several moments more, before she gave her spectacles a hard push, and returned to the library.

* * * * * * *

Peter paused in the doorway to the billiards room, for the moment unnoticed by his children. David was engaged in a game with his sister, Susan, a year his junior.

At sixteen, David looked the man, and acted the boy. Like his father, he was tall and handsome, the arrogant sensuality less blatant, but hard to miss anyway. He lacked, though, his father's edge of ruthlessness and his mother's austerity. He had a quality that was wanton, almost womanish, though he was in no way effeminate. He would not cut as hard, nor stand as unyieldingly, as either of his parents.

Peter had often wondered from whom the boy had inherited this side of his nature. He had hoped that David would outgrow it, but that had begun to seem unlikely. Perhaps it would have annoyed him less if he hadn't half suspected it had come down from his own family and not Lorna's. There was nothing soft anywhere in Lorna's family, including the bodies of their women. But it wasn't her body that he had married Lorna for.

Susan, a year younger and a woman already, seemed tougher than her brother. In a way, Peter regretted that she would not be the one to inherit PM Cosmetics, for there was little question that she would be competent to run the business. From the time they had been children, Peter had tried to involve them in the business operation, David because it would one day be his, Susan because David objected less to being dragged about the offices and the laboratories if his sister went along.

Always it had been Susan who listened and watched and asked perceptive questions, and David who was to be caught daydreaming, or looking for faces in the clouds outside the window.

Susan was the first to see their father standing in the doorway, though she waited until she'd finished her successful shot before signaling her brother.

"Hello, Father," David greeted him, managing to look cheery and unconcerned despite the wariness in his eyes. It occurred to Peter, not for the first time, that his son did not care a great deal for him. It was the first time, however, that another thought did occur to him—that perhaps he no longer cared so much for his son, either.

It was a disturbing thought, and Peter did not linger on it. He had not, in fact, planted the seed with the objective of becoming a parent, model or otherwise, but he had taken his responsibilities seriously. It had been his sincere desire to make his son as tough as he himself was, because he felt that there was no better preparation for surviving in a world of harsh realities. He was not a man who accepted—or concealed—disappointment well.

"This is rather a premature vacation, isn't it?" he said aloud.

Susan put aside her billiard cue. "I suppose I'm a bit *de trop,*" she said. "I'll remove myself."

"There's no need. If your brother will be good enough to join me in my study...?"

It was deliberately addressed to her, and not to David. Peter didn't wait for a response, but turned on his heel. David, rolling his eyes in his sister's direction, hurried after him.

David never failed to feel intimidated whenever he had to go into his father's study. It was a room without warmth or charm, the wood-paneled walls so dark that at night they seemed to recede into nothingness. Even the chairs were mercilessly hard. It was a room that, to his mind, perfectly reflected his father, with whom he was equally uncomfortable.

He was not told this time whether to stand or sit, and took the option of standing, in what he hoped was a properly contrite pose.

Peter sat behind a desk as big, David thought, as a boxcar. For a painfully long time he neither spoke to his son nor looked at him, but occupied himself instead with looking over the day's mail, always placed first in the box on his desk, regardless of to whom it was addressed.

David shifted his weight uncomfortably from one foot to the other. At first he kept his eyes glued to his father, wanting to be prepared for the inevitable moment when those dark eyes would turn up to stare unblinkingly at him, but after a while his gaze wandered. He studied a row of books, all elegantly if somberly bound; none of them, he was certain, had ever been opened, with the exception of one he'd taken down once himself to read. That mistake had earned him a sore bottom.

"Your fascination with books seems to have eluded your instructors at school," Peter said.

David jumped and blushed. *Caught again,* he thought, with a mixture of embarrassment and resentment. It always seemed as if his father deliberately waited to catch him when his attention had wandered.

"I like to read well enough, if it's the right book," David said.

"You like to do most things well enough," Peter said, "so long as it's to no profit."

"Not to argue the point, sir, but the school took rather the opposite view. A bit too profitable, if you take my meaning." He tried for a smile, but his nervousness made it look more like a grimace. He had begun to sweat, and was afraid to wipe his brow.

"Have you nothing to say for yourself?"

"Begging your pardon, but you've always stressed the importance of my learning to make money. Perhaps we could look at it that way."

Peter glowered at him for a moment, not quite sure if he had been made fun of or not. In fact, he was no more comfortable than David was.

"There are rules to making money, as there are to most things," Peter said.

"And have you never broken the rules?"

"There are rules, even, for breaking the rules," Peter snapped.

There was a tap at the door, and a maid came in to tell him that a Mr. Ramsey was outside to see him.

"Send him in," Peter said.

"Shall I go?" David asked when the maid had gone out again.

"Yes, but only to your room. I know the director of this school, a greedy little bastard. You'll return to school tomorrow, with a suitable check, and your own apologies, which you'll see are good enough to get you reinstated. I'll take the check out of your allowance. And the next time, it'll come out of your hide."

Though his father's manner seemed to dismiss him, David hesitated. Peter, who had returned his attention to his papers, looked up again.

"Yes?"

"I was wondering—you couldn't make the trip yourself, deliver the check in person, if you know what I mean?"

"I'm not in the habit of making deliveries," Peter said matter-of-factly. "I—we—are in the cosmetics business, a fact of which you seem woefully ignorant. And I'm through changing your diapers. The next time you'll have to wear them soiled. If you know what I mean."

The maid knocked again, and ushered Mr. Ramsey into the room. Peter looked at David and jerked his head in the direction of the door. Wordlessly, David went out.

"A fine-looking boy," Ramsey said, speaking around a cheap cigar that had quickly begun to spoil the air in the room. "Your son, I take it?"

"Yes," Peter replied, with neither pride nor joy.

Fitting his attitude to that of his host, Ramsey said, with a sigh, "They try a man, don't they? Children, I mean."

"I've no need to hire a detective to tell me about my own son, Ramsey. Sit down."

Unoffended, Ramsey sat in one of the tall, hard chairs. "Suppose you tell me what you did hire me for, then, and I'll get to it that much sooner."

"I want you to find someone," Peter said. "A woman."

Ramsey gave a sly chuckle, rolling the cigar from one side of his mouth to the other. "Shashay la femme, huh?" he said, mangling the French. "Who is she?"

"She's going under the name of Nightsong, Lydia Nightsong."

"Married?"

"I would say so. I knew her under a different name in the past, but I can't remember what it was. She's tall, reddish-yellow hair, the sort they describe as buxom."

"Sounds like a looker," Ramsey said with a knowing leer.

"She is," Peter said, ignoring the leer. "She would have come here from China, though perhaps not directly. That's about all I know—oh yes, she was riding in Walter Hanover's carriage today. There must be some sort of connection between the two of them. He's the Nob Hill Hanover."

"That's mighty little to go on," Ramsey said.

"You'll be paid well enough for your trouble."

Ramsey removed the cigar from his mouth. "Make any difference how I go about finding her?" he asked.

"Not to me. Except, of course, if you get into any trouble, keep my name out of it."

"You know me, Mr. MacNair, the very soul of discretion. Never you worry, if she's in the city, I'll find her for you. Want me to have her brought to you?"

"That won't be necessary. Just let me know what you find."

"You're the boss," Ramsey said, getting up. "I'll be getting back to you."

When he had gone, Peter rang for the maid. While he was waiting, he went to the liquor cabinet and poured himself a glass of Scotch, pausing for a moment to study the glass's contents, and adding another inch to them before stoppering the bottle.

"You rang, sir?" the maid asked, coming in.

"Yes, get rid of that," Peter said, indicating the cigar Ramsey had left smoldering in the ashtray. He waited until the girl had gone out, then walked to the window, and half emptied his glass.

That girl—to know that she was here, in this very city. He had all but forgotten her, and yet some inescapable memory had stayed with him down through all these years since that night in China. She had lingered at the far reaches of his consciousness, like a fragment of a dream that would not fade into the morning mists.

He gave a toss of his head, as though to dislodge his troublesome thoughts. It was not she that he wanted, but the perfume she had carried out of China. He must have it.

But first, he must find her.

CHAPTER TWENTY-THREE

"But you can't mean that you live here." Walter Hanover surveyed the tailor shop with an air of dismay.

"I'm afraid so," Lydia replied. "There was an incident aboard ship on our way back from China. We lost virtually everything. As a result, I arrived here pretty much at the mercy of my uncle. This is his shop."

Walter glanced up at the windows of the second floor. "But those rooms must be miniscule," he said. "There's hardly room to turn around in."

Lydia laughed lightly. "It is cramped but it's not quite that bad. No doubt you're used to grander accommodations than we are."

"And have you no other family?"

"None," Lydia said with a sigh.

Luncheon had been a thrilling experience. After living so long at the level of meanest existence, it was an indescribable joy to sit at a table covered with fine linen, to feel the smoothness of real silver in her hand, and to dine on haute cuisine. They had eaten cold poached salmon with a green mayonnaise and cucumber slices, and after that a delicate salad of watercress and tomato, and then raspberries with cream, accompanied by champagne and coffee to finish. The service had been flawless. Walter was obviously known to the maitre d'hotel, and she suspected this was the reason no one had seemed to notice her shabby costume.

After the months with her uncle, she could appreciate

Walter Hanover all the more. It was true, he was anything but a romantic figure, but when all was said and done, what did she care for romance? She had only to think what romance had cost her to be grateful to be done with it.

And in other respects, Walter was an acceptable companion. He was intelligent and charming, and a perfect gentleman. She was not a fool, and she certainly could read the message in the glances that he gave her, particularly when he thought she wasn't looking, but he did not force his hand.

He had even managed to make her almost forget the unfortunate meeting with Peter MacNair.

Like the passage of a dark cloud before the sun, the memory cast a shadow over her mood. That man. It had been so long that she had even managed to overcome much of the bitterness that had been his legacy to her. She had been sure that she would never see him again, and it had been much more important to concentrate her energies on simply getting through the day.

Like a ghost he had returned to haunt her. It had been one thing to look back upon him as a part of a distant past. But to know that he was here, in the same city, that any day their paths might cross, was more than she could bear.

Oh, how could she have been so silly? She had behaved as if she had been thrilled to see him, as if she still desired his kisses, his arms about her. She felt certain that if she but closed her eyes, she could remember every moment of the night they had spent together—the feel of his body against hers, the sound of the rain beyond the window of the little Chinese cottage, and on the wall, where she could just make it out beyond his shoulder, a painted bird, singing to a painted moon....

"Are you all right?" It was Walter's voice, solicitous, concerned, yanking her back to reality. With a shock, Lydia realized that she had indeed closed her eyes and been wafted back in time.

"Yes, I...thank you, I was remembering something."

She looked out of the window, as if to reassure herself that this was reality, and the other only a memory. Yes, they were still seated in Walter's carriage outside the tailor shop, the horses pawing the street nervously. Above them, the driver cleared his throat.

"You haven't yet told me what upset you so badly earlier, when you ran into me," he said. "If there's any trouble, I wish you'd let me help."

"It was nothing, a personal quarrel with someone," she said with a dismissive gesture. "I'm afraid I reacted badly. I must have seemed a perfect fool."

"You could never seem anything to me but a perfect angel," Walter said, clasping her hand.

"I'm anything but that," she said ruefully. The buoyant mood that had carried her through lunch had dissipated. "Perhaps I ought to go in."

Walter looked again at the shop, a slight curl of his lip revealing his disapproval. "This won't do at all," he said. "If we're going to be seeing one another, you can't go on living here—oh, I say, we *are* going to be seeing one another, aren't we?"

"Why, if you want to, of course."

"And you won't go disappearing again, like the last time?"

"I promise," Lydia said, flashing a smile at him. She did not add that this time she had nowhere to go.

His face suddenly brightened. "But of course, how foolish of me. These cosmetics of yours, the ones you were telling me about—are you sure that women will want to buy them?"

"I know that I would, if they were for sale, and I could afford them," Lydia said. "But I've already explained, the backing that I was hoping to obtain fell through, and it seems unlikely that I'll have the money for a great many years."

"Never mind about that. Come with me." He rapped for the driver, and told him to drive them home. Lydia offered no argument. Perhaps after all her prayers were going to be answered this time.

The carriage brought them virtually to the top of Nob Hill, slowing before a huge granite structure that made up in massive size and grandeur what it lacked in beauty. They turned into a porte cochere and stopped.

"Here we are," Walter said, helping her down. "This is home."

"Why, it's enormous," Lydia said, glancing up at three stories of leaded windows, with turrets above that. After living in the palaces of China, with their countless tiny bungalows, like so many precious gems in a perfectly sculpted setting, she found American mansions rather grim and forbidding, but she was hardly likely to tell Walter that.

As if reading her thoughts, he said, "Frankly, I find it a little grotesque, but my father had ambition, not taste. Anyway, it's more comfortable than it looks, or maybe I'm just used to it."

He took her arm and led her in. The door opened for them as if by magic, but as they came in Lydia saw that it was the work of a uniformed butler, whom Walter greeted offhandedly.

"Is my mother in?" Walter asked, handing the butler his hat and walking stick.

"She's in the parlor, sir," was the reply.

Walter led her along a corridor lined with oil paintings. They passed several rooms, and she had glimpses of heavy carved furniture and sofas covered in deep velvet. The atmosphere was moneyed and overpowering.

Walter's mother suited the mansion perfectly. She was as oversized and overdone as the Victorian furnishings, and quite as grim and forbidding as the house itself.

She acknowledged Lydia with a curt "How do you do," and a pointed glance at Lydia's worn dress. "You have rather an unusual name," she added.

"Only because people aren't used to hearing it," Lydia replied. "I'm sure that Hanover must once have sounded peculiar too."

Mrs. Hanover greeted this suggestion coolly, though Walter found it amusing. "I think she's got you there, Mother," he said.

"Walter, don't be foolish," his mother said. "Hanover is a very old and highly respected name, Miss Nightsong."

Walter said, "Miss Nightsong, have you got those cosmetic samples—that perfume you were telling me about, perhaps."

Lydia obediently produced the vial of perfume. Walter took it from her and handed it to his mother.

"What do you think of this?" he asked her.

"Really, Walter, I don't think...."

"Please, just sniff it and give us your honest opinion," he insisted.

"I would hardly give you any other kind," she said, taking the vial.

She removed the stopper and held the vial tentatively up to her nose, looking as if she were quite prepared to dislike the result. One eyebrow lifted slightly. She held the vial away to look at it for a moment, then brought it to her nose again.

"What do you think?" Walter asked impatiently.

"Why, it's very nice," she said, "though I can't quite place it. French, I should say, and very expensive—perhaps Lanvin, though it's even more subtle than their scents usually are."

"Would you buy it, if it were available?" Walter asked.

"Well, I don't know, I've worn the same perfume for years—but yes, I suppose I would. It's very unique. Do you mean to say this is something new?"

Walter gave a boyish whoop of glee. "So new, no one's even discovered it yet, but they will. Mother, we're going into the cosmetic business."

"Really, Walter, I can't see...," Mrs. Hanover began, but it was to Lydia that Walter turned. She had said nothing during all this, though she had been pleased to see her perfume impress the aloof Mrs. Hanover.

"There's your answer," Walter said to Lydia. "We'll finance your company—our very own cosmetic firm. You won't need to find other backers."

"But I can't just accept charity," Lydia said.

"I'm not talking about charity. We'll invest in your firm. You have the product, we'll put up the money. It's a straight business arrangement."

"Really, Walter...," his mother started to say, but she was interrupted by a high-pitched squeal from the hallway and a girl a year or two younger than April burst into the room, her long hair swinging.

"Daddy," she cried, "I'm home, and Aunt Augusta says to tell you I can come back in the fall if I want, and it's all right with you, oh, please say it is, please."

She threw herself at Walter, hugging him in a wild embrace. Laughing, Walter hugged her back.

"Whoa, slow down," he said. "That's too much to take in all at once. Anyway, I want you to meet someone."

She swung around, discovering Lydia, and though she continued to smile, her brown eyes seemed to harden. Lydia got the impression that the girl had had occasion to meet her father's lady friends before, and that she liked her no more than the others.

"Hello," she said.

"This is Miss Nightsong, my new business partner. My daughter, Kathy," Walter said, beaming at first one and then the other.

"How do you do," Lydia greeted her.

"What sort of business?" Kathy asked.

"A very fragrant one, which I'll tell you all about in due time. Now be a good girl and run along, and I'll come and see you in a little while."

"But I haven't seen you in a month," Kathy said. "Can't you come with me now?"

"Never mind, darling," Mrs. Hanover said. "Your father's engaged just now. Why don't you come along with me, and we'll see if cook hasn't got some fresh cookies especially for your homecoming."

She put her arm about the girl's shoulder and would have led her from the room, but Kathy resisted being gotten rid of so easily.

"Are you engaged, Father?" she asked, looking from him to Lydia, and back to her father again.

"Only on business, I'm sorry to say," Walter replied, winking at her. "But cross your fingers for me."

Lydia was embarrassed by the frank declaration, and it was readily apparent that neither Walter's mother nor his daughter found the remark much to their liking. Walter appeared not to notice, though Lydia could not tell if he was being deliberately obtuse or not. She had already discovered that he could be relentlessly cheerful, but surely he must know that her presence was resented.

Of course, so far their relationship had been merely platonic. Whatever his mother or daughter might think, she had not committed herself to anything more so far as Walter was concerned.

Not that she hadn't considered the various possibilities; but the question of April still remained. Obviously Walter would never accept her having a daughter who was half Chinese; but would April be willing to accept practicing a deception which must be humiliating, even painful to her? It was a great deal to ask, even if it did mean assuring their future.

"I must say, you don't look very pleased," Walter said when they were alone again. "I thought you had your heart set on this company of yours."

"I did," Lydia admitted. "But this is all so sudden. I don't know what to think."

"Mother liked your perfume," he said, "and I like your enthusiasm for it, and your determination. Don't worry, the money won't be a gift, only an investment. And the cash I put up now will allow you to find yourself more suitable living quarters—at least until I persuade you to consider the arrangements I really have in mind."

"If we can truly think of it as a loan," Lydia began hesitantly.

"Have no fears, I intend to get full return back on my investment," Walter said. "But enough of this. I think it's time we drank a toast to our new company."

He rang for the butler, and when he appeared, ordered him to bring a bottle of champagne and glasses. While they waited, he prattled on about various business details, contracts that would need to be drawn up, offices, laboratory facilities.

Lydia listened with half a mind. She was thinking ahead. She was certain that, with the right backing, she could make a success out of duplicating and marketing the items she had brought with her from China. Peter MacNair had brought back cosmetics far inferior to hers, and clearly he had established a prosperous business with them. She was certain to do as well. If that required practicing a little deception, why, surely that was not too much to ask of her daughter, when the rewards were so great.

Hadn't she herself made every sacrifice to get them out of China, to bring them here, and keep them alive thus far? Anything was preferable to continuing as they were in Richard's Whitley's home. His brutal assault on her was sure to be repeated. And how long would it be before April suffered the same fate?

No, she was being offered a golden opportunity. She would be foolish to let a few qualms of conscience stand in the way now, after all she had already gone through.

She would make April understand, somehow.

The butler returned with a cart, on which rested a bottle of champagne, set in a bucket of ice, and a tray with two crystal glasses.

Walter himself opened the wine and poured it, the sparkling bubbles spilling over the gilt-edged rims. He gave her one, and lifted the other in a toast.

"What shall we call our new firm?" he asked.

Lydia hesitated a moment. "In a way, we have a third partner," she said. "Perhaps we ought to dedicate it to her—the Dowager Empress of China."

"Excellent," Walter said, beaming. "Very well, then, here's to Empress Cosmetics—products fit for royalty."

CHAPTER TWENTY-FOUR

The amount of money that Walter proposed to invest seemed staggering to Lydia, and at first she was reluctant to accept so much.

"It's not merely a matter of generosity, you know," he explained. "If I'm going to invest, I want the company to be first class right from the start. There's psychology involved in marketing, you know. People want to deal with a firm that projects an image of success."

His arguments did indeed make sense, especially when he reminded her that, though the amount seemed large to her, it really was not in terms of his financial status.

"In plain English," he added, "I can afford it."

Before they left the house on Nob Hill, he gave her a check for five thousand dollars, and they agreed to meet the following day with the attorneys, to work out the details.

Lydia's elation began to fade, however, as Walter's carriage carried her back to Chinatown and the tailor shop.

There was her uncle to face, for one thing. She knew him well enough by now to know that he would not be pleased at their leaving him, especially when he was losing so much cheap labor. When he learned that they were going to better themselves, and improve their lot, he would no doubt expect to share in their good fortune, whether he was entitled to or not.

Even more worrisome, however, was April. Lydia knew that her daughter would be hurt to learn that she was expected to live a lie. But what other hope had they of escaping from the dreary existence they were now living?

"I've got just one request," Walter said as they stopped in front of the shop. "I want you to move out of here as soon as possible, into something a bit more suitable."

"I can hardly start spending the profits from a company that hasn't even been formed yet."

"The accountants can charge the expense to you, and deduct it from your share when the company actually does make a profit," Walter insisted. "Which I'm confident won't be too far in the future."

"You're very kind to me," she said.

He beamed like a small boy who's just done something very extraordinary. "Of course, I've got my motives," he said.

Lydia made no reply to the veiled suggestion. She was quite aware of Walter's feelings toward her.

Her own feelings were less clear. Certainly she thought him generous, and even pleasant company, but then, after living with Richard, almost anyone else would seem a relief. She couldn't imagine Walter in a romantic role, though it was obvious that that was the role he wished to play in her life.

Still, romance was unimportant to her. She knew that she would never again be sexually aroused by a man; that part of her life had long since been over. And in every other respect, Walter was a model companion.

Every respect but one, and that was his feelings toward people of Oriental blood.

Walter came into the shop with her briefly. Lydia was grateful, as she knew Richard would be angry that she had been gone so long without having told him anything in advance. She had a pang of guilt as she realized that April would have returned from her lessons some time ago, and no doubt had been frightened at being alone with Richard, but she was sure to have avoided his presence.

When Richard saw Lydia in the presence of an obvious gentleman, his initial scowl vanished, to be replaced by an obsequious manner she'd never seen in her uncle before. He fawned and flattered, and seemed not to notice Walter's shrinking away from him, nor the look of distaste on his face.

"I can see you're a man that likes his tailoring done very fine," Richard said, his greedy eyes devouring the cut of Walter's fine suit. "It's a shame you've not come in my shop before this. We do quality work here, as my niece can happily tell you, and it's not often we get to work for a man of real taste. Would you want to look at a piece of goods while you're here?"

"I think not," Walter said, wrinkling his nose slightly. He took Lydia's hand and walked to the door with her. "Don't be forgetting my request," he said, winking. "The sooner you get around to it, the better I'll like it."

"I'll look around first thing in the morning," she promised him.

He bent and kissed her hand before going. Lydia stayed by the door until his carriage pulled away, Walter leaning out to wave goodbye to her again.

She turned back to find Richard his usual self again, his dark eyes glinting angrily.

"That's quite a gentleman for you to be mucking about with, ain't it?" he asked sarcastically. "Just picked you off the streets, I suppose?"

"I met Mr. Hanover previously," she replied. "I just happened to run into him again today, and he invited me to lunch, if it's any of your business."

"Oh, you met him previously, did you?" he asked, mimicking her voice. "No doubt at the governor's ball. And it is my business, if a female of my family, living in my house, is going to start peddling her wares around town. I've got my own reputation to think about, you know."

"I can assure you, your reputation's in no danger from me," Lydia replied. "And as for our living in your house, that will be changed very soon. We'll be leaving here in a short while."

"What? Moving in with the fine gentleman, on such short notice as that?"

"If you must know, Mr. Hanover and I are going into business together, and he's advanced enough money so that April and I will be able to afford a place of our own, as soon as we find something suitable."

"What kind of business?" Richard demanded, blocking the doorway when she would have gone past him into the living quarters.

"Cosmetics," she replied. "We're forming a company, Empress Cosmetics."

"You mean all those bottles and jars you brought with you? He's paying you money for those?"

"Yes, exactly."

His eyes narrowed craftily. "And what about me?" he asked. "Don't I get nothing, after I took you and the brat in the way I did, looked after you like you was my own? Now I'm to be cut off without anything?"

"I wouldn't exactly say that," Lydia replied hotly. "You've had a year of our labor, for far less than you could hire anyone else. And more than that, besides."

"You wouldn't be referring to that little episode between us yesterday, now would you? I don't see no reason to be sore about a little tousle, it was bound to happen sooner or later, the two of us living here together the way we have been."

"All the more reason for April and me to move as quickly as we are able," Lydia said.

She brushed by him, half expecting him to try to grab her, but he made no move. Breathing more easily, she hurried up the stairs.

The door to April's room was locked. "Who's there?" April called when she knocked.

"It's your mother," Lydia replied.

The door opened in a moment, and April flew into her arms. "Thank heaven you're home," she cried.

"Has anything happened?" Lydia asked, her heart skipping a beat.

"No, it's just that I'm always frightened when I find out I'm here with him." April lifted a tear-stained face. "Oh, Mother, where have you been?" she demanded, fright giving way to anger.

Lydia felt a pang of guilt. She hadn't intended to be gone so long when she had left the house. Later, when she had met Walter, she had been too engrossed in exploring the possible benefits of his friendship to hurry home.

"I'm afraid I got tied up on business," she said aloud. "And I'm truly sorry you've been worried, dear, but I know you're going to be happy when you hear what I've been up to."

"Business?" April pulled free from her embrace and stepped back into her room. Her expression was hurt and petulant. "You mean for your uncle?"

"No, I mean for us," Lydia said brightly. "And it means you won't have to worry about him in the future. We're going to get a place of our own."

April looked skeptical. "When?"

"As soon as we can find a place. And we can start looking tomorrow—today, even, if you want to."

"Oh, do you mean it?" Her face broke into a smile, but she quickly sobered again. "But what kind of business do you mean?"

"Our very own cosmetics company, Empress Cosmetics. It's a long story, but anyway, I ran into Walter Hanover—you remember, the gentleman we met that first evening in town, who got the hotel room for us—and he was so impressed with the samples I have that he's advanced the money to start the business, and enough besides to find better living quarters."

"And he didn't even mind when you told him I was your daughter, and not your maid?" April asked.

Lydia turned away. "I haven't exactly told him that," she said. She saw her daughter's face fall. "Oh, I know it's unpleasant for you, but don't you see, it's our only hope of getting away from here. And aside from his prejudice, he's a very nice man, really."

"But there isn't any 'aside from his prejudice,' is there?" April asked angrily. "He'll be around all the time, won't he?"

"Not all the time," Lydia replied. "And it's not the worst sacrifice that could be asked. I'll have to do my share too, after all."

"Let him make love to you, you mean, the same as all the rest of them?"

Without thinking, Lydia slapped her face. At once she was horrified at what she had done, and at her daughter's anguished expression.

"Oh, darling, I'm sorry," she cried, grabbing April and hugging her tightly. "Please, please forgive me, I reacted without thinking."

"It's all right," April said after a moment. She squirmed free of her mother's embrace.

"If it matters so much to you," Lydia said, "I'll give Walter's check back to him and tell him I've changed my mind. Besides, if he was interested enough to invest money in Empress Cosmetics, then someone else will be too, someone without any romantic notions."

"No, don't do that," April said. She spoke calmly, and her face was devoid of any emotion. "You were right, it is our only hope of escaping from here. When can we look for a place to move?"

"Why, any time you like." Somehow, Lydia found her daughter's quiet resignation more bothersome than her anger had been a moment before. "But...."

"Let's do it right away, then," April said, interrupting her. "I am afraid of Uncle Richard."

PART FOUR

CHAPTER TWENTY-FIVE

"San Francisco certainly has the most unusual weather," Lydia said, taking off her bonnet as she came into the house. "It's sometimes freezing in the summer, and sometimes scorching in the winter."

"Father says San Francisco is like a woman," Kathy Hanover replied. "Always trying something different."

"Well, I know some women who won't change for anything," Lydia said, thinking of Kathy's grandmother, though she did not say so.

The house was pleasantly cool, at least. She had left the windows and curtains closed, against the unseasonable December heat, and the rooms were dark after the outside glare.

"Oh, hello." April, hearing their voices, had come in. She looked disappointed to find that Lydia was not alone, but in the company of Kathy.

Kathy, startled by her unexpected voice, jumped and whirled about.

"You little fool, don't you know better than to sneak up on people like that?"

"I'm sorry," April replied, without a trace of contrition. "It's the carpeted floors, I forget that they muffle footsteps."

"Your memory's not very good, it seems to me," Kathy said. "And don't stand there gawking like a fool. Get me something cold to drink, and be quick about it."

For a few seconds, April hesitated. Then, with a silent glance in Lydia's direction, she started from the room.

"Wait, dear," Lydia called, angry with Kathy, and with herself for permitting the outburst. "Come and see what I bought you."

"I'll just get Miss Kathy's drink," April said, and went out without pausing.

"Really, Kathy," Lydia said, turning on the younger girl. "Your rudeness was inexcusable."

"Well, I don't see how you can put up with that girl, she's arrogant, and hopelessly inefficient."

"She's my—" Lydia began, in her anger close to revealing the truth; but at the last moment, she thought better of it. "—problem," she finished lamely.

"All I can say is, servants must enjoy an entirely different station in China. In San Francisco, that girl wouldn't last two days working for anyone else. Certainly not for a Hanover. Why, my mother would take a switch to her before she threw her into the street."

"Then I'm quite glad she's not working for your mother," Lydia replied. The truth was, she cared no more for Kathy than April did. The child was a snob of the worst order, and though for Walter's sake the two of them had made an effort at being friendly, both were well aware that it was nothing more than a pretense, and a burdensome one at that.

Nor was Walter's mother any easier to get along with. It had been a difficult four months since Lydia had accepted Walter's offer to invest in Empress Cosmetics.

The company was progressing nicely. Offices had been found, and a laboratory for the manufacture of the products. Before they could be manufactured, however, they had to be duplicated, and a month ago Walter had had to invest another sizable sum to cover additional expenses. They had hired a chemist and five assistants, plus a secretary.

The chemists had gone on what seemed to Lydia a spending spree, except that their purchases were all chemicals and pieces of equipment. After a great many false starts, in the course of which Lydia had all but despaired, they had finally had a success: an almost perfect duplication of one of the lotions that had been used by the Empress of China to make wrinkles seem to vanish. The feel, the smell and look, even the results, were indistinguishable from the original.

After that, success had seemed to come swiftly. Only the finest of the items, the perfume that Lydia had already named Nightsong, eluded their best efforts.

"You need what the French call a *nez*," the chemist, a squat, intense man named Morris, had told her. "A nose, to translate it literally. They are to the blending of perfume what the great wine tasters are to the wine-makers."

"But can't you just analyze the perfume and learn what went into it?" Walter had asked.

"Of course. We can tell you what blossoms, in what proportions, what was used as the oil base—but we cannot make it smell the same, because no two flowers smell the same. You can't make a perfume formula by writing, one cup of rose petals, because yellow roses won't smell the same as red roses, and this batch of red roses won't smell the same as that batch of red roses. A *nez* determines how many of what blossoms he needs to duplicate the original scent. That's how all the great scents remain the same over the years."

"Then we must hire a *nez*," Lydia said.

Morris gave a little laugh. "I'm afraid that's easier to say than to do. Great ones are born, not made, and often the tradition is handed down from father to son, who carry on for generations with the same perfume makers. That is why so few new perfumes appear that are truly great, and why they so often fail so quickly."

"But surely there must be someone...."

Morris shrugged. "If I knew of anyone, madam, I would recommend him in a minute. But perhaps someone will appear in time—after all, more and more people are flocking to this country, and to California, people from every field of endeavor. Who is to say that a great *nez* will not appear here too?"

"And until then?"

"Until then, we will continue our work in the laboratory,"

Morris said, shrugging again.

"Never mind," Walter consoled her. "Even without the perfume, we can make a success of the company. And Morris is right. Somewhere there must be a qualified man who would like to come to America, particularly if the price is right. I'll put agents on it at once."

"But that sounds so expensive," Lydia protested. "And you've already invested so much."

"All the more reason to protect my investment," he assured her. "And look how well everything else is going, my pet."

But in truth, except for the work of Morris and his chemists, everything else was not going well.

She and April had found a house almost at once, on Van Ness Street, and though it was small and unimpressive, it was charming and comfortable, and infinitely better than life with Uncle Richard.

He had complained so much at their "deserting him" that Lydia had relented and given him a hundred dollars with which to hire himself a new assistant, though she knew perfectly well he would only hire another Chinese for slave wages, and use the money for other things.

Life in their new home ought to have been a great deal more pleasant, but though they both liked the house, Lydia was all too aware of April's unhappiness.

It didn't help that as she and Walter had grown closer, almost out of necessity, Lydia had spent more of her time not only in his company, but in the company of his mother and daughter as well.

It was apparent that Walter wanted them all to like one another, and especially wanted the two women of his family to approve of her. Privately, Lydia thought he was wasting his time; Kathy was no more than polite, and sometimes not even that, and Mrs. Hanover remained cool, but this did not stop Walter from throwing them together at every opportunity.

It was he who had practically insisted on the shopping trip that Lydia and Kathy had taken together today, a sojourn that neither of them had been particularly enthusiastic about. Lydia, however, was all too aware that without Walter's money, Empress Cosmetics would have to close its doors virtually before they were opened, and she made every effort to do what she knew pleased him.

Unfortunately, all too often, what pleased Walter plainly displeased April. Lydia could hardly blame April for being unhappy when treated rudely by the arrogant Miss Hanover. Still, she did seem at times to go out of her way to be antagonistic.

"If you'd only avoid her when she's around," Lydia insisted, but April's answer was invariably the same.

"A maid hardly has the right to avoid her mistress's guests."

"It's about time," Kathy said, interrupting Lydia's reverie as April reappeared with a cold glass of iced coffee.

"I had to chip the ice," April said.

Kathy pointedly turned to Lydia and said, "Chinks always have trouble with the ice. I suppose they know nothing of civilized conveniences in their primitive country."

Suddenly she gave a squeal, as the iced coffee sloshed across the front of her dotted Swiss. "Oh, damn you, you fool," she cried.

"I'm sorry, my foot slipped," April said.

"I ought to slap you," Kathy cried. "I think I will."

She moved a step toward April, who made no move to avoid her, but Lydia stepped between them. "No, I forbid it," she said. "This is my house, remember."

"Then you ought to learn how to run it," Kathy snapped, brushing at the stain with a dainty lace handkerchief.

"April, please hurry and get a towel," Lydia said.

"Don't bother, I'm going home, where servants know how to behave," Kathy said, snatching up her reticule. "I'll send you the bill for the dress." The door slammed loudly behind her.

Lydia turned on her daughter. "That was uncalled for," she snapped.

"She had it coming," April replied sullenly.

"You know how Walter dotes on that girl. And without Walter's backing, we have nothing. Do you want to go back to Richard's and the way we were living there?"

"What's the difference?" April asked, heading for the door. "I was a servant there, and I'm a servant here. At least in my father's house in China, I was a princess. I wish we'd never left there!"

"April!" Lydia cried, but it was too late. She had gone out in Kathy's wake, the door once again slamming loudly. The sound seemed to reverberate through the house.

For a moment Lydia considered going after her, but she knew that it would be futile. Her own child scarcely spoke to her any more, except in anger.

She sank down upon a divan. Her only hope was that Empress Cosmetics could soon begin the marketing of its line of cosmetics. Once she was able to repay Walter the money he'd invested, and begin showing a profit, it wouldn't matter if he pulled out or not. Then it wouldn't matter if she offended him, and she could afford to be honest.

Why wouldn't April understand?

There was a tap at the door. Thinking April had come back after all, and perhaps locked herself out, Lydia jumped up and ran to the door, flinging it open.

She found herself face to face once again with Peter MacNair.

CHAPTER TWENTY-SIX

"You!" Lydia cried.

He smiled, the same slightly lopsided smile that invariably caused an inexplicable quickening of her pulse, hate him though she might.

"Not a very warm welcome, considering how much trouble I've had finding you," he said.

"Wasted trouble," she replied, "since I don't want to see you."

"But I want to see you. May I come in?"

She hesitated briefly. A part of her wanted nothing but to slam the door in his face. She was almost surprised to find herself swinging it open.

"I can spare you a few minutes," she said, trying to keep her voice icy. She certainly didn't want to encourage him to call again. "I suppose you've come about the perfume sample?"

"Not entirely," he said. "It would be foolish to say it wasn't on my mind, since you've known all along how interested I was in that particular perfume. But more important, I wanted to see you again."

She turned to face him directly. "Why?" she asked.

"I should think that would be self evident. You are a beautiful woman, you know."

"A beauty that you once valued cheaply, as I recall," she replied.

"You mean that incident in China?" he asked.

Her eyes flashed with sudden anger. "That incident in China, as you so casually put it, left me a slave to a Chinese for many years. I might have spent the rest of my life there."

"But you didn't," he said. "And at least you have had a life, which is better than what might have happened. You might have been dead long ago, if not for what I did."

"Do you have the nerve to stand there and try to tell me that what you did was for my own good? You were thinking of saving your own skin."

"That's true, I was," he said. "But I was thinking of saving yours too. You were little more than a child then, but you're a grown woman now, and you must have some wits, or you'd never have survived, let alone escaped.

"Think back on what happened. We were in the middle of that accursed country, surrounded by millions of Chinese who'd been goaded by their Empress into killing every white person they could find. Your mother was dying, and even if she'd been well, there wasn't a chance that I could reach the coast if I took you with me. I barely made it as it was, and I had to hide from every Chinaman I encountered. I arrived little more than skin and bones, and so exhausted I could hardly walk. You'd have been dead before we got half way. If the Chinese hadn't spotted you and killed you, the journey alone would have done it. At least with that mandarin you had a chance to live, even if it was as a slave, as you put it.

"And by the way, you don't think he'd have just let you slip out of town without going after you, the way he wanted you? You ought to thank me that you're able to stand here today, instead of rotting in a Chinese grave."

Some of the fire had vanished from her eyes. Though she still looked angry, she knew that what he said was true.

"You make yourself sound quite the hero," she said caustically.

"Not a hero, just a man who wanted to save his skin, as you said, and at the same time do what seemed best for you. I'll bet if that father of yours was around right now, he'd tell you I did the best thing, under the circumstances."

"That we'll never know," she said, abashed. "Very well, then, you've had your say, and I'll even grant that what you say makes some sense, though I don't think you're entitled to quite so noble an interpretation of your actions. Was there something else you wanted?"

"How about a drink?" he asked, grinning again. It was maddening to her how nonplussed she felt when he grinned at her that way. She was tempted to refuse him the drink, but at the last minute, she relented.

"There's some Irish whiskey, and some wine," she said. "Sherry, I think."

"The poteen. Sherry's always seemed too womanish for me. Will you have one with me?"

"I think not. I prefer to keep my head fully clear while I'm around you. At least until I know what you've planned for me this time."

"If you really want to know, I was thinking of a quiet dinner together somewhere, where we could get caught up on all the years that have gotten away from us since then."

"Thrown away, you mean, not gotten away. Or better yet, traded away. How much did Ke Loo give you to betray me to him?"

"Not nearly enough."

"I'll give you credit for boldness," she said. She had gone to the trolley on which she kept the liquor and glasses; Walter liked a drink when he was there.

Peter watched her as she poured the drink. She was indeed a beautiful woman. His memory of her was of a girl little more than a child, astonishingly passionate, and pretty enough, but otherwise unremarkable. Their meeting a few months before, when she had accidentally crossed his path once more, had been too unexpected, and too much of a surprise, for him to gain much of an impression.

Who would have guessed that she would grow into a woman of such breathtaking loveliness? Her skin was like alabaster, with a glow that almost seemed lighted from within. Her eyes were bold and flashing. Her figure was the proverbial hourglass, the waist tiny, the bosom and the hips lusciously rounded. He wanted desperately to seize her in his arms, to tear the clothes from her body and make love to her right here on the floor of her parlor.

It was an effort of will to restrain himself from doing exactly as he'd imagined. He could practically picture her naked, her long legs spread wide, her ripe, full breasts trembling with the force of her breath.

She turned from the trolley, drink in hand, and caught his eyes upon her. Something of what he was thinking must have shown in his face, for her expression changed in a twinkling. A faint blush came to her cheeks, and she lowered her lashes with unexpected shyness. Unexpected, and touching.

Of course, it wasn't her beauty that had brought him here, it was something else that she had—that blasted perfume. He wanted it, wanted it with almost the same ardor that he wanted her. He longed to possess them both. His company was a success, and he had made a fortune, but he was too shrewd not to know that their line was second rate, and had little hope of getting any better.

But with that perfume—! What an incredible stroke of luck that she had it, and had come to him with it. If she hadn't been in such dire straits since coming from China, she might already be manufacturing and selling her own version of the perfume, and it would be too late for him to do anything about it. But so far Dame Fortune had been kind to him.

He knew all about Walter Hanover. Ramsey was a despicable man, but beyond peer as a detective. His report had left very little unsaid. Peter knew too that thus far Morris and the chemists that Empress had hired had been unable to duplicate the perfume, because they simply didn't have the man for that job. He knew this because one of Morris's assistants was being paid by the detective as well.

Peter, though, knew the man who could duplicate the perfume. The man was in Paris, but he could be bought. Peter had approached him once before, but PM Cosmetics hadn't had the prestige to tempt him; this perfume would. The man was a true *nez*. He would never be able to resist that challenge if it was presented to him, especially when combined with an offer too generous to turn down.

All he needed was the perfume, and this dazzling woman crossing the room now to bring him his drink had it in her possession. He fully intended to get it from her, and that faint blush when she'd seen him looking her over had confirmed for him the best way of accomplishing that goal.

"That's rather a frank look," she said, handing him the glass.

"Would you rather I looked at you less frankly? I thought you wanted honesty."

"Honesty, yes; lechery, no," she replied. "And as for dinner, I have other plans."

"Not with Walter Hanover, he's got a meeting tonight. And the way your daughter looked when she ran out of here a few minutes ago, I doubt that she'll be back too quickly."

Lydia raised her eyebrows. "You know quite a bit about me, it seems."

"I've made it a point to learn about you. If you knew how hard I've tried, through the years since that night in China, to find you again—China's an enormous country, you know, and still far from opened up to foreigners. You seemed to have disappeared."

"I did, in a way," she said, confused by this totally unexpected attitude from a man she had fully intended to hate for the rest of her life.

Had he really tried to find her? It could be true. There would have been no trail to follow, not for a foreigner, at least. And Kalgan was so isolated a city. A man might search for a lifetime, to no avail.

Certainly, from all that he knew about her, he must have gone to great lengths to find her here. But was that because of her, or something she had that he coveted for himself? When he'd first arrived, she had thought she knew, but now she wasn't sure.

"There is one thing," she said, with less antagonism than

before. "About my daughter...."

"You'd rather I didn't publicize the fact that she's your daughter," he said for her. "Everyone here believes she's your maid."

"You seem to know everything," she said.

"It was a fairly easy deduction. I knew about Ke Loo, which the others don't. And for anybody who knows that much, there's enough of you in the girl to be recognized. As for your not wanting me to tell anyone else, that's pretty evident in the fact that you haven't told anybody else yourself. Don't worry, you've got nothing to fear. I promise you I won't say anything."

"Not even if you don't get your way? About the perfume, I mean?"

He grinned again. "Getting my way may have nothing to do with the perfume. Was she the only child?"

"There is a boy," she said, lowering her eyes, but not before he saw the shadow of sadness darken them. "I wasn't able to bring him out of China."

There was a pause, both of them momentarily absorbed in their own thoughts. He was thinking again how desirable she was. It was not only the loveliness; there was something more, something harder to put his finger on. Despite her independence, and despite the intelligence and courage she must have needed to make her way here, against the odds, she had a touching vulnerability, which made him feel oddly as if he wanted to protect her, especially against unscrupulous men like himself.

He chided himself mentally for such foolishness, and said, "You still haven't given me an answer about dinner. Will you go with me? I'll promise not to talk business at all."

Lydia passed a hand wearily over her brow, as if trying to dislodge unhappy thoughts that had stuck there.

"Please, I—I think I'd better not," she replied. "I feel confused...."

"It's only prolonging the inevitable," he said. "If not tonight, then tomorrow night."

"I'll be busy."

"Or the night after, then." He paused, and added, in an entirely different voice, very softly, "Please."

It was that last that changed her mind. He sounded, and looked, so sincere, so eager to make amends.

"All right," she said. "Tomorrow night. But spare me the romantic approach, please. I'm too old and much too hard-hearted for that sort of thing. If there's anything I don't want, it's the sort of man who's good for nothing but throwing a woman on a bed and making love to her. Let it just be two old acquaintances, catching up on things."

Hardly that, he thought, but he smiled and did not argue the point aloud.

CHAPTER TWENTY-SEVEN

Lydia had expected Peter to take her somewhere grand. She knew that he knew all about her and Walter, and she knew that Peter had money, though probably not as much as Walter, and she thought surely he would try to outdo the other man.

To her surprise, he took her to a little Italian restaurant near the fishermen's wharf.

"It's not very impressive to look at," he apologized, "but the food's excellent, and the fish are just out of the water."

Everyone seemed to know him. The same had been true when Walter had taken her to the Palace Court for lunch, but somehow this seemed to be more impressive. For one thing, this was plainly a family-run restaurant, and they treated Peter like an old acquaintance and not merely a regular customer. At his suggestion, she had snapper, a fish, he told her, caught probably no more than a mile from where they were sitting, and probably no more than an hour or two earlier.

She found him easy to talk to, and was surprised; then surprised that she had been surprised; hadn't he talked well before? He was a sympathetic listener, and since he knew so much already about her background, and even her relationship with Walter, it seemed pointless to be coy about those things. It was a relief, in fact, to be with someone who already knew about China, and April, so that for once she did not have to be careful how she referred to either.

"It wasn't such a hard life," she answered to a question about the years in China. "Quite easy, in fact. He was a prince, after all, and women there aren't supposed to know anything. It's rather peculiar, isn't it, to think of those two great nations, England and China, run by strong-willed women, yet in both countries women are treated as chattel."

"There have always been women with the personality, or the will, to assert themselves," he said. "Look at Eleanor of Aquitaine, and she lived in a time when women were more subjugated than they are now. Look at yourself, a modern, independent woman, her own company taking shape, the sort of story that other women would envy."

"Not if they knew what it was to live it," she said. "I sometimes wonder what the world will be like for my daughter. I should like to think that by the time she reaches my age, women will be regarded as individuals in their own right, and not as mere appendages to males."

"Your daughter's very lovely. I doubt that life will prove very difficult for her."

"That's just my point," Lydia said. "Why should she need loveliness to buy her place in the world? As if that were an answer anyway—you say that I am lovely, but I can't see that it's been of help to me."

"You don't think Walter Hanover would be investing in your company if you were ugly, do you?" he asked, smiling as if he did not take her arguments very seriously.

"I would rather you had said, 'if you were a fool,'" she replied. "But what about you? You've told me nothing about what has happened with you since China."

"I'm afraid it's a far less exciting tale than yours. I returned from China with the items I'd picked up there—you remember, we talked of them that night. I looked around for backing—much the same as you've done—and I found it, much the same."

"Perhaps I should explain about Walter," Lydia said.

"You needn't explain, not to me. My wife's family is very wealthy, from the silver bonanza. I tried to obtain money from various banking institutions. It was Lorna who suggested that her father might give me the money I was looking for. Of course it wasn't said so in just those words, but the implication was, he'd be willing to invest in a son-in-law. She wanted me for a husband, I wanted the money. It seemed a fair enough arrangement. We married. The rest you know."

"And it's been successful, apparently."

He grinned ruefully. "Financially it's been a success. I repaid the money long ago, and I've tried my damnedest to make a success of the marriage too, but I'm not so big a fool as to think I have."

"You don't give the impression of a man who's suffered as a result of it," Lydia said drily.

"Oh, yes, I know, it must seem to you particularly as if life's been a bed of roses for me. But let me tell you, you've got no idea what it can be like, trapped in a loveless marriage. My wife despises me. She's as cold as an iceberg."

"Do you have children?"

"Yes, two boys and a girl. But she's managed to bring them up with her point of view. I'm like a pariah in my own home."

"You hardly seem to me like the sort who'd long endure anything unpleasant."

"I know, you think of me as a scoundrel, but I've got my principles too. It's been a great many years since that night in China, and even then, however it seemed to you, I was thinking of your best interests as well as my own."

"I think I'd rather not discuss that subject," Lydia said, sipping the thick black coffee with which the meal had ended.

"All right, then let's discuss another one," Peter said. "You and Walter Hanover. I hate to see you make the same mistake I made."

"Walter and I are just friends," she replied.

"Does Walter know this?" he asked with a mocking gesture.

"At any rate, I found myself with no more options than you had. Walter is my only hope for making a success of Empress Cosmetics."

"Not really," Peter said, leaning across the table to clasp her hand so tightly that it was almost painful. She found her eyes drawn to his, and she was frightened by the intensity of his gaze. "I already have a successful firm. I have the manufacturing facilities, the distribution—I even have what you don't—the man who could duplicate the Empress's perfume."

Lydia snatched her hand away as if it had been burned. "Your spies are very thorough," she said.

"Lydia, don't be a fool," he said. "I've not lied to you. I told you I'd learned everything I could about you and your company. I know that your chemists aren't able to duplicate that for you, and they never will be. But I can do it. If you came in with me, we could make a sensation of that perfume. You could have your own line, the Empress line. It would be exactly the same as having your own company, don't you see?"

"Except it wouldn't be my company," Lydia replied, the spell that he had managed to cast over her broken by this turn of the conversation. "It would be yours. I would be at your mercy."

"Better mine than Hanover's."

"I'm not so sure of that. Shall we go? My maid—I'm sorry, I'm so used to calling her that—my daughter is at home alone, and I promised her I wouldn't be late."

"Lydia...."

"Please."

Reluctantly, he signaled for their check. Lydia waited in silence while he paid it, thinking of how confusing her life had become. April was still angry. She had scarcely spoken since their quarrel the day before. Walter had hinted just this afternoon at the subject of marriage. And here she was with Peter MacNair, the one man she had sworn to hate to her dying day.

She still wanted to hate him, too, but somehow it was increasingly difficult. Another part of her wanted to believe the things he had told her, his explanation for his actions in China, his feelings for, and interest in her now. Yet she could not quiet the voice within her that whispered it was folly to trust this man, for all his handsome good looks, for all his charm, and the smile that played havoc with her heartbeat.

She looked up to find him studying her again, this time his

eyes surprisingly gentle. If only there weren't so many facets to him. It would be so much simpler if he were a scoundrel, plain and simple. Jeremy had been easier, because for all his kindness and generosity he was a wastrel, who drank to excess and smoked opium because he hadn't the backbone to deal with life on its own terms. Walter was wealthy and so far undemanding, and she felt secure in his affection for her.

But Peter MacNair? No woman could ever feel entirely secure in his affections. He was unlike any other man who had crossed her path, with one singular exception, Ke Loo.

They were alike in that they were both cruel and arrogant, and neither would stop at anything to get what they wanted. But unlike Ke Loo, Peter MacNair had a softer side too. He would take a woman by force, if necessary, she supposed, but he would be a tender as well as a passionate lover. It might have been only last night when she lay in his arms and felt the heat of his mouth upon her, his hands searching, discovering, his body hard against hers....

She blushed to realize that he was looking at her exactly as if he read her thoughts; or perhaps he was only having similar ones himself.

If so, his wishes were in vain. She wondered if she should tell him that it was no longer possible for her to respond to a man sexually. Would that erase that bothersome smile from his face?

For a moment, she actually toyed with the idea of letting him have his way, solely for the satisfaction of seeing his expression when he realized that the fires he had kindled in a sixteen year old girl were no longer his to command.

She dismissed that idea at once. There was no point in borrowing trouble.

* * * * * * *

Van Ness was quiet as Peter helped her from his carriage a short while later. "No need to wait, Joseph," Peter informed his driver. "I'll stroll home."

Lydia was surprised when he took her hand in his to cross the street, but she offered no objection. It had been a far more pleasant evening than she had expected, though his very presence caused her some uneasiness.

The moonlight turned the leaves of the linden trees to pewter. It was one of those magical nights when the air had the tang of the sea. Somewhere not too distant a tenor was singing a song about Sorrento in a voice so light and free that it seemed no more than a whisper of the breeze. The clip-clop of the horses' hooves faded as Peter's carriage disappeared down the street.

Suddenly, as if erupting from a cannon, another carriage was speeding along the street. Black, with horses that might have been dark shadows, it raced pell-mell toward them.

"Watch out, you fool," Peter shouted, but the driver, cloaked in raiment as dark as his horses, did not hear him.

They had paused frozen in the middle of the street, watching in horror as the carriage bore down upon them, as transfixed as the snake by the eye of his fakir.

"He's going to run us down!" Peter cried, and as if a light had been kindled before her eyes, Lydia had an image of a dour-faced woman with a fur cap, and cold, merciless eyes, who had reason to wish her dead.

CHAPTER TWENTY-EIGHT

For several seconds, which might have been an eternity, it seemed that they were doomed. Had Lydia been alone in the street, she would surely, she realized afterward, have fallen beneath the hooves of those charging horses, for her body refused to respond.

Peter acted for both of them. He threw her aside with such violence that she not only fell to the ground, but rolled over and over until she came to an abrupt stop against the curb. Even at that it was so close a call that the wheels of the carriage, as it passed, threw dirt in her face.

She lay dazed and battered, still terrified. She heard footsteps and thought that someone had leaped down from the carriage and was coming for her.

"No," she gasped, trying to struggle to her feet.

Strong hands grabbed her and she was lifted from the ground, still struggling, until she turned her head and saw that it was Peter who held her. In the distance, the carriage clattered around a corner, rocking dangerously, and was gone from sight, though they could hear the racket for a lingering moment.

"Are you all right?" he asked, and she saw that his face was white with concern—or was it only fear for his own safety?

"Yes, I'm just shaken up a bit," she replied. "I can walk now, I'm sure."

He did not put her down, though, nor did she take her arms from about his neck, where she had flung them when she saw who was holding her.

Suddenly, she did not want to be free of his arms. She closed her eyes and lay her head against his strong chest, where she could feel the beat of his heart, slowing, but still pounding.

How strange that she had remembered everything but the scent of him, as strong and sure and clear, though in no way like, the perfume she had smuggled from China. Yet now that she was close to him again, now that her nostrils were filled with the essence of his scent, she knew that she would know it anywhere; even if he were hidden from all her other senses, she would recognize him ever after.

And again, as if they had established a rapport between them, at the same time he said, "You smell so lovely."

How had it happened that he was kissing her? Afterward, she could never remember, and yet, there were his lips, crushing hers with such force that she wanted to cry out, though with pain or with pleasure, she couldn't say. And now his heart—or was it hers!—was quickening again, rising to what must surely be an unbearable crescendo of excitement.

He took his mouth from hers, and she gasped for air like a drowning person, and felt her breast aching, and a tingling in her limbs. He turned and began to walk swiftly toward her house.

"What are you doing?" she asked, as he fumbled with the door, and flung it open.

"I'm going to throw you upon the bed and make love to you," he said in a hoarse voice. "You were right, that's exactly the sort of man that I am, and I mean to do it whether you agree or not, so you'll save us both a great deal of bother if you don't try to fight me."

She did not try to fight him. The house was dark. April would be in bed by now, and her bedroom was on the floor above. Lydia's was on the ground floor. Oddly, as if he had rehearsed this very scene, Peter went straight to it.

He did not throw her upon the bed, but put her down gently, as if she were a doll that might be easily broken.

"Please," she murmured, and seemed to hear her own voice as

if from a great distance. "The fall in the street—let me freshen myself."

"You're beautiful," he whispered, already deftly opening the fasteners at the back of her dress. "You need nothing. No, wait—the perfume. Since the day you came into my office, I've dreamed of smelling that scent on you. It was made for you."

Without hesitation she slipped from the bed, and went into the dressing room that adjoined. She was back in a moment, bearing the precious vial.

"Let me put it on you," he asked. She handed him the vial, but he did not open it at once. Instead, he took her in his arms again; his kisses fell like a torrid rain upon her lips, her throat, her earlobes, while his practiced hands removed her garments one by one, until she was naked before him.

The curtains were drawn back from the windows and the brilliant moonlight flooded the room, making a lamp unnecessary. It turned her pale skin to alabaster, her hair to spun gold. She was as dazzling as a Chinese porcelain.

He slipped off his jacket, but when he went to unbutton his shirt she stepped closer, and brushing aside his hands, began to do it for him. While he stood motionless, feet wide planted, she undressed him as he had undressed her, even kneeling to draw his trousers downward, and his undergarments as well, until he had stepped from them, and stood as naked as she.

She could not explain the urge that had prompted her to do this. It was a sudden urge, too powerful to be denied. The memory of his body, as she had known it, burned like a holy vision before her eyes, until she wanted—needed—to see him in the flesh, superimposed upon the other.

And he was splendid, destroying her memories in a stroke, for she saw now that they had failed her. The broad, powerful shoulders with the muscled arms, the deeply sculpted chest with the rippling belly and the faint trail of hair that began at his navel, leading the eye downward, bursting into a thicket of dark, wiry hair....

"Your eyes are very lovely," he said, reaching for her, "But I want more than their gaze."

She felt as though the very bones within her were melting, until she was not an entity herself, but only a flow of desire and passion, swept against him, along with him, in a floodtide of white heat.

"You're trembling," he murmured.

"Am I? I couldn't tell."

His answer was a soft laugh against her ear, even its echoes sending flashes of excitement, like lightning, zigzagging up and down her spine.

He lowered her to the bed, while she clung to him with a need that was desperate. Someone somewhere was moaning softly, little animal sounds of terrible delight, and she knew that it was herself, only not herself, but some savage creature that he had awakened within her, a woman she hadn't known existed, and was frightened by, but powerless to control.

"Yes, yes," she gasped, and then, a long shuddering, "Ohhhhh," as his mouth burned a trail downwards, igniting the tips of her breasts, sending flames leaping over the mound of her belly. Her legs yearned wide for him, then spasmed tightly about his shoulders as he went still lower, and he discovered her there, lips that had never known lips before.

She cried aloud, writhing and squirming, oblivious to everything but the sensations that he was creating within her, until the ecstasy was more than she could bear, and she found herself begging him to stop, even while her body thrust and struggled against him.

Finally he was upon her, in her, and all of the coldness that she had known since then with men, all the disappointment that had convinced her she was no longer capable of responding to such acts, vanished, and again she discovered the thrill, yielding with an aching joy as she felt him moving deep within her, deeper and still deeper. She welcomed him, not only in her mind, but in her flesh as well, enveloping him, clinging wetly to him as if she could not bear to let him draw back, sobbing helplessly as a new rush of delirium swept through her, making her body shudder and arch, her senses reeling in the throes of what might have been death, or a birth into a new life, and only dimly did she feel the last, brutal thrust, and the quaking of his hard, glorious body upon hers....

* * * * * *

He did not leave until dawn had begun to wash the ceiling with a pastel glow, and the mockingbird that came to drink from the basin in the garden sang to their pleasure.

They made love, and dozed, and made love again, throughout the all too fleeting minutes of the night, and when at last he rose from the bed, she slept with her crimson yellow hair in a splendor of disarray upon the pillows, and a smile upon her lips.

The scent of her body, a fresh, natural, womanly scent, blended with that most intoxicating of all perfumes. He had dabbed it on her breasts, and buried his face between them. He had dabbed it on her thighs, and soared to new heights of passion at the blending of perfumes there.

He had not lied to her about that; of all the women in the world, she was the one for whom a divine wisdom had created that perfume, for she alone was a perfume to equal, to complement, rather than to conflict, with it.

He smiled to himself, for her surrender had been complete, a surrender not only of her body; had she not given him the vial herself, putting it into his hands?

He walked around the bed, to the little table where the vial had stood while they made love, its essence making an aphrodisiac of the very air about them—and came to a dead stop.

The vial was gone. But when...how...?

He felt a pang of annoyance, even anger, but in a twinkling, he was laughing softly to himself. He was not yet in possession of what he had come for. What was in the vial was a treasure, but he knew too, now, that it was no more precious than the treasures she had yielded to him through the hours of the night.

And, in time, that one too she would give him, he was confident. In return, he would deny her nothing, this goddess with the flaming hair.

But first, he would have his way.

* * * * * *

Three men sat in a dingy room behind a laundry in Chinatown. They spoke in Chinese, in the Manchu dialect, and one of them, whose name was Ling Ta, was very angry.

"She is not dead?" he demanded. "Not even hurt?"

The man nearest him said nothing, but watched, his eyes darting like a lizard's, from one to the other. The third man sat with head bowed. A faint shudder made the collar of his tunic tremble like a leaf in the wind.

"He carried her inside," he said. He did not raise his eyes.

Ling Ta rose from his chair so abruptly that it toppled over with a crash. The frightened man jumped, but did not get up.

Ling Ta motioned to the other. He too rose, and went around the table. The one with bowed head still did not move, though he knew perfectly well what was coming. Only at the last, as the hand dropped about his head and the knife blade slashed the air toward his throat, did he lift his head, perhaps to beg, though the gesture had the look of a sacrificial offering.

There was a gasp and a sudden, acrid stench.

Ling Ta looked away. He felt no sympathy for the man who had just been slain; he was a bungler, he was lucky that his death was so swift.

Swifter than my death will be, if I fail, Ling Ta thought.

He would not fail, though. He had sworn an oath on the graves of his ancestors, an oath to his Empress. He was the instrument of her vengeance. He had failed, once before, in the legation in Peking, but this time he would succeed. It was for this purpose that he had traveled across the great ocean to this ugly, coarse land. He despised it here, yet there was a certain pleasure to be taken from its unpleasantness.

"Take it away" he said of the fallen bundle that had once

been his henchman. "I will do the deed myself."

CHAPTER TWENTY-NINE

"But I don't understand," Walter was saying, his voice taking on an unpleasant whining quality, "what your connection is with this MacNair."

What a confusion life was, Lydia thought morosely. She made an attempt at a nonchalant shrug. "I've told you already," she replied. "I knew him years ago, in China. There's really not much more than that."

"Well, there's certainly the business side of it," Walter argued. "Putting it as simply as possible, he is our competition. And while I don't mean to insult your considerable charms, I'd say that might have something to do with his powerful interest in you."

"You're quite right, of course," Lydia said. "Peter would like to obtain Nightsong, by hook or by crook."

She thought of that night, a month before, when Peter had spent the entire night making love to her. How thrilling it had been—and how close she had come to letting him make a fool of her once again. She had awakened with the dawn, half opening her eyes and then almost closing them again when she saw Peter stealing around the bed. Through eyes opened to mere slits, she had seen him approach the table on which the Nightsong perfume had been left earlier. She saw his look of disappointment and anger when he found the vial gone. Thank heaven she had slipped it under her pillow earlier.

She had closed her eyes fully then, to hide the tears that had begun to sting. It was still the perfume, after all, that he wanted.

With his scheme a failure, she had expected him to lose interest in her after that, but oddly enough, he seemed to have gotten over his disappointment. He had continued seeing her nearly every day, and though they had made love often since then, the perfume had never again been mentioned, not even as an adjunct to their lovemaking.

Was he only being patient, waiting for the right moment to try to obtain it? Or was the interest that he showed in her genuine, quite apart from the other? It was a question that she couldn't answer.

In fact, her own feelings were no less confusing. She had been hurt after that incident, and had attempted to be cool to him, but to no avail. Despite all her firm promises to herself, they both knew full well that he had only to smile at her in that certain way, or indeed, only to reach for her and take her in his arms, and all her resistance vanished in a twinkling.

"If you know what he's after," Walter was saying, "why do you continue to see him constantly? You act as if you're in love with him. I must say, Mother has made quite a few remarks to the same effect."

"I should think your mother would be relieved to think that I might be in love with someone else," Lydia said, and immediately regretted speaking so brutally.

Walter's face reddened. "It's a matter of consideration for my feelings," he said, turning petulant. "After all, I would hardly want to be business partners with someone who didn't give a snap of her fingers for my feelings."

"But I do care about your feelings, Walter," Lydia said, reaching across to clasp his hand. "And you may assure your mother that I'm not in love with Peter MacNair."

She was relieved to see the quick smile that brightened his face, though her conscience nagged at her. She was no longer sure about her feelings. Was she in love with Peter? At times she could still be certain that she hated him, all the more so because he had tried once again to deceive her, and had very nearly succeeded. At other times, though, she felt quite the opposite.

Was it possible, she wondered, to love someone and hate him as well? She suppressed a sigh, and managed to give Walter a reassuring smile.

They were seated on a bench in the park. No more than a hundred feet away, a gentleman on another bench rustled the paper that he was ostensibly reading, and glanced over its edge to see what Lydia and Walter were doing.

Ramsey, the detective who had located Lydia for MacNair, was thinking that, at his current rate, he could make a career out of checking up on this one woman.

He had no sooner made his report, and a good report it was, too, with enough information to fill a good-sized biography, than he had been called back to the MacNair house again. He had arrived half expecting some sort of complaint regarding his work, and this he was prepared to argue to the limit. He took pride in few things, but his work was one of them. He liked to boast that there wasn't anyone living that he couldn't find, and no piece of information that he couldn't obtain—given, of course, the necessary incentive, meaning money, and the necessary means, also money.

To his surprise, this time, however, it hadn't been Mr. MacNair who had sent for him, but the Missus. Now there, he thought, grinning lasciviously to himself, was a fine piece of woman, a subject of which he considered himself no mean judge. Enough, he would have thought, to keep most men well satisfied.

It had been hard to disguise his surprise when he'd learned that she wanted him to check up on her husband and another woman—and even more of a surprise to discover that it was the very same woman he had just tracked down for the husband, a fact she already knew.

"That's why I've turned to you," she said, speaking in that snooty way that women of her class, especially women of strong appetites, liked to take with a fellow like him. "It would be foolish to start from scratch with someone who knows nothing about this woman, when you've already learned so much."

"Quite a bit," he admitted.

"I've read your report to my husband," she said, taking the report from a drawer in case he didn't believe her. He recognized his own handwriting on the cover page. "You did a good job—" He beamed, but his smile vanished as she continued, "—but not good enough for my purposes."

"I take it," he said, a trifle less warmly, "that there's some specific information you want to know. Maybe if you'd tell me just what it is...."

"I'm afraid I don't know myself," she said. "But you're right, of course, there is something."

"Not to beat a dead horse, but it makes it kind of difficult if I don't know what I'm looking for."

"I should think it is obvious I'm not looking for evidence of sainthood. I want something scandalous."

"Suppose it involved your husband?" he asked quietly.

She gave him a particularly frosty look. "Let's not waste time beating around the bush, Mr. Ramsey. I take it for granted that my husband is having an affair with this woman, though I want you to confirm that for me, if you can. But that's not what I'm looking for. This woman is altogether too mysterious—and that name, it's positively silly. I can't believe she didn't make that up. I want to know about her background. You're certain this child who's with her is her daughter?"

"No mistake about that," he said. "I checked it out thoroughly. That's how she brought the kid into the country, as her own daughter. I saw the passport myself."

She did not ask how he had managed that. "And you're certain of the Chinese blood?"

He grinned and said, "If you saw the kid, you wouldn't ask."

"Then there has to be a Chinaman, doesn't there? Find out what Chinaman, and when, and where."

"That might be expensive," he said. "Could be he's still in China."

"Our firm has a representative in China. I'll give you access to him. And I don't care how expensive it is. But I want results fast."

"And my fee?"

"Whatever you think reasonable."

He lifted an eyebrow. "What if it was something more than money?"

For a moment she seemed not to comprehend. Then he saw a slow blush color her face, but she did not look away from his steady gaze.

"I'll pay any price, if you find what I'm looking for," she said.

* * * * * *

For Peter it had been a puzzling month since the night when he had carried Lydia into her house after a runaway carriage had nearly run them down.

He had begun his affair with her with confidence. He had planned nothing more than an enjoyable frolic, in the course of which he intended to get his hands on the perfume, or at the very least persuade her to join with his own company.

Thus far, nothing had been quite what he planned. It was true that the "frolic" was indeed enjoyable, far more so than he could ever have dreamed, though frolic no longer seemed the right word to describe their relationship.

Damn, he didn't know himself what the right word was. As much as he enjoyed Lydia, both in and out of bed, there was something disturbing about her, something he couldn't seem to define.

He found her never out of his thoughts for long. He had realized in the course of a meeting just the day before that he had been daydreaming about her, and had not even heard a question directed at him by his sales manager.

As for the perfume, he had not seen the vial since that first night, though she had worn it at one other time when he was making love to her. The worst of it was, when he was with her, the perfume seemed to fade in importance. The last few times, he had scarcely thought of it at all. The desirability of her, his urge to hold her in his arms and feel her soft flesh yielding to his flesh, eclipsed all other considerations. Later, he invariably cursed himself for a fool, but each time it was the same.

It occurred to him, quite unexpectedly, that maybe he had fallen in love with her.

Peter was not a man given to romance, nor to self-analysis, but he paused now to analyze what he felt for Lydia.

It was not only her physical allure that captivated him, though her beauty and desirability never failed to take his breath away. There was more to it than that.

He admired the courage and the strength of will that had enabled her not only to survive what should have been a life sentence to that mandarin, but to escape it as well, and bring her daughter here to San Francisco. She had a toughness about her that many a man could envy, and she wore it like a shield to protect her from the blows that the world had inflicted upon her.

Yet beneath that brittle exterior was a heart that was tender and gentle. She poured out all of her love on her daughter, a daughter who did not seem to notice or appreciate it.

Would that love ever be poured like a river of happiness upon him? Was that what he wanted—her love?

It would be a fortunate man who received that love, for he knew instinctively that it would be unwavering, unflagging, strong and protective and loyal to the end. The sort of love any man wanted to find in a woman, especially in a beautiful woman whose body inflamed his senses, whose lovely face haunted his dreams.

He had started out intending to make a fool of her and get what he wanted. Was it possible that he was the fool, who hadn't even known what he wanted?

Years before, she had called a curse down on him, had sworn that he would suffer from love, as she was suffering.

Had her curse come true?

CHAPTER THIRTY

"What are those men bringing in?" Lydia asked, indicating the movers struggling up the stairs.

"Some new desks," Mrs. Clary, her secretary, said.

"But we've already got an entire office full of furniture," Lydia cried. "More than we can use."

"These were ordered by Mr. Hanover," Mrs. Clary said, with a note of disapproval in her voice.

Lydia hesitated; she disliked countermanding anything Walter had done, not wanting to offend him when she needed him so badly just now. Still, it made no sense to buy things they didn't need, at a time when they still weren't even ready to start making money from the firm.

Sometimes it actually seemed as if Walter deliberately tried to keep their fledgling company short of money. He had insisted on having an entire suite of offices, when so far they had no office employees other than Mrs. Clary, who functioned not only as secretary, but as receptionist, bookkeeper, and general factotum—an arrangement the two women had worked out to their mutual satisfaction when Lydia had explained that there wasn't money enough yet to hire a full staff, and Mrs. Clary had replied that she didn't mind doing multiple duty, if she could be sure of her place as the company grew.

Why, Lydia wondered, couldn't Walter be equally practical? Of course, it was his money, and she realized he had never had to worry about money, but surely he didn't treat all his investments so extravagantly.

The walls, paneled in mahogany, were covered with expensive paintings, and the rugs on the floor had cost a thousand dollars alone, though Lydia had seen nothing wrong with plain wood floors, at least for the time being.

And now this, a half-dozen brand new desks, which would remain unused for months yet, judging from the progress they were making. At a time, too, when their available cash was very nearly exhausted.

"Tell them to take the desks back," she said, deciding on the spur of the moment.

"Won't Mr. Hanover be angry?" Mrs. Clary asked.

"Not nearly so angry as that furniture maker will be if he finds out he can't be paid for all that," Lydia said. "Which reminds me, did you get all those bills paid?"

"Not all," Mrs. Clary replied, meeting her gaze with frank blue eyes. "There wasn't enough in the bank account. As a matter of fact—but perhaps you'd rather wait until we can go over everything in detail?"

"No, you'd better tell me the worst of it now," Lydia replied.

"As a matter of fact, it appears we aren't going to be able to pay everyone tomorrow. We're just short of enough to meet the payroll—you remember, I said last week we were cutting it awfully thin. However, I don't mind waiting a few days for my salary, if that will help."

"No, that won't be necessary," Lydia replied. "I'll speak to Mr. Hanover."

There was nothing else for it. She would have to speak to Walter about yet another advance of money, though she had promised herself that the last time would be final. At this rate, she would owe him all the profits of the firm for a year or more.

She paused thoughtfully. Was that what Walter had in mind? Not actually taking all the money from her, but keeping her tied to him, dependent upon him, for as long as possible?

It was entirely likely, she realized. He still hinted at marriage every opportunity he got, though lately his hints had been more petulant than sly, as his jealousy of Peter had taken root and grown in his mind. At times she was sure that Walter went so far as to spy on her relationship with Peter; he seemed to know every time she saw him, everywhere they went, what they did.

She blushed, hoping that Walter was not privy to everything she and Peter did, though that would account for his growing jealousy.

"I'll go see Mr. Hanover at once," she said aloud. "And you see that those desks are sent back. Tell them we'll be in touch when we need more furniture."

* * * * * * *

She went first to her own house. At the door, she heard girlish laughter, and stopped to listen. It had been so long, she realized suddenly, since she had heard April laugh. My poor child, she thought, feeling guilty as she so often did where April was concerned, have I robbed you of so much? She renewed her promise to herself that as soon as she was financially independent, she would give up the pretense regarding her daughter.

But when would that be? Unless she could curb Walter's reckless spending, April would have to pose as her maid indefinitely.

She heard a man's voice, muted by the door so that she couldn't identify it. It could not be Walter, she knew. April would never be so carefree with him, or with any of the men from the company.

Lydia went in, to find April and Peter MacNair laughing together at some joke. For a moment, Lydia felt a pang of anxiety. April was so lovely, and Peter so unscrupulous. Surely he wasn't trying to seduce her.

At once she rejected the thought as unworthy. Their faces, as they turned to greet her, were too innocent. Am I becoming jealous of my own daughter? Lydia asked herself. In a burst of insight, she realized how deeply she had fallen in love with this man she had sworn repeatedly to hate. At the same time, she knew she could never trust him enough to tell him how she felt.

Love was dangerous, for it gave another person the power to

hurt and to control. She could not afford the luxury of love, and especially not with a man like Peter, who could be trusted only to serve his own greedy interests.

"Something seems very funny," she said, smiling brightly as she came into the room.

"Your daughter's very amusing," Peter said.

"Is she?" Lydia replied, and realized as she said it how distant she and her daughter had become, that someone else should have to extoll her virtues. "Tell me, I could use a laugh myself."

"It's not the sort of thing that bears repeating," April said, her laughter fading to be replaced by her usual distant manner. "Excuse me, I have to be going."

"There's no need to run away," Lydia said anxiously, trying to recapture the fleeting moment, but it was gone already.

"I'll be late for my lessons," April said, and was gone before Lydia could protest further.

"I seem to have spoiled everyone's fun," Lydia said, taking off her hat and tossing it on a chair. She felt despondent. Why wouldn't things go right? Hadn't she worked hard enough, sacrificed enough? Why must life always be unfair?

"You could hardly spoil anything for me by coming in," Peter said, in an uncommonly tender voice. "Your daughter's just feeling put upon. I'm the only person she knows that she doesn't have to put on an act for."

"Not quite the only person," Lydia replied. "She does have a mother, after all."

"And a father too, but for the present, she finds that they're both rather distant and hard to reach."

Lydia's temper flared; she was in no mood to be lectured now, especially not by Peter.

"And who has been close to me?" she demanded. "I work and struggle to provide for us. Of course I am distant, but not so far that I can't be touched, if someone were only to reach out."

For an answer, Peter reached out a hand toward her. It was a surprising gesture, and for some reason it caused tears to well up in Lydia's eyes. For a fleeting second, she forgot her antagonism toward Peter, and saw in his eyes a light that had never been there before—or had she only failed to see it before?

She took a step toward him, but at that precise moment, Walter said from behind her, "I'm not intruding, I trust?"

She had forgotten that she had given him a key to use to drop off some items a few days before. He had used it now, at this inconvenient moment, to let himself in without knocking— probably, Lydia thought, hoping to catch her in some embarrassing scene with Peter, to further fuel his jealousy.

She saw Peter's glance dart to the key still in Walter's hand. When he looked at Lydia again, the tenderness she had glimpsed in his eyes had vanished, to be replaced by a mocking cynicism. She wanted to cry out, to explain to him, but the moment had gone, and it couldn't be brought back.

"There's nothing to intrude upon," he said. "I was just leaving."

She came very close to asking him to stay. It was not only pride that held her back, but fear, not so much of him, but of herself; to do so would have been to make herself vulnerable to him once again, and she hadn't quite the courage for that.

He did not glance back as he went, though she thought she saw him pause ever so slightly at the door. Or had her vanity gratuitously imagined that touch of need for her, a need he himself was probably incapable of feeling, let alone expressing?

Peter MacNair was not a man who needed anyone, least of all a woman. Even his urge to fornicate was in some way an expression of his lack of need for them. "You see," he seemed to say, "would I use and discard them so casually if they were necessary to me?"

It was almost with a sense of shock that she realized that Walter was still there, waiting and watching, not Peter's departure, but her reaction to it.

"I don't like your seeing that man," he said unnecessarily.

"I may not again," she said.

"Have you quarreled?"

She saw his nostrils flare with anticipatory pleasure; it filled her with disgust.

"I'm glad you've come by," she said, ignoring the question. "It saves me a trip. I wanted to talk to you about business."

"Why can't it ever be anything else?" he asked querulously.

"I've no time for anything else in my life," she answered flatly. "I sent back those desks you ordered."

"I can't imagine why," he said, his face darkening as it did when his desires were challenged. Unbidden, the thought came to her that Peter would have told her to do as she wished, or suggested she go to hell, and reinstated the order for the desks, never resorting to quibbling and picking at the decision.

"Can't you?" she asked, refusing to be dragged into justifying her actions. "We haven't the money. We haven't the money, in fact, to pay all the salaries."

"And you want me to provide the needed cash, I suppose."

She looked at him steadily for nearly a minute. It was he who blinked finally, and glanced away.

"Don't you think it's rather unfair," he said, "that I am the one who's making everything possible for you, all the things you want, and the one thing that I want, you deny me, and give to a man who isn't worthy?"

"What is it that you want, Walter?" she asked, already knowing the answer.

He looked back at her, his eyes as bright and greedy as a dog coveting a bone.

"I want to make love to you," he said, the words tumbling out hastily, fairly tripping over one another.

She did not need to hesitate, to consider, having already done that.

"Here?" she asked. "Now?"

He nodded, as if not quite trusting his voice to speak. Lydia followed his example, eschewing words for action. She went quickly past him toward the bedroom, not even looking back to see if he followed.

Stupidly, he lingered for a moment as if awaiting an invitation. But only for a moment. Then, as if realizing the invitation would not be spoken, and afraid she might change her mind if given time to consider, he came after her, hurrying too much, looking altogether too eager.

* * * * * * *

It was surprisingly simple, perhaps because so uneventful. A minute of two of inexpert groping, a little thrusting and panting, rubbing his body against hers. He had scarcely penetrated her before she felt the wetness and realized he had spent. She wondered fleetingly how such an abortive act had produced a child for him, particularly one as strong-willed as Kathy.

To her dismay, he lifted himself above her and, looking down into her face, asked, "Was it—was it satisfactory?"

Again she thought of Peter, carrying her masterfully to the bed, brooking no argument, fully aware before it had begun that her satisfaction was part of the bargain. How had he known that, which was a mystery to the others?

She was suddenly frightened by a possibility: could that be a part of love?

Walter was waiting with the look of a beggar. She managed a smile. "It was lovely," she lied. She found that the lie cost her no more than the act had. Sin, she wondered? Or kindness? But she was not so vain as to ascribe motives to herself that she was not entitled to. Her kindness in lying to him was kindness to herself, and to April. Except for the effect it might have on them, she found that she cared very little how he felt about what had transpired.

He accepted her lie altogether too easily, too completely. The begging, humble look left his face, and when he got up to begin donning his clothes, he had assumed his usual look of arrogance, of disdain.

She got up too, in a hurry to clothe herself. It made her uncomfortable to have him glance at her occasionally while he buttoned his shirt, looking pleased with himself, as if he had mastered some difficult colt.

She was dressed before he was, and left him to finish alone, returning to the parlor. She told herself she was afraid April might come back, and be hurt to see them in the bedroom, but the truth was, she found it difficult to be in Walter's company now that she had given him the use of her body. She was afraid that he would now expect it again and again, at his convenience. It would be harder to refuse him now.

There was more than that that he wanted, however. He said without preamble, as he came into the room, "I think it's time we got married."

She hadn't expected this, and she saw that the extent of her surprise annoyed him. His eyes narrowed and his mouth set in that stubborn way he had when he was prepared to insist on being indulged.

"I don't see why that's necessary," she said.

"Perhaps because I want to stake a claim on you," he replied. "I want MacNair to be served notice that you are mine."

"I should have thought I was my own," she said, "only on loan to others, but never theirs to possess. Is that how you see me, Walter, like a horse you've bought and paid for?"

"You must admit, I've put out quite a lot of cash. Far more than would be needed to buy a horse."

"And does that indicate the depth of your desire for me?"

He had the grace to blush, but the stubborn lines remained at his mouth. "You know how much I care for you. I'd hardly ask you to marry me otherwise."

"I—I can't marry you, Walter," she said.

"Why? Because of that MacNair?"

She shrugged. "Does the reason matter?" she asked.

He was silent for a long moment. When he spoke, it was coldly, unfeelingly. "Only to this extent—if you won't marry me as my wife, I won't marry you as a business partner either. I shall withdraw my money from Empress Cosmetics."

"But you can't be serious!" Lydia cried.

Walter's face was set in a stubborn expression. "I am quite serious," he replied.

"But Walter, what you're saying is blackmail."

"Nonsense," he said, unmoved by the accusation. "You must see that I'm offering you the only possible solution to our dilemma. Surely you can understand that otherwise it would be impossible for us to continue our association. There would simply be too much hard feeling, on my part initially, I'll admit—but in time, you would feel guilty for having led me on as you did. Eventually we would be at one another's throats. No, if we are to continue as business partners, I think we must be marital partners as well. Otherwise, I think we must give up everything."

Lydia stood for a moment in stunned silence. Every hope that she had was invested in Empress Cosmetics, hopes far more precious than the money Walter had invested. For the sake of the company, and the security it meant in the future, she had forced her own daughter to live a humiliating lie. She had given up a home with her Uncle Richard, admittedly a despicable one, but a roof over their heads nevertheless. She had even submitted to Walter sexually, giving him her body to use without consideration for her own feelings.

And now she was faced once again with losing everything, unless she submitted to this new threat.

Yet what else could she do? If Walter withdrew now, she would indeed lose everything that had been built up in the company. She could not even pay the overdue salaries, and she knew full well she had no way of raising the money herself to continue without Walter. Nor could she, after her haughty refusal of Peter's offer, go back to him now and tell him she would be his partner, even if that alternative was acceptable to her.

Even if she were willing to do so, the end result would be the same: she would be expected to prostitute herself to Peter; and strangely enough, though she found Peter sexually stimulating, she felt that it would be harder to give herself to Peter for financial gain than to Walter. Just as she resented the fact that Peter's interest in her was based on his desire for the perfume that she alone possessed, she was loathe to give herself to him as part of a business arrangement.

Walter meant less to her. From the moment his threat had escaped his lips, the affection and friendship she had felt for him had withered and died. She would feel no qualms over expecting him to pay for her favors, because he would never otherwise be entitled to them. With him, she could think of it as a business arrangement pure and simple—and by the same token, one that could be terminated when the circumstances that had warranted it no longer existed. When Empress Cosmetics had proven a success, and she had money of her own, she would feel entirely justified in separating from Walter.

It was, she knew, a heartless way of looking at things, but the only view that she had been permitted by the men who influenced her life.

"Very well," she said slowly. "I accept your proposal of marriage, Walter, unromantic though it may have been."

His face, so cold a moment before, was now wreathed in smiles. He came to her, seizing her in a fervid embrace.

"My darling," he murmured, "I'm sorry to have been so brutally frank, but it's for the best, believe me. I know I can make you love me in time, once you're free of that odious scoundrel. Trust me, I will see that you're happy. He won't dare bother you once you're my wife."

Lydia smiled past Walter's shoulder. He knew little about a woman's feelings, and less about Peter MacNair, she thought. From this moment forward, she knew that she would always despise Walter for a fool.

"We must make the arrangements for the wedding," he said, stepping back and beaming at her. "It must be the biggest event of the season...."

"No," Lydia said. "It must be my way, or not at all. It will be a civil ceremony, nothing more, and if we're to do it, let it be as quickly as possible."

His face fell, but Lydia remained adamant. She did not tell him that she was afraid to publicize the wedding lest someone who happened to know of her marriage to Ke Loo would learn of it, and come forward. It was unlikely, but she was certain that her background was known to someone here in the city who was in the employ of the Empress of China. She was still convinced that it had been no accident that a carriage had nearly run her down some time ago; she had thought then, and still thought, that it had been an attempt to kill her for taking the Empress's perfume.

A civil wedding might escape the notice of a Chinatown resident; many of them, she knew, read little English. But a big, splashy wedding might come to their attention anyway. The doings of the Nob Hill families were common gossip throughout the city, for there was hardly a neighborhood that was not touched by their influence.

When it became clear that she did not intend to give in on this point, Walter accepted her decision, though with obvious reluctance.

"Mother and Kathy will be disappointed," he said, sulking a little.

Once again, Lydia thought how unrealistic Walter was, or at least how little he understood the women in his life, but she kept that opinion to herself. In the future, she promised herself, Walter would hear only as much as she wanted him to hear.

* * * * * * *

An engagement to one of the Nob Hill Hanovers could not be kept secret for long, however, nor was Walter's mother willing to let her son be married "as if we were ashamed." An announcement had to be made, however unobtrusively, in the local papers.

To Lydia's surprise, Mrs. Hanover made no serious objection. It was almost as if she realized that the wedding had been arranged over Lydia's objections, and sympathized.

Or perhaps, Lydia mused, she understood that to resist would only increase her son's stubbornness. It was ironic that the woman should be cooperative at the one time when her disapproval might have been welcome.

It was the daughters who provided the objections. Kathy Hanover went into a sulk, refusing to speak to her father, who only shrugged it off.

"She'll get used to it," was all Walter said.

Lydia was more concerned for April, but even she seemed to accept the matter philosophically, perhaps because she had guessed beforehand that the relationship would lead to this.

"Am I to continue to pretend to be your maid?" was all she asked.

"Only until the wedding," was Lydia's reply. "I promise you, once Walter and I are married, I'll tell him the truth. It won't matter then if he approves or not."

It gave Lydia a perverse satisfaction to know that, having been forced into this marriage, she could exact so fitting a revenge. She found herself looking forward to the moment when she could end the sham regarding her daughter. It was the only satisfaction that she could take out of the impending wedding.

Indeed, it seemed remarkable that so significant a wedding could be taking place without pleasing anyone but Walter, whose pleasure, she knew, would end when he learned about April. Surely there had never been a wedding so designed to displease everyone!

* * * * * * *

Lorna MacNair, however, was pleased to read of the impending marriage, for it gave her the opportunity she had been waiting for.

She read the announcement on the very day that Ramsey brought his report to her. It was a wonderful report, exactly the sort of thing she had been hoping to learn, and it fitted in perfectly with a scheme taking shape in her mind.

"This is magnificent," Lorna purred, scanning the sheaf of papers for the third time. She glanced up at the detective.

"You're sure of your information?"

"Absolutely," he replied. "You could print that story in the newspapers without any fears."

Lorna gave a little laugh of pleasure. "My dear man," she said, "that's exactly what I intend to do."

"What about our agreement?"

She fixed her gaze upon him. To his surprise, there was something in her eyes akin to sexual excitement. Power, he thought, was sometimes the most powerful aphrodisiac of all.

"You need have no fears on that score, either," she said, smiling for the first time with genuine warmth. "You will be paid in full."

He returned her smile; her excitement was contagious. He felt a swelling in his trousers, and wanted to take her there and then, but he knew that she was the sort who would have to call the tune. For such a reward, though, he could afford to wait.

As if she had been entertaining the same thoughts, she said, "Tomorrow, when the story breaks."

It was as if she were promising him that the excitement would be even greater then.

"I can wait," he said. Though his business was sometimes a dangerous one, Ramsey himself was a cautious man; he had no wish to tangle with an irate husband, certainly not one who looked as formidable as Peter MacNair.

* * * * * * *

At that exact moment, Peter was reading the same news item in his office. He scanned the story quickly, then read it over again to be sure there wasn't some mistake. Swearing aloud, he leaped to his feet and headed out of the office.

"I'll be gone for the afternoon," he told Miss Adams.

"But you have an appointment with...." Miss Adams stopped, realizing that she was already speaking to an empty room.

"Must be very important," she murmured to herself, staring after her employer.

Lydia knew, the moment she opened the door and saw Peter's face, why he had come.

"You read the announcement, I suppose," she said, holding the door wide for him to come in.

"That nonsense about your marrying Hanover? Yes, I read it."

"I don't know why it's such nonsense," she replied coolly. "Walter's very eligible, very pleasant."

"And very rich."

"I should hardly think you are entitled to criticize me for that, though yes, of course, you're right, that does enter into it."

"Anyway, you're not exactly eligible yourself, are you? Aren't you forgetting someone?" he demanded angrily.

"Ke Loo? No, I haven't forgotten him," she said.

"Well? I don't know about China, but there are laws here against having more than one husband."

"Yes, I know. But you must know there's not a chance in a thousand of anyone's ever learning about Ke Loo. And I can hardly arrange to divorce him, now can I? Besides, I'm Lydia Nightsong now. There's really nothing to connect me with that girl who was married against her will all those years ago, even if anyone knew or remembered that except you. Ke Loo will never be coming to San Francisco, and Walter certainly won't be going to China. I've thought about it a great deal, but aside from your revealing the truth, I can't see that there's any danger of it coming out."

"I won't let you do this," Peter said, standing directly before her. "You're not in love with Hanover."

"I can't see why that should possibly concern you," Lydia replied.

"You little fool."

Suddenly he seized her in a crushing embrace, covering her lips with his own, in a kiss that left her weak and breathless.

"You little fool," he murmured into her hair, "don't you know that I love you?"

Lydia's heart seemed to skip a beat. She had dreamed lately

of somehow magically hearing him speak those words, but in her heart she had never believed it was possible. She was too stunned to answer, to say anything more than, "Oh, Peter," as she clung to him.

"If you insist on committing bigamy, I'll marry you myself," he said, holding her tight against him.

"And make bigamists of both of us?" she asked, laughing with pleasure.

"I'll divorce Lorna. I'll give her anything she wants, everything, even the company. It doesn't matter, we'll build up a new company, our own company, just the two of us...."

He felt her stiffen in his arms. She pulled back from him, her green eyes flashing as she looked up into his.

"The perfume," she said, speaking slowly and with a voice that grew colder with each syllable. "That's what this is all about, isn't it? You want me to give you the perfume."

"Don't be a fool," he said, angry again. "Of course I want that, I've always wanted it, but what does that matter, as long as it's the two of us, together?"

"That's why you don't want me to marry Walter, because you know that once I do, you'll never be able to obtain Nightsong. And you'll go to any lengths, even to promising me marriage— only you've really no intention of going through with your promises, do you, any more than you meant your promises all those years ago in China?"

"You're talking nonsense," he said, letting her go abruptly. "I love you. Doesn't that count for anything?"

"You never told me that before."

"Because I never knew it before. I've been blind, until just a moment ago."

"Until you had to think of some argument to prevent my marrying Walter," Lydia said drily. "Get out of here."

Rejection fanned the flames of Peter's anger, and he spoke now without thinking. "Why don't you at least be honest?" he demanded. "The truth is, you lost interest in me when I suggested giving Lorna all my fortune, because then I'd be coming to you a poor man, dependent upon what we could build together. And why should you settle for that, when you can have the wealthy Walter Hanover?"

Lydia strode to the door and flung it open. "Get out," she repeated, her voice rising.

"I'll go. Save your dramatic gestures for your future husband. I'm only sorry you didn't save the rest of it for him too. I'm afraid he's getting some badly worn merchandise."

He went past her without even another glance. Lydia, tears stinging her eyes, had an impulse to call his name, to run after him. Suddenly the prospect of marrying Walter no longer seemed desirable to her.

She took a step forward, but her fear held her back—fear of Peter's real motives. How could she believe him, when she knew better than anyone what a scoundrel he was?

Everyone knew leopards didn't change their spots. She would only be begging Peter to hurt her again, as he had hurt her before.

While she stood framed in the doorway, torn by indecision, he had reached the curb and in one swift movement leaped into his waiting carriage, barking an order at the driver. In another moment, it was gone.

Slowly, the tears now streaming freely down her cheeks, Lydia turned back to the room. It was too late to change her mind now. Peter was gone from her life, this time for good, and soon she would be Mrs. Walter Hanover.

CHAPTER THIRTY-ONE

"Nob Hill Bigamy?" Lydia read the newspaper headline aloud, a feeling of dismay engulfing her. She knew, without even reading the rest of the article, that the front page story was about her engagement to Walter.

"But who could have told them?" April asked. "No one knew but us. Unless they just guessed."

"No. It's all here—the names, the cities—even my parents' background. No one could have guessed that much," Lydia said, rapidly scanning the print.

With an ugly oath, she threw the paper aside. "And I know exactly who told them. No one knew but us—and Mr. Peter MacNair."

"Mr. MacNair? I can't believe it," April said. "He always seemed so nice."

"Nice? Like a snake," Lydia said, pacing angrily back and forth. "This isn't the first time he's betrayed my trust. This is his revenge because I wouldn't give him what he wanted."

There was a knock at the front door. "Don't answer it," April said.

For a moment Lydia hesitated. Heaven knew she didn't want to face anyone just now, not till she'd had time to sort out her thoughts.

No, she wouldn't hide like a craven coward. She went to the door and threw it boldly open, to find the last person she had expected to see standing there, hat in hand.

"Uncle Richard," she exclaimed, too surprised even to object to his presence, as she might have done at another time.

"Hope I'm not intruding," he said, looking so humble that Lydia found herself wondering if he were up to some trick. "I read that newspaper piece, and I figured you'd be upset. So I says to myself, no matter what private fights we've had, it's times like these that family ought to stick together."

"Why, that's very kind of you, Uncle," Lydia said, unable to conceal her astonishment. This was certainly a far different man from the one who'd used and taunted them so cruelly when they had lived with him.

"If you don't want me to come in, I'll go and not trouble you further."

Lydia felt a pang of conscience. Perhaps she was being too harsh, and at any rate, at the moment, a sympathetic face, even Richard's, was most welcome.

"No, come in, please," she said, stepping aside to let him enter.

He looked around the room, the familiar greed gleaming in his eyes as he noted the furnishings; though they were modest, they were grand indeed compared to the shabby pieces with which his quarters were furnished.

"Very nice," he said, his gaze, sober and friendly, returning to Lydia. He glanced toward April, nodding his head in greeting, but his eyes did not rake over the contours of her body as they used to do.

"I suppose this queers things," he said, indicating the newspaper that Lydia had thrown to the floor.

"So far as the wedding, I'm afraid it does," she said. "I don't know how Walter is going to feel about the company now."

"You mean your perfume business might be out the window with the rest?" Richard asked.

Lydia sighed and said, "I think it's likely. I'm going to go see Walter as soon as I've gotten dressed. There's no point in putting it off, and it's unfair to wait for him to come to me."

Richard twisted his hat in his hand, and looked down at his shoes nervously. "I don't know how you'll take this," he said, "seeing as how we got along before, but, well, you know I did take you in then, when you needed a place, and like I said, a family ought to stick together when things go bad. Anyway, what I'm trying to say is, you can always move back in above the shop, if you want—and I won't even ask you to work for your board, just to show my heart's in the right place."

"Why, that's very kind of you," Lydia said, surprised yet again; she was tempted to take a cynical view of this new Uncle Richard, and yet he seemed sincere. He no longer looked at them with that lustful longing she had always seen in his eyes before, and she could think of no other motive for his actions but the one he had given. Maybe his conscience had been bothering him over his previous behavior; or again, maybe he only wanted to move them back in so that he could force himself on them, as he had done before with her. She couldn't say which.

"I'll come," April said.

Startled by this new development, Lydia turned to her. "But, don't you think we should discuss this before we make any decision?" she asked.

"I don't see why," April replied, giving her hair a toss. "I can't see that I was treated worse there than I have been here, and at least I didn't have that horrible Kathy treating me like scum."

"Kathy is hardly likely to come around here in the future," Lydia reminded her. "Even if we stay. And there's no longer any need for us to pretend that you're anyone but who you are."

"Who is that, Mother, can you tell me?" April asked. "I've been a princess of China, and a fugitive, and an outcast—on the boat, we had to hide in our cabins like rodents afraid of the sunlight. And here I've been your maid, and a foreigner, a Chink, they call me."

"You're my daughter," Lydia said.

April's eyes flashed. "Shouldn't you have thought about that sooner?" she asked. She did not wait for a reply, but turned and ran from the room.

"April!" Lydia cried, but her only answer was the slamming

of a door.

"There," Richard said, reminding Lydia of his presence. "I came to help, and here I've caused more trouble, it looks like, the last thing I wanted to do."

"It's not your fault," Lydia said, brushing a wisp of hair back from her forehead with a weary gesture. So much had happened, so swiftly, it was difficult to sort out her thoughts. "And I do thank you for your offer. I'm not quite sure how things stand just now, to be honest."

"Well, no matter," Richard said, shuffling toward the door. "The invitation's been extended. Let's just leave it at that, why don't we, and if you want to come, go right ahead and come, the old rooms are ready for you."

At the door he paused, and again looked embarrassed. "I'm ashamed to ask this," he said, speaking hesitantly.

"Whatever it is, you needn't be," Lydia replied, only half paying attention; her thoughts had already jumped ahead, to facing Walter.

"I know I sort of took advantage that one time—for what it's worth, it was the liquor had me riled up—and I've given that up, you've got my word on that. But, what I was wondering is, I'd feel a bunch better if we could patch things up between us."

"Very well, then let's agree to forget all of it, and start afresh," Lydia said.

He lifted his face, grinning foolishly. "Could we seal that with a kiss? Just a peck, that's all I mean."

For a second, Lydia hesitated. Was this another of his old tricks? But he looked so eager, and so kindly, that she came to him and stretched up to give him a kiss. She was grateful that he stuck to his word and made nothing more of it than a quick, perfectly innocent peck.

"Now I feel that you've really forgiven me for making such an ass of myself before," he said.

Outside, with the door closed behind him, his expression changed as abruptly as if a mask had fallen from his face. He chuckled slyly to himself as he went down the steps to the street.

Fooled 'em right proper, I did, he told himself. A man needed to be clever, he did, if he wanted to get ahead in the world. Women. What fools they were, always ready to believe the first sweet talk they heard.

His heart had ached with resentment from the day he'd learned that Miss High-and-Mighty and her Chink brat had landed themselves a rich sucker, and he was cut out of all of it. It might have been different if she had found some way of cutting him in, but no, she was selfish, plain and simple.

Of course, he hadn't forgotten that inheritance, and what the lawyer had told him. If anything happened to her and the kid, then that money belonged to him, and a right tidy sum it was by now, what with the interest accumulating all these years.

First, though, something had to happen to them. When he'd read that she meant to marry that swell, he'd been certain it meant his plans were hopeless. Fat chance he'd have of arranging anything accidental with her living in some Nob Hill mansion.

Today, though, when he'd read that her secret was out and the marriage sure to be off, he had seen at once that it was like he'd been given another chance. Why, with them living back at his place, he could arrange things any way he wanted to, as easy as pie; and this time he wouldn't hold back on account of family sentiment.

No sir, he'd learned his lesson on that score!

CHAPTER THIRTY-TWO

The Hanovers' butler delivered Lydia to the parlor, not the study where she was usually shown. She took that as a sign of Walter's anger.

While she was waiting, she walked to one of the tall, heavily curtained windows that overlooked the street. It was peculiar, but she was sure she had seen the same Chinese man, in the traditional trousers and tunic, walking behind her twice as she had climbed the hill to Walter's house. Since the incident with the carriage that had nearly run her down, she had more than once had the feeling that she was being followed or observed, though she had never been able to confirm it.

She had not forgotten that the influence of the Empress of China reached even to San Francisco, nor that she was a target of the Empress's anger. She would like to think that time would have lessened that old woman's ire, but she could not be sure.

There was no sign of the Chinese man on the street outside. Probably she had been mistaken. I mustn't turn into one of those women afraid of her own shadow, she scolded herself, but nonetheless she stood for several minutes, watching.

"Is there something unusual about the view?"

Lydia jumped and turned to find not Walter but his mother, standing in the doorway.

"I thought I saw someone I knew," Lydia said. "A Chinese fellow."

"A family member, perhaps?" Mrs. Hanover asked, her voice cutting.

Lydia blushed, but refused to back down. "I wonder if I might have a word with Walter?" she said.

"I'm afraid not. Walter is indisposed, but he has asked me to take care of his business with you in the future."

"It wasn't entirely on business that I wanted to see him," Lydia said.

"That, I'm afraid, is all that need be discussed. There is nothing else he wishes to talk with you about."

"I see." Lydia paused, considering whether it would do her any good to insist upon seeing Walter; but it took little consideration to decide that it would be futile. Walter could be both stubborn and petulant, and he would not have sent his mother to do his bidding if he had any intention of changing his mind.

"Very well, then," Lydia said aloud. "Let us discuss business. I do need to know just what Walter intends. As he may have told you, we are once again short of money to cover expenses."

"I'm afraid that is no longer our concern," Mrs. Hanover replied. "In view of your recently discovered perfidy, we have decided we must withdraw from Empress Cosmetics as active partners. To make it even plainer, we no longer wish to be involved in the same business with you."

"But you've not even given me a chance to explain," Lydia cried.

"Are you suggesting that newspaper story isn't true?" Mrs. Hanover asked, lifting one eyebrow. "If that is the case, then you must be prepared to sue for libel."

"I—I can't do that," Lydia admitted, embarrassed all over again, "But there are circumstances...."

"We are not interested in 'circumstances,'" was the frosty reply.

"Then can't you at least consider the personal situation and the business as separate matters?" Lydia asked, a note of pleading creeping into her voice. "There are other people to be considered now, people that I hired at Walter's suggestion. How am I to pay them?"

"That no longer concerns us. We are interested solely in the return of the money we loaned you to form your company."

"But that money was invested in Empress Cosmetics as a straightforward business deal. It wasn't simply loaned to me."

"I think if you'll have your attorney look at the papers you signed, you'll find that the loans took the form of demand notes. We are demanding repayment of those notes. It's a fairly simple arrangement."

"But...." Lydia stopped, at a loss. She knew nothing about such matters. She had simply taken Walter's word on everything. She had signed where he said to sign, without a thought for repayment, other than out of the company's eventual profits. Yet she knew Mrs. Hanover well enough to know that the woman was probably right. Of course, she ought to have known, people like the Hanovers would not get into any sort of business deal without protecting their interests in every way.

"I think that about covers everything we have to discuss," Mrs. Hanover said, looking and sounding quite satisfied with herself. "Our lawyers will be in touch with you, *Mrs.* Nightsong. Anything else you wish to discuss can be taken up with them. And now, if you'll excuse me, Roberts will show you to the door."

"That won't be necessary," Lydia said. "I know the way out."

"I'm afraid you do not even know the way in. Hereafter, should there be any reason to call, please present yourself at the rear door. I do not know what the custom is in China, but in San Francisco the front door is for social calls, the rear door for trades people."

Her face burning, Lydia brushed quickly past the woman and hurried from the house. She would not give her the satisfaction of begging, nor of showing how deeply she had been offended.

By the time she had reached the street, however, anger had given way to despair. What was she to do? The situation was hopeless so far as Empress Cosmetics was concerned. She could not even pay the overdue salaries with the money left, and it would be necessary to sell everything to repay even part of the money that Walter had advanced. She could not even keep the house on Van Ness Street.

Like it or not, she had no choice but to return to her Uncle Richard's house, until she could get back on her feet again.

Once again her life seemed to have fallen in ruins about her feet. Her heart still ached from the pain of Peter's betrayal. Her attempt to buy financial security for herself and April by marrying a man she did not love had backfired; even April seemed to despise her for her efforts.

She had nothing left but the perfume. Nightsong! It almost seemed to be cursed, as if within that haunting fragrance lay some power for evil, the blossom of some dark flower as destructive as it was intoxicating.

Perhaps, she thought, that was the secret of its desirability. Perhaps she would be better off to get rid of it. She could sell it to Peter and use the money to buy some new life for herself and April, somewhere far from here.

As quickly as the idea came, she rejected it. No, she had come this far, she had dared so much, she would not quit now, not until she had seen it through. There had to be a way. And if she had to endure more hardships, more pain, why, she had endured so much already, what could a little more matter?

Even with Uncle Richard, she had already endured the worst that he could do to her; she had nothing more to fear from him. She made up her mind that she would not put off the inevitable. She would return home and begin packing at once to move to Richard's.

She crossed the street, dodging the afternoon traffic. A hundred yards behind her, a Chinese man in tunic and trousers watched, and followed.

* * * * * *

"That's the last of it, Miss Nightsong," Mrs. Clary said, handing Lydia a stack of letters. "Everything else has been answered."

"Thank you, I'll take care of these myself," Lydia said, dropping the letters into the large bag she had brought to empty out the desks.

She glanced around the office. The furnishings had gone already, sold for a disappointing half of what she had paid for them only a short while before. In the past week, since her unfortunate break with Walter, she had learned a great many business lessons, one of them being that buying and selling the same items involved different prices.

"I've certainly learned about business the hard way," she said aloud.

Mrs. Clary gave her a sympathetic smile. "Men don't make it any easier for a woman to learn, do they? Sometimes you'd think they're afraid of us."

"Perhaps they are," Lydia agreed. "Though I can't imagine myself as a threat to anyone. Everyone's gotten their severance pay?"

"Yes, and I've got mine right here." Mrs. Clary held up the check made out to herself.

Lydia smiled ruefully. "I promise you, I'll manage some day to make up the difference in what I owe you. Empress Cosmetics isn't dead, just in temporary retirement. And I do thank you for staying to help me finish things up."

"Just so long as you promise I can have my job back when you start up again," Mrs. Clary said.

"I promise—if you still want it, that is." Lydia paused for one final glance around the room. It was empty now but for the desk at which Mrs. Clary had been working. "Well, I suppose we may as well go."

"You go ahead," Mrs. Clary said. "I'll lock up on my way out. Oh, I forgot to tell you, that Mr. MacNair called again. He sounded really unhappy."

"You needn't worry about Mr. MacNair's feelings," Lydia assured her. "He hasn't got any."

"He's certainly persistent, isn't he?"

"Like a rat, gnawing its way through a wall. Goodbye, Mrs. Clary, and thank you again."

Lydia shook hands with her former secretary and left the office quickly, not wanting to take time to get sentimental. If she started thinking about how close she had come to realizing her dream at last, it would only bring on more tears, and she had shed enough of them lately, in the privacy of her own bedroom. At least she would spare herself the humiliation of shedding them publicly.

It gave her an odd mixture of feelings to know that Peter was still trying to get in touch with her. It annoyed her, and yet, in another sense, it gave her a peculiar feeling of—she didn't quite know what. Happiness was hardly the word, though it did please her, perversely, to think that he cared so much.

What foolishness, she chided herself. It wasn't she he cared for, it was a perfume she had stolen from the Empress of China. And that was a theft for which she had certainly suffered ample punishment!

Peter had come to the house half a dozen times before she had moved out of it. The first time, she had slammed the door in his face as soon as she had seen him, and had refused to open it again, though he pounded on it for a good ten minutes. After that, she hadn't opened it at all, no matter how long or how loudly he had knocked.

She knew herself well enough to know that she couldn't trust herself with him. Scoundrel that he was, she loved him, and that she could do nothing about. But she needn't be such a fool as to give him yet another opportunity to mock her and use her, as he had done every time she submitted to her feelings for him. She could not tear him from her heart, but at least she could see that he remained there, securely locked away where he could do no more mischief. Someday, she might even be able to get through a night without yearning for him.

* * * * * * *

In the office she had just quitted, Mrs. Clary prepared to leave, and remembered suddenly that she had not mentioned to

Mrs. Nightsong that Chinaman who had been hanging around the last few days.

Oh, well, poor dear, she thought, she's got enough on her mind as it is. And it can't be anything important, or the fellow would have come in and stated his business.

Mrs. Clary went out, locking the office door for the last time. She did notice as she left the building that the man had disappeared. Probably, she thought, someone who had been trying to get up courage to ask about a job. Well, he must by now know that there was no hope of that.

With a shrug of her shoulders, she dismissed the matter from her mind.

CHAPTER THIRTY-THREE

For Richard Whitley, it had been a frustrating week. It seemed to him as if his niece's daughter had grown into a woman overnight. Hardly an hour went by that he wasn't aware of her tantalizing young loveliness. He had always wanted her, but now it was an obsession with him.

He had been trying to concoct a scheme that would enable him to rid himself of the two of them and collect the inheritance that he regarded as rightfully his; but first, he had made up his mind that he wanted to have a go at the young one—and maybe her mother too—before he finished them off.

He had come in from some errands only a few minutes before, thinking that the house was empty. Not until he had climbed the stairs to his bedroom had the sound of water splashing alerted him to the fact that someone was bathing.

He listened outside the door to the young one's bedroom. Yes, she was in there. He heard her humming a little tune to herself.

Kneeling, he put his eye to the keyhole. Inside, he saw the big tin tub from the laundry room, and the girl seated in it, having a bath. As he watched, she raised her arm and he caught a glimpse of one upturned breast, just budding into womanhood. He felt an instant stiffening of his manhood.

For a moment he had the urge to burst into the room and take her there and then; but he knew full well what a tigress the other one could be, especially when she was protecting her daughter. He didn't want her sneaking up on him with a butcher knife, not if he could help it.

He stole quickly down the hall, to be sure Lydia was not in her room. He even went down to the shop, which was still shuttered and closed.

Good enough; of course, she might come back, but chances were he'd be finished with it before she did. The way he felt, with trousers tented out in front of him, it wasn't going to take but a minute or two to have it over with.

Evening was falling. He put out all the lights, locking the back door, then made his way quickly and silently back up the stairs. He paused at his room to get the gun he kept there—just in case the she-wolf came back before he was done.

April was just stepping from the tub when the door to her room was suddenly flung open with such force that the flimsy latch broke. She gave a squeal of fright and turned to see Richard lunge at her, his face contorted with lust.

He had been so changed in his attitude that she had actually lost a great deal of her fear of him; otherwise, she would never have risked bathing without being certain her mother was in the house. Now she saw how foolish she had been in thinking that he had reformed.

It was too late for second thoughts. There was not even time to cry out before he had seized her. For a second or two he threatened to topple both of them into the warm, soapy water.

"Don't, I beg you!" she cried, squirming to free herself from his arms.

"It'll do you no good to beg," he said, his voice hoarse and rasping. He tried to plant a kiss on her lips, but she shook her head to and fro, avoiding him. In horror and revulsion, she felt his hand, rough and hairy, pawing between her thighs, trying to force them apart. She fought to keep them pinned together and at the same time to maintain her balance. If she fell, she knew instinctively that he would be upon her in a moment.

She tried to scream, but she had no more than opened her mouth than he brought his fist back and struck her brutally, snapping her head back and all but rendering her unconscious.

In a daze, she felt him sweep her up into his arms and carry her toward the bed in the corner.

* * * * * * *

Lydia was surprised to see that the shop and the house were dark except for the lamp burning in April's window on the second floor. Surely Richard ought to be home at this hour.

She came around to the rear of the house, to come in the back way, as she usually did when the shop was closed. To her surprise, that door was locked. It was usually open, with the result that she had no key for it, only for the shop door in front. Growing suddenly frightened, she began to hurry around to the front again.

She was running by the time she reached the shop door, but in her anxiety her fingers were trembling so badly that she dropped the key and had to fumble for it on the steps before she found it and could open the door. She did not take time to light a lamp, but left the door open and ran through the shop by the light that spilled through.

There was no sign of anyone in the kitchen, but as she paused in the doorway, there was a clatter from above, as of something being thrown loudly to the floor.

Lydia fairly flew up the stairs, instinct guiding her through the darkness. At the landing, she saw that there was a light in her daughter's room, and running toward it, she saw the latch hanging ineffectually, torn from the wall by force.

In the doorway, she paused as the horror of the scene before her registered on her consciousness.

She saw the tub, first, and the trail of water that led across the room to the bed. Only then did she fully comprehend the sight of April, limp upon the bed, and Richard, his trousers on the floor where he had flung them a moment before, kneeling between her parted legs, about to thrust his rigid member between April's defenseless thighs.

So aroused was he that Richard had not even heard her run up the stairs, though he need only have turned his head the slightest bit to have seen her standing in the doorway.

Lydia's eyes raked the room and fell upon the heavy earthenware pitcher with which April had carried hot water up from the kitchen.

Dashing into the room, Lydia seized the pitcher. Richard heard her then, his head jerking around, and at the last minute he raised a hand protectively, but he was too late to defend himself. With a strength she hadn't known she possessed, Lydia brought the pitcher crashing down upon his head, breaking it into a thousand pieces.

Richard gave a low groan and slumped across April's naked body.

"Mother," April murmured dazedly, struggling to free herself from the dead weight pinning her to the bed.

"My darling, it's all right now," Lydia sobbed, tugging at Richard to roll him out of the way. "He won't harm you now."

"He broke in," April said, shaking her head to try to clear it.

"Don't try to talk, help me get him over there," Lydia said. "Quickly, your robe, before he comes around."

As if on cue, Richard gave another groan, and stirred slightly.

"Hurry," Lydia cried, helping her daughter to her feet. April was still wobbly, and had to cling to Lydia for support. Lydia grabbed a robe from the back of a chair where April had thrown it earlier when she had started to bathe, and together they hurried from the room.

They had just reached the top of the stairs when they heard a bellow of rage from the room they had just fled.

"Damn you, I'll kill you for that!" Richard shouted. Lydia looked over her shoulder in time to see him burst from the room.

They tried to flee down the stairs, but near the bottom, April stumbled and fell to her knees.

"Oh, get up, hurry," Lydia cried, tugging at her arm, but it was too late; Richard was upon them.

Lydia felt herself grabbed by powerful hands, and in the next instant she was thrown hard against the wall, the breath knocked from her.

"Run, April, run," she managed to gasp.

April staggered to her feet. Richard turned as if he would seize her, and at once Lydia was upon him, pounding his back and his head with her fists.

With an oath he turned on her again, grabbing her throat. In horror, Lydia saw that he held a gun in one hand. He brandished it in her face. "I'm going to kill you!" he said.

April had gotten up, and suddenly she darted toward the doorway to the shop. She ran into a chair, knocking it over. The noise startled Richard, and he whirled in that direction.

As he did so, Lydia brought her foot back and kicked him hard in the shins. He gave a yelp of pain and she heard a clatter as the gun slipped from his hand and fell to the floor.

Lydia spun free of his grasp and tried to run in the other direction, but he was faster, seizing her again before she had gone more than a few feet.

"I don't need the gun," he said in a low, menacing voice. This time she felt both hands on her throat, squeezing cruelly. His face was close enough that even in the darkness she could see the maniacal gleam in his eyes.

The room tilted and spun around her. This time, she knew, she was going to die.

* * * * * * *

Ling Ta stood hidden in the shadows, trying to unravel the mystery of what was happening. The foreign words were unintelligible to him, but it was obvious that the man was furious, and the two females frightened. It almost looked as if the man meant to kill the woman.

For a few seconds more, Ling Ta hesitated. Perhaps it would not be necessary after all for him to kill her, perhaps the job would be done for him. It had seemed a stroke of good fortune when the woman had run into the house, leaving the door standing open for him to follow. Even the darkness was a blessing. And now this—was it more good fortune?

He dismissed that idea at once. He could not be sure, in the darkness, even if the woman collapsed, as she seemed on the verge of doing, if she were really dead, or only unconscious.

More important than that, however, was the oath that he had sworn to kill this woman who had betrayed the Empress of China. To watch her die at someone else's hands would not fulfill the oath he had sworn on the graves of his ancestors. It had been a mistake before to have arranged for someone else to do it—and so it had failed.

Her back was toward him. Still concealed by the darkness, Ling Ta raised a hand in which he held one of the deadly war hatchets of the Chinese tongs. It sailed through the air with a faint hiss when he threw it.

Then something incredible happened. The woman, still struggling though by now the fight should have been ended, stumbled and dropped to her knees. Clutching her throat, the man leaned over her, turning slightly, at the very instant that the hatchet struck.

There was a slashing sound, like a melon being split, and an eerie, high-pitched gurgle from the man as the hatchet split his skull open.

* * * * * * *

The pressure was suddenly gone from her throat, and a second later Richard collapsed heavily over her. Lydia felt a stream of something warm and wet, and with a shock realized it was blood.

Not until she had pushed Richard aside did she see the ugly hatchet protruding from the top of his head. She attempted to scream, but the sound came out a moan of horror.

Something moved across the room, and she looked, to see a Chinese man advancing toward her. He passed the window, and the pale light revealed the dagger in his hand.

It revealed his face too, and she knew in a twinkling that he was the one who had been following her, and knew too why he was here.

"You are from the Empress, are you not?" she asked, speaking in the Manchu dialect.

His own tongue, coming unexpectedly from the woman, startled him, and he stopped.

"Yes," he said. "I have come to kill you."

"How do you know I am the woman you seek?" she asked. While she spoke, she ran her hands over the floor, searching for the gun Richard had dropped a few minutes before. It must be here somewhere—but where? She leaned back, practically lying down, and felt farther around.

"You are the one," he said. He glanced at Richard's crumpled body. "I am sorry I had to kill the man."

"Don't be sorry, he was evil," she said.

He began to walk toward her again. She saw the dagger lifted up. He was so close now that she could smell his sweat and hear the rustling of his silk trousers.

Her fingers touched the cold metal. Was it loaded? She could only hope....

He suddenly leaped at her. Lydia snatched the gun from the floor, and without a chance to aim, fired point blank. The face, contorted in what might have been a grimace, or a grin, seemed to explode from within, the shot echoing painfully in the small room. The knife thudded into the floor, no more than an inch from her shoulder.

"Mother?" April's voice was little more than a tiny whisper.

"It's all right," Lydia managed to say, though she was still trembling so much that she could not move. "It's all over."

CHAPTER THIRTY-FOUR

"There's a letter for you, Mother."

Lydia took the letter from her daughter, and glanced down at the handwriting. Yet another note from Peter. Having come to realize that she would not see him, he had made use of the mail to beg her to talk with him.

Without bothering to open it, Lydia crumpled the letter up, envelope and all, and threw it into the fire burning in the stove. Twice she had made the mistake of trusting Peter MacNair, and twice he had betrayed her. She would not make that mistake again, no matter how her heart ached.

Nor would she ever again be in a position where she would have to accept the terms dictated to her by a man—any man. It had come as a great shock to learn that Richard's death had left her financially secure for the first time in her life. As his only heir, she had inherited the shop with the apartment, which she had sold. To her surprise, she had learned that Richard had been something of a miser; for all his unending complaints of poverty, his savings account had represented a tidy sum.

More than that, she had learned only a few days ago that there had, after all, been an inheritance from her mother's family, an inheritance left to her mother, and rightfully hers upon her mother's death, which Richard had kept a secret from her.

All in all, there had been more than enough to buy a modest home for herself and April, only a few doors down from the house they had been renting on Van Ness, and plenty besides to insure the launching of Empress Cosmetics.

Finally, just the day before, had come the best news of all. Morris, the chemist who had happily returned to work for the firm as soon as he had learned of her good fortune, had come to her in a state of excitement, with the best news of all: he had found an authentic French *nez,* a recent immigrant to California who had worked since childhood in a perfume factory, and was confident that he could duplicate Lydia's Nightsong perfume.

At last, Lydia thought, things were going her way.

But not everything, a voice within her seemed to say. Her glance went to the stove. The letter she had thrown into the flames had vanished in them. For a moment she wished that she had read it after all. Perhaps....

She gave her head a shake. No, it was futile to dwell on something that was so plainly hopeless. Even if she could believe what Peter had to say, what could he possibly offer her? He had a wife, children of his own—he could never be hers.

At the thought of children, Lydia turned to where April had been standing, meaning to say something to her, but April had gone.

She felt another pang of regret. It had been a long time since there had been any closeness between herself and her daughter. April still had not forgiven her for the deception she had been forced to practice.

What else could I have done? Lydia asked herself for perhaps the hundredth time. She too had been forced by circumstances to practice deception, and she had suffered for it; but it had come out right in the end, hadn't it?

The question lingered in her mind, but she brushed it aside. She had done what had to be done. April was still young, and her life had been sheltered compared to Lydia's own. In time she would come to understand. Lydia was sure of it. She too had once been young and she had seen the world through enchanted eyes; but the world was not enchanted simply because a girl saw it so. It was deadly earnest, and it made no concessions to dreamers or fools.

Someday, April would fall in love with a man, and she would

know pain, and she would see the world as a different place. With luck, she would look back, and see her mother's actions differently, and perhaps then she would forgive.

* * * * * * *

April made her way to Chinatown, as she did at every opportunity. It was still only here that she could feel at all comfortable. Here she could be herself, for she still thought of herself as Chinese and not Caucasian. As a Caucasian, as her mother's daughter, as an American, she had known only unhappiness and pain. In China, she had been a princess; a girl, true, and condemned to a woman's lot, but it had been a life of luxury, of elegance and grandeur of a type that would be incomprehensible to the girls she passed on the streets of San Francisco. Kathy Hanover would be shocked, she knew, to be informed how coarse, how primitive, was the life that her father's wealth afforded her.

Someday she would return to China—to *her* China, her native land. She never spoke of this with her mother, knowing that her mother would never understand.

It was hard sometimes to believe that she had sprung from her mother's womb, so unlike did they seem. It was not that she did not love her mother, for she did, and she understood, at least in part, some of what her mother had done for her.

They did not think alike, though; perhaps it was that her mother's heart had always been here, in the land that had been hers as a child, while her own resided in a distant palace, scented with almond blossoms, and watched over by the great mountains of Asia.

She felt a loyalty, an attachment to her mother, but she could not love where her heart was not.

So engrossed was she in her reveries that April did not see the young man emerging from the shop that sold Chinese tea until she had run into him, and found herself in his arms.

"I'm so sorry," he said, holding her just a second or two

longer than was necessary to keep her from falling. "I ought to look where I'm going."

"Please, it was my fault," she said, embarrassed. "Oh, your package...."

He had dropped his bundles, and a package of tea had broken open, spilling its contents. She knelt quickly, gathering the others.

"How dreadful of me," she said.

He knelt too, gathering the rest of the packages. "It's nothing," he said, "Look, only a little of it spilled, the rest is all right. The Chinese say that—oh, how stupid of me, you're Chinese."

"Half Chinese," she said, smiling at his lack of pretense. "But how is it that you know what the Chinese say?"

"This is my favorite part of the city," he said. "I come here whenever I'm in town."

"You're not from San Francisco, then?" For some peculiar reason, the thought gave her a little pang of disappointment.

"Well, yes, officially I live here," he said, with a wry grin. "But my father keeps me out of his hair by keeping me away at school as much as possible. He really hates times like this, when I'm on break. Do you live here?"

"Yes—that is, not here exactly, but in the city."

There was an awkward silence. At almost the same time, both realized that they were still kneeling on the sidewalk, forcing passersby to go around them. Laughing simultaneously, they got up. April handed him the rest of his packages.

"My name's David," he said. "David MacNair."

She started. "You've heard of me?" he asked.

"I—I've heard the name."

He grimaced and said, "My father, I suppose. Everybody knows him, most of them far better than I, I'd guess. What's your name?"

"April." She waited for a reaction, but there was none. Was it possible he had heard nothing about her and her mother, despite his father's involvement in all that had happened? But he had said he was out of the city most of the time; and he wasn't friendly with his father, he'd made that much clear.

"That's very pretty."

There was another silence, though this one was less awkward. He seemed perfectly content to stand and smile at her.

"I must be going," she said, afraid that if she said more, he might realize who she was, and this lovely rapport between them would be spoiled.

"Wait—I'd like to see you again sometime."

"You will, if you come here often," she replied. "I'm always somewhere about Chinatown."

"Listen...."

"Please," she said, interrupting him, "I must go now."

"What about next time?"

"We'll speak then," she said, adding mysteriously, "If you still want to."

Then she was gone, running lightly away down the street and leaving him to think that he couldn't imagine not wanting to speak to her again. He watched her go, the blue and yellow of her dress like a spray of flowers—the first flowers that bloom in April, he thought.

How lovely her name was! How lovely she was! He had never before seen anyone so dazzling, so...but the words would not come to express what she had inspired in him.

Suddenly he realized—love at first sight. How silly he'd always thought that sounded before, and now he saw that it was the most natural, the most beautiful experience in the world.

She came to Chinatown; then he would come to Chinatown too, until he found her again. He would haunt the streets and the shops, he would ask about her—but all at once he grinned, because he knew somehow, with a certainty that defied question, that he would find her again. He knew that they had been fated to meet.

Until now, returning to San Francisco had always been an unpleasant ordeal for him, because it meant confronting his father. Now, however, his return to school, though it was not for another month, already loomed far too large on the horizon. What if he did not find her for a week, or even two weeks? There would never be enough time.

His mother was in the hall when he arrived home. To her astonishment, he grabbed her about the waist and gave her a whirl.

"David," she gasped, disapproving because the nurse had been in the hall and seen what was surely a vulgar display. "What's gotten into you? You haven't been drinking, have you?"

He laughed, and whirled her again. "Oh, Mother, I *am* drunk, but not on Father's liquor."

"Really, David, I don't understand...."

"The most wonderful thing, Mother!" he cried, so happy that not even her primness could dampen his spirits.

"David...."

"I've just met the girl I'm going to marry!"

ABOUT THE AUTHOR

V. J. Banis is the critically acclaimed author ("the master's touch in storytelling..."—*Publishers Weekly*) of more than 200 published books and numerous short stories in a career spanning nearly a half century. A native of Ohio and a longtime Californian, he lives and writes now in West Virginia's beautiful Blue Ridge.

You can visit him at http://www.vjbanis.com

www.ingramcontent.com/pod-product-compliance
Lightning Source LLC
Chambersburg PA
CBHW021321250626
47155CB00002B/579